Love,
California Style
• BOOK 1 •

Heart of DESIGN

ELLEN BUTLER

CRIMSON
ROMANCE
F+W Media, Inc.

Published by
Crimson Romance
an imprint of F+W Media, Inc.
10151 Carver Road, Suite 200
Blue Ash, OH 45242. U.S.A.
www.crimsonromance.com

ISBN 10: 1-4405-8363-3
ISBN 13: 978-1-4405-8363-6
eISBN 10: 1-4405-8364-1
eISBN 13: 978-1-4405-8364-3

Cover art © 123RF/nyul

To my boys, Clator, Alex, and Andrew.

Acknowledgments

Thanks to an old high school friend, Juan Loeza, for providing translation services. A hearty thanks and shout-out to all my author friends on my Yahoo groups, at BRLA, and in my local writing chapters. Your excellent advice keeps me going when writer's block stands on my shoulder like a two-ton elephant. You've made me laugh at the lowest of times when the rejections rolled in. And, your unerring support keeps me moving forward in this highly competitive and daunting profession. You are the best. I don't know what I'd do without you.

Chapter 1

"Sophia Hartland, put that tray down and come with me right now!" Poppy hopped from one foot to another, her face agitated.

"But Hannah said they need more shrimp." I tried to carry the heavy-laden tray past her.

"Oh, bother Hannah!" Poppy grabbed the tray out of my hands and shoved it into the hands of a passing waiter, hired for the night. "Pedro, take these out to the main buffet table and replace the empty."

The surprised Pedro nodded and headed back out into the throng of party guests.

"Here, put some of this on." Poppy handed me a tube of lip gloss from her pocket. She reached behind my head, and, undoing the alligator clip, allowed the heavy, dark tresses to fall down my back. She ruffled the locks with her fingers.

"What are you doing?" I stood with an opened tube of gloss in my right hand and tried ineffectually to grab with my left the clip Poppy had removed from my hair and attached to her pants. "I need that! It gets too hot with my hair down."

She grabbed me by the shoulders, and, with a hearty shake, got my full attention. "Sophie! Ian O'Connor wants to meet you!" Her hazel-green eyes bore into me.

"Okay. Who's Ian O'Connor and why does he want to meet me?"

"What! Are you kidding? Do you live in a hole? Ian O'Connor! You know, Eeeaann Oh-Coonnneerr." She said it like I was deaf and could read her lips if she spoke nice and slow.

I shook my head, completely lost.

"He's one of the hunks on the hottest new cop show this year, *LA Heat.* It was a mid-season replacement in the spring, and it's been picked up for a full season this fall. He's so smokin' hot, women throw their bras at him. You know, he plays Ryder McKay."

"Nope." I shook my head. "Sorry. Not one of the shows I watch. Why does he want to meet me?"

"He said he liked the painting in the front hall and asked who did it. I was pseudo-stalking him, and thus in hearing distance, so I cozied up and explained all the credit went to you, my best friend and interior designer," Poppy said in a rush. "And he said he'd like to meet you sometime. And I said, 'well she's here tonight' and if he was serious I could introduce you two." She bounced up and down like a rabbit and squealed, "And he said, 'sure.'"

I rolled my eyes, always the cynic. "Poppy, he probably happened to mention it in passing, and then when you attacked, he was just being nice. This guy has likely made a beeline to another part of the house by now to get away from you, crazy stalker woman. We'll be lucky if he didn't already bolt from the party."

I loved Poppy dearly. She was my best friend in LA, and as the owner of Poppy's Party Planning, she gave me jobs that helped supplement my income when times were slow, and I was between design contracts. I met my intelligent, crimson-haired friend at a party six years ago, early in her career. This job was for a director's birthday party, and Poppy had come up with the idea of going old Hollywood and asked for my help with the party décor. I decided nothing screamed old Hollywood like art deco and created an entire theme around it. Unfortunately, Poppy had a quirky tendency to fall in and out of love with TV and movie actors as often as she changed her socks. I feared Ian O'Connor was her latest fixation.

"Please tell me we aren't doing 2 a.m. drive-bys with this Ian fellow."

"Sophie!" she exclaimed. "You have it all wrong. Ian's not my latest crush. Seriously, he wants to meet you. Do you have one of your business cards?"

I always carried business cards with me, especially to Poppy's Hollywood parties. I hoped to break into the A-listers and dreamed of becoming the "it" designer. So far, my business saw mild success, but I had yet to work on a big director's or actor's home.

Pulling a card out of my pocket, I fluttered it in front of her face. "Okay, stalker lady, if this guy is still around, take me to him."

"Here. Use this on your nose. It's shiny." Poppy handed me a small compact and to please her, I powdered my straight nose, wiped a black glob of mascara from beneath my blue-eyed lashes, and slicked on strawberry-flavored lip gloss. My dark hair was ruffled, giving me a slight bedhead look.

"Have you got a comb? My hair is a mess."

"It looks good. You know, sexy messy, like one of those Victoria's Secret models."

I rolled my eyes again. I was about as far from a Victoria's Secret model as you could get. My wavy hair fell just above my bra line when it was down, which was rarely. I was about five seven and currently wore a size eight, which was thin for me. However, in LA, a size eight was pretty much comparable to a rhinoceros when a majority of the women prancing around wore a size two. Poppy, her patience finally at an end, snapped the compact shut, grabbed my hand, and dragged me into the party mob to search for the elusive Ian.

Ian apparently wasn't that elusive; Poppy ran him to the ground at the bar. All I could see was a head of dark, wavy hair and an incredible set of broad shoulders. His back was to us, and he was engaged in a conversation with a sylph-like creature barely wearing a white dress.

I jerked back from Poppy's grasping hand. "I don't think now is a good time. He's busy talking with someone. Maybe I'll meet him later tonight."

"C'mon. Don't be a chicken. Mr. O'Connor. Ian, yoohoo." Poppy waved a hand, her bracelets jingling merrily.

Ian turned and caught Poppy's eye. She crooked her black polished finger, and, much to my surprise, he disengaged himself from the sylph and strolled our way.

Taking a gander at Ian from the front was even better than seeing him from the back. He was one of the many "beautiful people" inhabiting the LA-Hollywood scene. I couldn't see the color of his eyes in the gloom, but the face was well worth looking at. A chiseled jaw and strong cheekbones flexed as he took a drink from the dark beer bottle and licked his lips. He clearly worked out on a regular basis, because his pectorals were perfectly formed and part of a tattoo peeked out from beneath the tight blue T-shirt, which clung to a rock-hard bicep. The air pressure surrounding me dropped, and my mouth went arid as his six-foot-plus frame approached.

"Ian O'Connor, meet my good friend Sophia Hartland, designer extraordinaire."

I blushed at Poppy's intro and subtly wiped a sweaty hand on my pants before taking his warm, caressing grip.

"It's lovely to meet you, designer extraordinaire." He spoke with a slight Irish brogue. He held my hand a moment longer than necessary.

Oh, lord, it wasn't enough that the looks made my heart speed up; the accent was going to put me over the edge. I could see why Poppy was crushing on this dude. I cleared my throat. "You, too, Mr. O'Connor. Poppy's a big fan of your show. She was telling me all about it."

"What about Sophia Hartland? Do you watch my show?" He flashed a perfect, white, toothy Hollywood grin.

I shook my head. "No, I don't care for cop shows."

That got a rumbly laugh. "Ouch. You're the quite the foil to an actor's ego."

Oh, geez. I grimaced. Twenty seconds with this guy and I'd insulted him. I was completely thrown off my game and saying whatever popped into my head. Generally, I had more tact. I knew better at these swanky parties. I needed to be all smiles and ingratiating to get more clients. Unfortunately, toad-eating didn't come naturally to me.

"Sorry. What network is it on? I'll set my DVR to record it. I'm sure I'll love it." I glanced around for Poppy to save me from myself.

She must have wandered off or been called away. Suddenly, I was in a crowded room one on one with this handsome Irish thespian, making an utter fool of myself.

"No, no. Don't apologize. Your first answer was best." His chuckling died down.

"Umm … listen, Poppy said you liked the art deco theme I put together. So … um … here's my card." I thrust the little piece of cardstock at him. Yikes, this was so unusual for me. I never lost my cool over a guy, especially an actor. I mean come on, an actor? What was it was about this dude that was making me behave like a stuttering idiot?

"That'd be grand. I just moved into a new place and figure it needs a lady's touch, so I could have a fancy party like this." His Irish accent pulled out the a's and rolled around in a singsong lilt.

I was relieved to be on a topic where I couldn't fail. "Sure. I'd love to see your place and work with you to create a luxurious space that makes you feel comfortable and yet is great for entertaining. If you want to give me a call, we can set up an initial consultation. I can see your home, and we can determine your style."

He smirked. "Not sure I've got a style, luv."

Back on my A-game, I put on my ingratiating business smile. "Oh, everyone has a style. Sometimes it just needs to be developed and refined. Maybe you're right, and a lady's touch is just what you need." I lightly tapped his solid forearm.

A very tall, very thin Barbie doll blonde with long, flat-ironed hair, wearing a strapless red dress and five-inch heels minced up and cooed at us. "Ian, honey, a group of us are gathering in the billiard room to play pool. Come play with us." She pouted. The way she hung on Ian's arm shouted possessive girlfriend, and the glare she sent my way declared, "hands off."

"Who's this?" Barbie simpered.

"Tanqueray, this is Sophia."

Tanqueray? Really? I did a mental head slap.

Tanqueray thrust an empty champagne glass into my hand. "Sophia, why don't you be a sweetheart and get me a refill. Can you bring it to the billiard room?"

"Hold up, Tanqueray. Sophia's an interior designer. She's not the waitress."

Barbie doll eyed my black pants, sturdy black shoes, and tailored white button-down, which clearly identified me as one of the wait staff. Her eyebrow rose in disdain.

I stuck on a honeyed smile. "Actually, I am working tonight. I help Poppy when she's short on staff." I laid the champagne glass on a passing waiter's tray and shifted my gaze back to Tanqueray, speaking directly to her with my faux smile.

"Tanqueray, Tommy the bartender is right behind you," I pointed over her shoulder. "*He* can get you whatever you need."

She made a tsking sound as her jaw dropped. Dismissing her, my eyes locked back to Ian. A muscle twitched at the corner of his mouth, and an eyebrow rose. *Oh crap.* I couldn't tell if he was irritated or amused by my dismissal of his girlfriend. I decided I'd better try to make nice and get the hell out of his presence before producing any further *faux pas*.

"Mr. O'Connor, why don't I put together a tray from the buffet and have it sent to the billiard room? It was nice meeting you." With that, I turned on my heel and strode out of sight.

Ten minutes later Poppy found me in the kitchen banging my head against the pantry door.

"Hey, Soph, what's wrong? Why are you abusing the pantry?"

"I royally screwed that up. This could have been my big chance to get into the Hollywood crowd."

"Uh-oh. What happened?"

"I allowed Ian's girlfriend to get under my skin and I was rude to her, right in front of him. I don't think he was impressed." Clunk, clunk went my head.

"Okay, honey. Stop that. You're going to leave a bruise on your forehead." She pulled me away. "C'mon. It couldn't have been that bad."

I explained our conversation.

"Ugh. Tanqueray? Seriously?" Poppy peered at me.

"Seriously."

"Gee whiz, I would've given Ian more credit than to date a woman named Tanqueray. I mean really, who the hell names their kid after a bottle of gin?" Her throaty laugh lightened my mood.

"It's probably a stage name. She looks like a slasher." Slasher is the title Poppy and I'd given to the hundreds of wannabe model slash actresses who crawled the streets of LA like cockroaches.

"Don't beat yourself up over it. There are other Hollywood schmoozers here. Why don't you take half an hour to do some networking? I'm sure you'll score a new client."

So, I handed out five more cards. Two were to Hollywood spouses, one to the wife of a producer and the other to a director. The rest ended up in the clutches of trophy girlfriends, what Poppy and I called hangers-on, also known as "entourage" to bigwigs, the people actually making the money. I didn't hold high hopes of obtaining an actual client out of anyone except possibly one of the trophy girls.

Poppy sent me home around two in the morning when the party had wound down to about two dozen older guests. All the young starlets and actors gathered their entourages around midnight and moved onto the latest "it" club to see and be seen. The maneuverings of the Hollywood grind made me glad I wasn't trying to become a slasher. There was too much relying on looks, weight, and whether or not you were liked by certain producers and directors. I was content to have my business, good friends, and my dog. Anything else was overrated. Or at least that's what I liked to tell myself.

Chapter 2

Monday morning I sat in front of my computer doing the thing I hated most about my job: paperwork. Paperwork consisted of tracking all my receipts, inputting hours, and billing clients. It also meant reviewing my subcontractors' hours and paying them. Math wasn't one of my stronger subjects in school, and I thanked God on a regular basis for calculators and computer programs that tabulated everything into precise little columns for you. With a sigh, I typed in the last numbers and closed out of the program. My reading glasses clattered on the black lacquered table as I flipped them off and rubbed my eyes. Stretching, I leaned back in my ugly ergonomic desk chair, put my bare feet up, and rubbed my neck to release the tension knots.

The peace was interrupted by my cell phone ring, and I answered automatically without looking at the caller ID. "Hello, Hartland Interior Designs."

"Sophia, luv, is that you?" The sexy Irish accent played across the phone lines, sending shivers down my spine.

My chair slammed back down onto four legs, and I promptly dropped the phone. *Crap!* "Ian! Just a minute!" I fumbled, shoving the chair back, and scrambled to get the cell, which had skidded along the hardwood floor underneath my desk. Sirius, my black Lab, sensing a game, jumped up to get in on the action. Tail wagging and barking, he thrust under the desk next to me in search of the toy. "Ian, I'm coming! Minor technical difficulties. Don't hang up!" I shoved Sirius back, taking a few excited licks along the way, and finally found the red mobile in the far corner behind the wastebasket. "Hello, are you still there?" I held it to my ear. Fortunately, it hadn't landed upside down and hung up on him.

"Still here, luv."

As I clambered out from underneath the desk, I came up too early and cracked my skull on the underside. "Oof!"

"Is everything okay? Maybe I should ring back later."

"No, no. It's fine." *When did my life turn into a Lucy skit?* Rubbing my head, I gave up trying to play it cool and decided to level with him. "Sorry about that. The phone slipped out of my hand and slid into the deepest dark corner under my desk, and I'm such a klutz I whacked my head crawling out from underneath it." I sucked in a breath and worked to get my act together. "Enough about me, what can I do for you, Mr. O'Connor?"

"Why so formal, Sophia? I prefer you call me Ian."

I swore I heard laughter in his voice. *Great, he probably thinks I'm a total dork.*

"Okay, Ian, then please call me Sophie. Only my mom calls me Sophia, and when she does, it usually means I'm in trouble."

"Are you trouble, Sophie?"

The opening was the size of a Mack truck, and I drove on through. "I can be trouble. Are you looking for some?" I said in a sultry voice.

"Are you flirting with me?"

I sat up straighter. *What was I thinking? This is a potential client, not a date! An actor for crying out loud.*

"I apologize. That was inappropriate. Are you calling to set up a consultation?" I crossed my fingers.

There was a pause. "Ah, back to business I see. Very well. Yes, I'd like to set up a consultation."

"Great." I kept my professional voice on while bouncing like a kid in my chair. "When were you thinking? I have some dates open next week." I swiveled back to the desk and tapped open the calendar on my iPad.

"Well, the sooner the better. My manager told me to hire a publicist. When the publicist came by the other day, she said I need to fix the house so it looks like a grown-up lives here."

"Ouch. Did you hire her?"

His laughter tumbled across the line, sending shivers across my shoulders. "No. She's right, though. I moved from a three-bedroom flat I shared with another bloke, and I don't have much furniture. Now I have this big house, I guess I need to fill it with the required toggery. Isn't that the American way?"

I smiled at that. "Yes. You're right. We Americans like our stuff."

"So, where should we meet?"

"I'll come to your house. We'll look at what needs to be done. I'll bring my portfolio so you can see some of the things I've designed. We'll discuss my fee structure, and if you're interested in what I have to say, I'll start drawing up the plans."

"Sounds good, luv."

My toes curled at the way he called me love. "How about next Wednesday? Say six?"

"Can you make it seven?"

"Seven it is. Why don't you text me your address?"

"Sure. See you on Wednesday … Sophie." He rang off.

I stared at my phone for a few minutes, still unable to believe Ian O'Connor actually called me, and I was going to meet him. He could be my next client. *Booyah!*

Uh oh, I forgot to apologize for insulting Tanqueray. I smacked my forehead. Undoubtedly, I would to run into her. It was even possible that she'd have a say in Ian's decorative choices. Criminy, I was going to have to play nice. It really chapped my ass, having to pretend to respect people like that. Was I ever going to survive in this skinny, botoxed, lip-inflated town?

I called Poppy to tell her the good news.

She answered on the third ring. "What's up, girlfriend?"

"Ian O'Connor called, and I have a meeting with him next week. If he likes my ideas, he might hire me," I said in one big rush.

"Ian, the guy from the party whose girlfriend you insulted? The hottie on *LA Heat?*"

My mood deflated slightly at the girlfriend insult reminder. "Yes, the hottie on *LA Heat.*"

Poppy squealed on the other end. "When are we doing a drive-by?"

"Poppy! He's a potential client. We're not stalking him."

"But you have his address."

"He texted it to me. We're meeting at his house."

"So, we could accidently drive by."

"He lives in the hills of Bel Air. There's no way we'd just be 'driving by.'"

"You're no fun. Where's your sense of adventure?"

"I left my sense of adventure behind after my stinkin' ex-husband cheated on me." I sighed, "Sorry, girlfriend, it's strictly business with Ian. This is one drive-by we aren't doing."

"Have you watched his show at least?"

"Crap. No, I forgot. I should probably do that. What night is it on?"

"I can't believe you haven't watched it yet. His Ryder character is a tough as nails, former Navy Seal with a deep conflicted past. It's on Friday nights at nine. You should check it out."

"I'll set the DVR so I can have an idea what he's doing."

"He's totally hot right now. I read in one of the rags that Ian's being considered to play the next James Bond."

I let that one stew in my brain for a moment. "Wouldn't it be cool if I could say I decorated a James Bond house? I wonder if he likes it shaken or stirred."

"I'll be he likes it hot and heavy and up against the wall."

"Poppy!" I giggled. "You're so crude."

"Don't tell me you haven't thought about getting into that boy's pants. I watched your reaction to him at the party. I don't blame you. He's one fine-looking man."

"I hate to burst your bubble, but it's strictly business. Besides, I don't have time for games with a player like him."

"Girlfriend, one of these days you're going to have to get back onto the dating wagon. You know, if you don't get some action, things'll shrivel up down there. I read about it in a magazine."

A gurgle of disbelief burst out. "You're so full of it. My lady parts are just fine. Don't you worry about me."

She snorted. "Whatever. This could be your ticket into the big leagues."

"So, basically, what you're saying is, I'd better not screw this up?"

"Exactly. Which means you'll have to play nice with that Barbie character."

"Tanqueray. Don't remind me. I wonder if she'll be at the meeting."

"I don't know. Listen, I've got to run, but you owe me a drink. I've got Sunday night open, how does that work for you? We can plan your strategy to deal with the skinny, blonde Tanqueray."

I scrolled through my calendar. "Sunday sounds good. Where should we meet?"

"Tres Hermanos. Seven thirty."

"See you then."

• • •

Sunday arrived sunny and warm, reaching the low seventies. I luxuriated in my Sundays since it was the only day of the week I refused to work. The difficulty with having a home business was it was easy to become a seven-day-a-week workaholic. About three years ago, I was working every day and almost forgot my sister's wedding. If my mom hadn't called the night before the rehearsal dinner to find out what time I was arriving, I would have missed my flight. As it was, I rearranged two client meetings, threw clothes in my bag, and purchased a wedding gift on the way to the airport. So now client meetings were off limits. If I shopped, it was for my own pleasure, and I never answered the phone or e-mails. Everything waited until Monday. In the morning, Sirius and I took a long walk through our mid-century community in Lake Balboa. He sniffed and peed on everything from mailboxes to trees. I grocery shopped in the afternoon then lazily lounged on the back brick patio painting my toenails and reading a trashy romance novel. The shadows grew long and the light waned. I had decompressed and was ready to enjoy my evening out.

It was Sirius's fault I was late to the restaurant. He chose my fuchsia peep toe pumps for dinner over doggie kibble. It took me an extra fifteen minutes to find a shoe that would satisfy my outfit. In the end, my red jeans and fluttery blue top were paired with lime green wedges, and Sirius was banished to the backyard while I went out.

The scent of sizzling fajitas assailed my nose as I bypassed the hostess station and headed straight for the bar. I approached an open space and my eyes ping-ponged back and forth, searching for Poppy. However, my normally punctual friend wasn't bellied up to the bar, margarita in hand. I parked my stuff, claiming two seats at the far end, and sent a finger wave to the bartender; then I dug around in my purse, searching for my phone to see if Poppy had left a message.

"Excuse me." A petite, dark-haired waitress tapped me on the shoulder.

"Yes?"

"Are you Sophie?"

"Yes, I am."

"Your redheaded friend has a table for you, if you'll please follow me." She gestured over her shoulder.

Well, this was unusual. Normally we declined the tables and spent the evening at the bar, eating chips and drinking our dinner.

I followed the hostess around the corner to an area separated from the main seating.

"Surprise!"

Startled, I stepped back and put a hand to my chest.

A table for eight was set up with party streamers, two pitchers of margaritas, a few open beer bottles, and a Mexican inspired table-scape with a colorful sombrero as the centerpiece. Poppy was wrapped around her latest boyfriend, a biker named Angel, who looked anything but his moniker. He had wild dark hair, brooding eyes, and was perpetually decked out in leather, denim, and black T-shirts. My design assistant, Michelle Murphy, a petite brunette with brown eyes, was a recent college graduate with a degree in English who came to Hollywood with "The Dream" and soon found reality. Although Michelle bore a certain prettiness, her temperament was too sweet, and she couldn't compete with the cut-throat LA starlets. Next to Michelle stood my electrician, Enrique Vargas, with his wife, Sancha, both Puerto Ricans with dark skin and eyes. However, where Enrique's hair was thick and black, Sancha insisted on dying hers red, which faded into magenta tones soon after coloring. Enrique's squat, solid girth came up to my nose and his acne-scarred face held a rugged attraction. Sancha, a round apple-cheeked Latino, stood a few inches shorter than Enrique and taught high school Spanish. Speaking to Sancha were my lanky, sandy-haired general contractor and carpenter, Jack Blumberg and his rotund, bleached blonde wife, Jodie. Jack and Jodie were in their mid-thirties, and Jodie was a stay-at-home mom raising three kids, ages six, eight, and ten. Getting out for an adult evening was a treat for her.

Enrique, or Ricky as I called him, and Jack were indispensable to my business. Ricky had been with me for five years and Jack almost four. They were excellent at their jobs, and on more than one occasion, had bent over backward to meet a time-crunched deadline to satisfy a picky client.

Poppy strode over, handed me a bowl-o-margarita and gave me a one-armed hug to keep our drinks from spilling. "Happy Birthday, Soph!"

"Did we surprise you, *niña*?" Sancha elbowed Poppy out of the way. Her plump be-ringed hands pulled me down to her height for a smack on the lips.

"Yes, you did." I grinned over her head at Poppy. "You really pulled it off this time, my friend. I had no idea."

"I know it's not your birthday yet, but I've got a wedding and a bat mitzvah back to back next weekend, and I figured holding the party early would throw you off the scent."

My thirtieth birthday wasn't until Saturday, and to be honest, I wasn't looking forward to it. Originally, I hoped it would pass quietly into the night without fanfare. However, I appreciated Poppy's effort. This was a fun group of people with whom to celebrate another year.

The waiter appeared with a loaded tray.

"Okay, everyone, take a seat. Dinner has arrived," Poppy hollered above the din of conversation. She placed me at the head of the table and sat directly on my right, with Angel on her other side. Jack sat on my left, and everyone else shuffled into a spot while the waiter laid steaming platters of food down the center of the table. We shared the meal family style. Poppy had ordered a variety of dishes, ranging from quesadillas, tacos, and a massive bowl of refried beans to enchiladas and chile rellenos, all rounded out with fresh chips and salsa. I couldn't have asked for a better surprise party.

Once we filled our plates, I turned to Jack. "Hey, I thought you should know I have a new client consultation planned for Wednesday. It's an actor by the name of Ian O'Connor."

He nodded. "Poppy was telling us about it before you arrived. She says it's the guy who plays Ryder on *LA Heat*. Is that true?"

"Yup. Poppy introduced us at one of her parties."

Jack whistled. "This could be really big for the company."

"I know. What does your schedule look like over the next month?"

"We have a few one- to two-day carpentry jobs on the horizon, and in about two weeks, one of my painting crews will be out of a job if I don't find something soon."

"I'm sure we'll be painting, so I'll get in touch after the consult to let you know."

"That would be great. I hate when I don't have work for the guys." As a general contractor, Jack supplied me with carpenters, painters, dry-wallers, plumbers, and flooring installers.

Jodie, sitting on the other side of Jack, said, "Hey, hey, this is a party. No more work talk. I want to know about Ian, though. That man is smokin'. If you end up working on his house, you better get me an autographed photo." She elbowed her husband.

Jack shook his head, affronted. "I'm not getting my wife some photo of a Hollywood hunk."

"Sophie will get one for me, won't you, Soph?" Her overly made-up eyes glared at her husband as she leaned around him toward me.

Sancha, who sat across from Jodie, spoke up. "Who is this Ian? Why do you want his photo, Jodie? You have a handsome husband. Why you need photos of another man?"

"He's the main character on *LA Heat*."

"The cop show?" Her dark eyes sparked with recognition.

Am I the only one who doesn't watch the show?

"Yes," Jodie responded.

"Which one is he?" Sancha asked.

Poppy leaned past Angel to answer Sancha. "He's the main detective. You know, the hot one, the one with dark hair and blue, blue eyes."

"The one who comes out of the ocean wearing nothing but water and swim trunks during the opening credits," Jodie mooned.

Sancha started fanning her face with a dinner napkin. "Oh my. *Ese hombre es varonil y muy sexy.* Sophie," she said, "Can you get me a photo, too? Maybe without his shirt on, eh?" She winked.

Ricky, who sat at the foot of the table, got in on the conversation. "Hey, why you need pictures of a half-naked man? You have a handsome husband, too!" He playfully threw Sancha's words back at her.

We laughed, and I promised to get autographed photos for all the ladies.

After dinner, the plates were removed and our waiter brought out a colorful cake. Along with four of his compatriots, they sang "Happy Birthday" in Spanish. At least, I think it was "Happy Birthday." Margaritas flowed down my throat like a river, and at the end of the night, after prolonged hugs and confessions of undying love to all my friends, Enrique and Sancha drove me home.

I vaguely remembered lying in the backseat of Sancha's Toyota singing "These Shoes Were Made for Walking," while doing a soft shoe on the window. In the rear of my mind, I knew the next morning would be painful, but the margaritas accomplished their job well, and I just didn't care. All of a sudden, thirty wasn't looking so bad. I had outstanding friends, and a yummy looking potential client who could help me make it into the big leagues.

Chapter 3

The doorbell tolled through the 1960s architecturally styled home, and I subconsciously wiped a palm down my black linen pants. Gripping a red iPad case, I shifted my Coach tote higher up on my shoulder. It was cool under the covered portico, but nerves made me sweat.

"Get a grip," I whispered down to my pink toenails peeping out of black sandals. I sucked in a lungful of air and consciously made an effort to slow my heartbeat. I was about to do a breath check when the door popped open. My eyes zoomed up to meet Ian's lash-fringed azure gaze. He wore jeans and a snug black T-shirt that outlined the perfection of his chest, and his feet were bare. He held a cell phone to his ear.

"Sophie, excellent timing! C'mon on in. Listen mate, my new decorator showed up, so I've got to bugger off." Ian stood aside to allow me to enter. "Of course she's beautiful, but she's also trouble." Ian winked at me. "She told me so herself. Gotta dash. I'll ring you tomorrow."

My cheeks burned.

"Go find your own decorator, mate. Sophie's mine." He chuckled and hung up. "Cheeky fellow."

The air shifted, and as I passed by, his musky male scent played havoc with my senses. However, the shocking design calamity that met my eyes as I walked through the foyer into the main living space was enough to draw my attention away from the marvelous male specimen sending me a heart-dropping smile. The kitchen had been recently renovated. It held modern stainless appliances, European style cabinetry with clean lines, and recycled green and gray glass countertops. It flowed into a large great room with vaulted ceilings and floor-to-ceiling windows that provided a stunning vista of rocky hills. Unfortunately, the vile color combination was tough to get past. The kitchen was painted neon orange, and when combined with the aqua and red striped wall in the great room and the lime green in the dining room, it was enough to give an epileptic a seizure.

With straight-faced tact I asked, "So, Ian, did you choose the paint colors?"

I always asked new clients this question before making any sort of observations about the current décor. Early in my career, I made an off-hand comment about an unattractive ocher yellow in a client's kitchen; I was mortified when she told me she had chosen it. The client wasn't best pleased with me, and her manner remained chilly throughout the rest of the job. It was a learning experience I refused to repeat.

"Lord luv you, no. After a while, the color gives me a headache. Clearly it's the reason I'm desperate for your help."

"It does seem to be a bit over the top. I wonder what kind of furniture the former owner put with these colors?"

"Wouldn't know." Ian shrugged. "The house was empty when I looked at it. I got a great deal because it had been sitting on the market for a couple of months."

I nodded. "I imagine the color palette was a deterrent to buyers."

"I bought the house because the kitchen was new and because of what's out back. Let me show you."

Ian lightly gripped my upper arm. Tingly feelings shot directly to my belly. He led me through a nine-foot sliding door to reveal a kidney-shaped pool with attached hot tub and splashing river rock fountain. The curved terracotta stained concrete patio was stamped to resemble tile, and it was complemented by an outdoor kitchen complete with grill, sink, double burners, and granite countertops. The kitchen was shaded by a second floor deck. Palm trees and native landscaping completed the resort-inspired oasis. The only furniture on the vast courtyard consisted of a green plastic table with two chairs and a ratty aluminum lounger set up near the pool. How did it hold together under Ian's weight? The new patio seemed at odds with the modernist architecture of the 1960s home, with its sharp lines and blocky construction. However, upon further consideration, the curvature of the pool and veranda softened the angular edges and created a pleasing juxtaposition.

"It's beautiful." I wandered over to the pool, disturbing the water with my fingers. "I assume you want to design an outdoor space for entertaining?" I shaded my eyes as I looked at him.

Ian scratched his five o'clock shadow. "Yes. Do you think we can do something like that?"

"Of course." I smiled. "That's what I'm here for. Why don't we go back inside and talk about what you want, and I'll look over the house and see what we can do."

Ian led me back into the great room. I took a seat on the well-worn couch as he headed into the kitchen.

"Do you want a beer?"

"No, thank you."

"Soda? Orange juice?" He bent over, searching the fridge, while I sat mesmerized by a pair of well-fitting jeans that outlined his fine backside. Ian caught me staring and shot a roguish grin over his shoulder.

My face burned and I dragged my eyes away. "Orange juice will be fine."

While Ian fixed the drinks, I steadied my nerves by getting down to business. I pulled a notebook and pen out of my case, fired up my iPad, and began a rough sketch of the space. Furniture was sparse. Besides the couch, the great room comprised of a stained wooden coffee table, a pathetic standing lamp, and an enormous flat screen TV that sat on a squat, unattractive stand in front of the fireplace.

"Does that fireplace work?"

"I think so." Ian handed me a drink. The couch shifted as he took his seat, and I slid closer to him.

I cleared my throat and put on my professional façade. "I assume the first thing you want is paint."

"Absolutely."

"I see the kitchen cabinetry and appliances are new. Do you want to leave them?"

"Yes."

"As for the great room, you need paint, furniture, lighting, and possibly a built-in for your TV."

"Sure." Ian took a long drink of beer, and my eyes followed his Adam's apple as it bobbed up and down.

"Curtains?" I whispered, cleared my throat, and tried again. "Curtains?"

He nodded. "If you say so."

I smiled. "Let's take a moment to figure out your style, shall we?"

"Like I told you at the party, I don't really have one."

"Well, the kitchen is fairly stylized. Looking beyond the hideous color, do you like its clean, modern lines?"

Ian squinted. "Sure."

"Okay, tell me about this couch; this is not a modern style."

"It's comfortable." He shrugged.

"So you like the comfort of the couch. Do you prefer material or leather sofas?"

"Material. I think."

Either Ian was a man of few words, or decorating was simply beyond his scope of concerns. "Of the things in this room, your TV is likely the most expensive item, so it's important to you?"

Ian glanced around the striped nightmare. "Everything can go, but the TV stays."

I nodded. "And the couch?"

"You can chuck the couch, but you have to replace it with something comfortable. Not leather. Too slippery."

"Is the sofa an important item to you?"

"Hell, yeah! I want to be able to kick my feet up and watch the game with my mates."

The room remained silent as I scribbled some notes. Ian was either going to be one of the easiest clients I'd ever dealt with or one of the hardest. If he truly didn't care, I could design whatever I thought would look good, and he'd go with the flow. It was the clients who didn't know what they wanted that became a challenge. Invariably, there would be a learning curve as they discovered their options. Then they'd spend weeks waffling back and forth and basically becoming a designer's nightmare. "Okay, let's assess what type of relationship we're going to have."

"We're having a relationship?" Ian sat forward with wiggling eyebrows and a cunning grin.

It took all my willpower not to roll my eyes at the immature come-on. Instead, I pushed him back with a firm hand. "A professional relationship. Now, after I present my recommendations, some clients don't want to speak again until the renovations are complete. Others want to shop with me, pick out their tile, paint color, etcetera. Some clients are in between. How involved do you wish to be?"

"I want to pick out the sofa."

"The sofa? That's it?"

"That's all I need."

I evaluated him for a moment. I didn't want to get my hopes up too high, but he was turning into a designer's dream by providing free reign. If only he would keep his flirty, delectable self out of my way, I just might be able to turn this place into something worthy of the cover of *House Beautiful*. The creative juices were already flowing, and the home's potential had me figuratively rubbing my hands in delight. "Hmm … okay, let's get started. Can you help me with some of the measurements?"

We spent the next half hour measuring the room dimensions and the exterior patio before heading upstairs to the master bedroom. "Let me guess, more stripes?"

Ian cringed. "Bright yellow and black. It looked like a bloody bee. I couldn't stand it so I put up this white. Two coats," Ian held up two long fingers, "and you can still see the black paint."

I laughed.

A pair of sliding doors led out to the upper deck, which was empty of furnishings. I poked my head into the *en suite*. "What was the bathroom painted?"

"Black. All of it."

What were the first owners thinking? "It must have been like living in a cave."

Ian snapped his fingers and pointed at me. "Exactly!"

I sat on the bed. The mattress was comfortable, not too firm. "Your mattress seems to be in good shape."

"It better be. I just spent a bleedin' fortune on it." He stood, arms crossed, examining me as I took notes and measured.

"What do you want in your bedroom?" I asked with pen poised.

Ian's eyebrow quirked and his grin was playful. "You."

I rolled my eyes at the blatant flirtation. *Seriously, did this guy just think I'd strip and go for it right now?* "I *mean*, what kind of design do you want? Calm, neutral oasis, Moroccan vibe, Old-world Tuscan? Or do you just want me to come up with something?"

"Hmm," he scratched his chin, "I might like the Tuscan thing. Can you swing that?"

"Honey, I can do anything," I answered in a distracted tone and drifted around the room, scratching fervently on my notebook.

"Anything?" Ian's warm voice murmured over my shoulder, startling me.

The pen sailed across the room as my shoulder made contact with Ian's granite jaw, shooting pain down my arm. His teeth closed with an audible snap.

"Yeowch!" I rubbed my shoulder and turned. "Oh, Ian, I'm so sorry. I didn't realize you were there. Are you okay?"

Ian shifted his chin back and forth with a rueful grin. "No problem, luv. All my fault. I guess I snuck up on you. How about you? Okay?"

"I'll be fine."

We stared at each other, rubbing our injured parts. A crackle of tension sliced through the air, and a chill zipped down my spine. My nipples hardened to pebbles, pressing against the thin silk of my white blouse. Ian's light manner abruptly changed, his gaze shifted to my breasts, and his eyes darkened. Nervously, I licked my lips and my breath hitched. Ian's gaze returned to clash with mine, and he stepped toward me. His movement snapped me out of my erotic trance. *This isn't a date; it's business.* I gave myself a mental head-shake. Pulling the notebook to my chest, I hustled out of Ian's bedroom.

"Why don't we finish up downstairs?" I spoke over my shoulder.

It was a few minutes before Ian followed. He retrieved his half-empty beer from the coffee table and chugged it before joining me on a stool at the kitchen counter, where I had materials spread out for his review. I showed him samples of my work and determined that he liked a variety of styles with clean lines; however, not at the expense of comfort. Then we talked about his budget and my fee schedule.

Closing the iPad cover, I wrapped up the consultation. "So, here's what happens next. I'll come up with a design plan for you to review, and if you like it, we'll move forward. It'll take about a week. How does next Friday look?"

Ian pulled a phone out of his pocket and scrolled through his apps. "I should be free Friday any time after six."

"How about six thirty?"

"Six thirty it is." His thumbs tapped in our appointment.

I packed up my materials and then Ian escorted me to the front door.

"I'll see you Friday." I offered my hand.

Ian's large warm hand enveloped mine, and with a light tug, drew me closer. The yeasty scent of beer drifted past my nostrils, as he leaned in to brush a delicate kiss upon my cheek. A breath whispered against my ear. "I look forward to it, Sophie."

"Umm … me, too," I mumbled.

I was already out the door when I turned back to find Ian scrutinizing me with narrowed eyes. The look disappeared in a blink, and I wondered if I'd imagined it.

"Yes?"

"Um … I … uh … I just wanted to ask, how many other designers will you be interviewing?"

His eyebrows scrunched into puzzlement. "Why would I interview other designers? I thought you were my designer."

"Well, some people like to have multiple decorators present them with ideas. Like an audition."

"Nope. I want you. That's it."

I blinked. There were so many meanings underlying such a simple statement. "Okay then. I look forward to working with you, and I promise I won't let you down."

"I don't think that's possible, Sophie." He said my name like it was a caress.

As I exited Ian's gate, I let out a hoot of glee and called Poppy on my Bluetooth.

She answered on the second ring. "What's up, girl? How was your meeting with Mr. Hottie?"

"He hired me," I squealed. "He's not even interviewing anyone else. I'm it!"

"Of course you are. You're the best. He'd be crazy to want anyone else."

"I'm so thrilled. This could be my ticket into the big leagues. If I do an awesome job, maybe he'll introduce me to his friends. Maybe he'll give me a recommendation."

"That's fantastic! I'm sure he'll recommend you. So, tell me about Ian."

"What about him?"

"What was he like? Dish."

"Oh, him." I swished my hand. "He's a big flirt. Don't get me wrong, he is super hot and he makes my knees weak, but you know his type. He flirts with everything in a skirt."

"He didn't flirt with me," Poppy said in a sad voice.

"Sure he did. He's gorgeous, and I bet every woman who crosses his path falls all over him. No wonder Tanqueray was so possessive at the party. She probably spent the night fending off every woman in sight. I kind of feel sorry for her. He'd be a hard man to pin down."

"Was she there?"

"No."

"Does she live there? Was any of her stuff there?"

I paused to review the house in my mind. Only one toothbrush in the bathroom, no Tampax boxes, no women's clothes hanging in the closet, and no scent of perfume lingered in the house. "I don't think so. At least I didn't see signs of a woman living with him, but the house is pretty Spartan."

"So, it must not be too serious."

"Maybe not."

"Tell me about the flirting."

"Oh, you know, little innuendos, that kind of thing."

"No, I don't know. Details."

"He told his friend on the phone that I was beautiful and to go find his own designer. You know … flattery. And there was a moment … " I mumbled.

"A moment?"

"It was nothing."

"Tell me about the moment."

"We were in his bedroom … "

"His bedroom." Poppy drawled.

"Yes." I firmly tamped down her innuendo. "As in, he wants me to decorate his bedroom."

"Okay, then what?"

"Then … I don't know… there was a moment of … tension."

"Sexual tension?"

I let out a deep sigh. "Yes."

"Whoop, there it is! What happened next?"

"Nothing!" I bellowed.

"What do you mean nothing?"

"Just what I said. There was a moment and nothing happened. I went back downstairs to work up some ideas."

"I think he's attracted to you."

"I think he's into Barbie doll, and flirting is his natural form of communication with women."

A deep sigh blew at me. "If you say so. When is your next appointment?"

"Next Friday."

"Be sure to wear something sexy, like a push-up bra, and put your red platform pumps on. They make your legs look long."

"Poppy! It's a business meeting, not a date. Besides, he's with Tanqueray."

"All's fair in love and war."

• • •

A decidedly randy grin split his face as he watched Sophie's car roll away from the gate. She'd looked even better to him today than when they'd first met at the party. The sexy sandals she wore made her taller, and he'd enjoyed watching her backside as she'd minced around his house with her serious demeanor and cute glasses, taking notes and scribbling down measurements. For the most part he didn't give a damn about what she decided to do about fixing up his home. As long as the noxious colors were neutralized and a comfortable couch set up so he could have a place to kick back and watch the game, he'd be happy.

He closed the door and returned to the living area where her empty drink sat on the kitchen counter. A red lipstick mark made a U shape along the rim. He fingered the glass. When they met at the party there'd been so many people pulling him in different directions, he'd been surprised when the planner flagged him down to introduce Sophie. He never considered hiring an interior designer; he just figured he'd hire some painters, buy some furniture and maybe a picture or two to spruce up the place. However, when her friend thrust Sophie's curvaceous body forward with all of that wonderful hair tumbling around her shoulders, and he looked into her nervous blue eyes, his body had immediately reacted, and he suddenly realized an interior designer was *exactly* what he needed. She'd intrigued him even more when she'd been forthright and honest about never seeing his show. So different from the ego strokes he was accustomed to hearing from most people.

She was different from most of the girls he usually dated. First of all, she had curves where a woman should have them, and they clearly weren't fake. It was a trait he'd been admiring the entire evening. He hoped it meant that she ate like a normal person. He was weary of dating rail-thin women whose idea of a meal consisted of water and two bites of salad and a cigarette to dull the appetite.

Secondly, she'd successfully dodged all of his advances. Even in his bedroom, when the sexual tension had crackled between them, her mouth slightly ajar and her eyes gazing hungrily at him. For sure, he thought he'd get a kiss from those luscious red lips, but something spooked her, and she'd skittered out of the room like a ghost crab on the beach. It would be his mission to find out why she fled at the slightest provocation, even though he could tell she was attracted to him.

He wiped the lipstick from the glass with his thumb. She was smart too; calculating measurements in her head and talking about different architecture and design features that sounded like Greek to him. Although, that Tuscan thing she mentioned seemed intriguing. She ran her own company and seemed to be fairly successful, not an easy task. Clearly, Sophie was going to be more of a challenge than he'd expected. Unlike women in his past, she didn't throw herself at him, nor take advantage when he made it abundantly clear that he was interested. Wooing women came easy to him, in large part, because of his looks. He was confident it wouldn't take long before Sophie wasn't just decorating his house by day, but keeping him warm in bed at night. After all, he could be as stubborn as the next Irishman; he'd just have to change his tactics a little bit to get what he wanted.

Chapter 4

"Squawk! Pick up the phone. Come on, pick up the phone." The high-pitched whistle of my mother's African Grey parrot, Reggie, woke me from a wonderful dream. I'd been sitting on a beach, where a fine-looking Polynesian brought me a fluffy drink and offered to apply suntan lotion.

"Squawk! Pick up the phone. Come on, pick up the phone." I rolled over and slapped my hand around the bedside table in search of the offending noise.

"Woof, woof!" Sirius decided to get in on the action. A wet nose pushed against my arm as his tail ricocheted back and forth between the bed and wall. Thwack, thwack, thwack.

Originally, I thought it would be amusing to use one of Reggie's clever sayings as my mom's ringtone. At 7:07 on a Saturday morning, its charm was lost to me.

I wiped slobber off my hand onto Sirius's head, which calmed him down and rasped, "Hello, Mom."

"Happy, happy birthday! Happy, happy birthday! Happy birthday, my dearest Sophia. Today you are thirty. Wake up, sleepyhead." Dorothy Hartland's sunny voice bounced off I don't know how many satellites to bring me my regularly scheduled birthday greeting. Every year, without fail, Mom called at exactly the time I was born on October second. She did the same to my sister on her birthday. Luckily for Holly, she was born at 2:23 in the afternoon. Luckily for me, Arizona didn't observe daylight saving, or the phone would be ringing an hour earlier.

Scrubbing the sleep from my eyes, I yawned. "Thanks, Mom."

"Did you get my card?" Mom's voice was anxious.

"Yes, it came yesterday, but I haven't opened it yet."

"Well, there's a gift card for Nordstrom in there, so go buy yourself something nice."

I yawned again. "Gee, Mom, thanks. That's great." My mother might have some annoying quirks, but she had a generous heart. The Nordstrom card was liable to be $200 or $300, and worth quite a bit of her receptionist paycheck.

"What are you doing for your birthday?"

"Nothing much. Poppy held a surprise party for me last week, so I don't have any plans."

There was a pause. "So … are you seeing anybody?"

I cringed. It must have been a record, a whole sixty seconds before she asked about men. "No, Mom. I'm not seeing anyone right now."

"What about that nice man who took you out to the movies last month?"

Puzzled, I yawned. "I don't know who you're talking about."

"Last month. You told me you went to the movies with some friends."

I combed my brain to determine whom she referenced. "Greg?"

"Yes, Greg. What happened to him?"

"Mom, Greg was dating my assistant, Michelle. A bunch of us went out to see the new Matt Damon movie. It wasn't a date."

"Well, if Michelle isn't dating him anymore, why don't you ask him out?"

"Maybe because he's at least a half dozen years younger than I am and comes up to my chin."

"Don't knock short men. I hear they can be very generous in bed." Her voice dropped to a whisper, "You know, like they're trying to make up for something."

I choked back a laugh. "I'll give it some thought."

"It's been four years since you and Michael divorced."

"Five," I corrected.

"Well, you should find yourself a new man. Sign up on that Internet dating site and find someone who'll take care of you."

After my divorce from Michael, he left me $10,000 in credit card debt, struggling to pay the mortgage, without health insurance, and my self-confidence in tatters. I removed myself from the dating-go-round and determined never to "allow a man to take care of me" again. I was able to take care of myself just fine, thank you.

"Work's real busy right now. I don't have time for dating."

"You can't snuggle up with your laptop at night, Sophia. Besides, you're thirty. Don't you want to try again to have a child? Your eggs are starting to get dusty."

I ground my teeth. First Poppy, now Mom. *Why is everyone suddenly so worried about my reproductive nether regions?*

"Are *you* dating anyone?"

Mom's gusty sigh came across the line. "No. But Peggy wants me to get on that new dating site Ourtime.com, you know for fifty and older. I just don't know if I'm ready."

My gut twisted with remorse for putting her on the spot, but I knew if Mom found someone else to focus her maternal urges on, she'd leave me alone. So, I pressed onward. "Daddy's been gone for two years, and you're only fifty-seven. Maybe Peggy's on the right track. I bet a lot of men on Ourtime are looking for companionship."

"Don't you believe it. Men at that age only want two things: a woman to clean their house and Viagra sex."

"Mom!"

"Besides, men on those sites aren't looking for women their own age. They're looking for a plastically enhanced woman twenty years younger than they are. I'll be getting messages from seventy year olds with saggy butts, a hearing aid, and prostate issues."

I couldn't contain my laughter. She was undoubtedly correct. Immediately after Michael and I split, I perused the singles ads, thinking I'd find someone to have meaningless sex with, to get back at him for cheating. The women sought men in their age range or slightly older. The men searched for women younger and in "fit condition."

"All right, Mom. Let's make a deal. I won't bother you about Ourtime, and you stop bothering me about dating."

"But, Sophie, you're young. Like any mother, I only want what's best for you. Don't you want to give me grandkids before I get too old to play with them?"

"Mom," my voice warned.

She heaved a sigh. "Okay, I'll stop."

"Besides, you can look to Holly for more grandkids."

"Mmmhmm. Perhaps."

That sounded loaded. My sister had a beautiful little girl named Eva. Mom doted on Eva, and I had hoped her birth would keep my mother's constant matchmaking at bay.

"Speaking of Holly, have you heard from her?" Mom asked.

"No, not recently."

"When was the last time you two spoke?"

"Like on the phone?"

"Yes."

"I don't know. Maybe a few weeks. Why? When was the last time you spoke to her?"

"Two months." My mother's voice was solemn.

"Two months? Haven't you called?" I was shocked. Mom and I spoke every week, and I assumed she and Holly did, too. Now that I thought about it, I wasn't at all sure when I'd last spoken with my sister. Between Twitter, Facebook, and texts, it was easy to keep up with someone's life with little or no verbal interaction. However, my mother didn't text, wasn't on Facebook and thought Twitter was a bird call.

"Of course, I called." She sounded indignant. "Every time I call I get the answering machine. Except the one time I got Omar.

Eva was crying. Omar said it wasn't a good time, but Holly never called back."

"Well, I'm sure she's just busy. Eva's a two year old, and you can remember what a handful a toddler can be."

Mom was silent.

"Right?"

"If you say so."

"What aren't you telling me?"

"Nothing. It's just … I can't put my finger on it, but the last time I visited things were odd."

"Odd in what way?"

"It started out with Holly suggesting I stay at a hotel because Eva wasn't sleeping through the night."

"Really? Where did you stay?"

"At Omar's hotel. He got me a nice suite and picked up the tab."

"Oh." Mom was probably overreacting. Omar worked security for a swanky hotel and casino in Vegas. He probably wanted his privacy. Mom could be a little overpowering. "Did you use the spa?"

"Yes, as a matter of fact, I got a massage and mani-pedi. Anyway, Holly seemed jumpy and strange."

"Perhaps she was sleep deprived."

"That's what I figured. Time and again, I told her I could take Eva to the pool at the hotel and let her have an afternoon to nap. She wouldn't have it. One day I puttered around the house baking and preparing a nice dinner, and she did get a nap on the couch, but it's like she wouldn't trust me alone with Eva."

"I'm sure she was just exhausted. When did you go?"

"At Easter during Eva's birthday."

Easter was six months ago. "You haven't been back since?"

"No. I was planning to go out at Labor Day, but Holly never returned my calls."

It sounded strange. On the other hand, Holly was a very sweet person and didn't like conflict. If she was overburdened by her job, toddler, and new marriage, it suited her personality to avoid my mother's probing questions.

"Tell you what, I bet she'll call to wish me a happy birthday today. If she doesn't, I'll call her tomorrow and check up on her. Okay?"

"Thanks, sweetie, I appreciate that. Have a relaxing birthday."

Sad to say the rest of my birthday was uneventful. I spent the morning shopping for one of my smaller clients who was redesigning her master bedroom. In the afternoon, I tackled the design plan for Ian's main living area. Like a teenager waiting for a boy to call, I checked my phone hourly waiting for a text, e-mail, or phone message from my sister. Nothing. Friends called and Facebooked with well-wishes, and I missed a call from Ian confirming our next meeting while I chased Sirius around the house in an effort to rescue one of my favorite ballet flats from his slobbery mouth. The late afternoon still brought nothing from my sister. I wasn't overly concerned by the evening because I figured she'd call after the baby was in bed for the night.

At half past eight, with a glass of wine and a bag of potato chips, I hunkered down in front of the TV and fired up *LA Heat*. The program followed the usual cop show formula. Jodie was right; the credits showed a beautiful beefcake shot of Ian, a.k.a Ryder, coming out of the ocean wearing tight board shorts dripping wet. I paused the recording for a moment to enjoy the perfection of his hairless six-pack abs. Ryder's colleagues included a curvaceous Hispanic detective named Maria, who reminded me of Selma Hayek, and a pair of uniformed cops, Birk and Diego, who provided comic relief. As for the episode, it was fascinating to watch Ian drop his Irish accent and become an American. After one episode, I was hooked. Believe it or not, my client almost looked better on TV than in person. Ryder's personality came off as a high-risk, larger-than-life cop. Additionally, the director must have used special camera tricks to highlight Ian's aqua eyes, giving them a luminosity that popped off the screen. I fell asleep in front of a *Friends* rerun around eleven thirty.

The whiffling of a cold nose in my ear awoke me the next morning. I rolled over to be greeted by Sirius's happy doggie eyes; he licked his chops and lifted my arm with his snout. This was dog speak for one of a few things: "pet me," "get up, I need to go out," or "feed me." Since it was almost nine, I interpreted it as, "I need to go out." Stiffly, I rolled off the couch and shuffled to the back door. Sirius barely took two steps off the back patio before lifting his leg, and our morning routine began. I poured kibble into his silver dog dish to the gurgle of the coffeemaker. Once the dog was fed, I dropped a piece of bread in the toaster and browsed the fridge for a fruit product that wasn't growing a green beard. No such luck, so I settled for a cup of yogurt—a food I only ate when desperate. While I slurped down the slimy breakfast, I scrolled through my calls and texts once again, looking for something, anything from my sister. Nothing.

A niggling concern started to itch at the back of my brain—Mom's anxieties must have been rubbing off. At ten, I called Holly. Her home phone went straight to voice mail. I hung up and called her cell.

"Hello," she answered breathlessly after the first ring.

"Holly?"

"Soph! Oh damn, I forgot to call yesterday didn't I? Happy birthday, big sis! Sorry I'm late."

"It's okay. I just wanted to check on you. How's everything going?"

"Oh, you know. It's fine. Eva's growing up so fast. Walking and talking."

"Is she sleeping through the night now?"

"Eva? Oh yes, she's a good sleeper."

I was stumped. "Mom told me she was having trouble sleeping when she visited at Easter."

Holly paused. "Right. The doctor said it was night terrors. All toddlers go through it."

"Good, good. So, how are things at the gallery?"

"Oh. I quit the gallery."

"I thought you were still part-time."

"No. Omar felt it would be better for Eva if I stayed home with her until she goes to school."

I was stunned. My sister loved her job at the gallery and was really upset when they cut her back to part-time soon after she married Omar. "I thought your job was important to you. What do you think, Holly?"

"Oh, I agree with Omar. What's best for Eva is what's most important. You don't have kids. You don't understand."

I felt as though I'd been sucker punched. During my divorce from Michael, I'd been relieved my one pregnancy had ended in a miscarriage. It was hard enough terminating the marriage; I couldn't imagine tearing a family apart and becoming a single mother. However, it didn't mean I never wanted children.

Realization must have hit her. "Soph, I'm sorry. That came out wrong. That's not what I meant. Seriously, I'm really sorry."

"I know what you meant. Forget it."

There was silence. I had a strange feeling my sister was holding back.

"Listen, Omar just drove up. I gotta go. We'll talk later." Click.

I stared at the phone, shocked by my sister's rudeness. I couldn't decide whether Mom was right and something strange was going on with Holly, or if she was just being incredibly selfish and inconsiderate.

An hour later, "Squawk! Pick up the phone. Come on, pick up the phone," interrupted my commune with the fridge as the last unidentifiable vegetable landed in the trash with a satisfying splat.

"Hi, Mom."

"Did you talk with your sister?"

"I sure did."

"And?"

"And nothing. She's fine. Just busy with Eva. By the way, did you know she quit the gallery?"

"Hmm, I wondered. At Easter she told me she took time off."

"Mom, what exactly are you worried about?"

No answer.

"Mom?"

"I don't know exactly. I thought she might be taking something."

"Taking something?"

"Her behavior was jumpy and erratic. Omar watched her and she got frazzled. I'm worried she's taking drugs."

"Drugs? Are you kidding? What kind of drugs?"

"I don't know. I thought maybe some prescription meds."

Mom's suspicions seemed so far out of left field, I had a hard time believing them.

"Have you called Omar directly?"

"No. I've thought about it but don't know what to say. Omar never really warmed up to me. I feel like he puts up with me because I'm Holly's mom."

I'm embarrassed to say, my relationship with Omar was non-existent. I'd seen him rarely and remembered him as a medium height, stocky, guy with mahogany hair and deep-set eyes so dark they were almost black. He worked odd hours at the casino and was a bit straight-laced for my taste. "Okay. Mom. I'll start calling her regularly. I've just landed an important account, so it's impossible for me to get away right now. I'll make some plans to fly out in a month or so. The next time I talk to Holly, I'll make sure to tell her to call you."

Chapter 5

"Hello?"

"Hi, it's Sophie Hartland. I have an appointment with Ian O'Connor." Her voice sounded tinny and distorted through the new security call box at the bottom of the drive.

"Sophie, come on up." Ian replied and pressed the gate release.

Taping for him had wrapped early today, and he'd just finished a workout when Sophie arrived. He met her at the top of the drive, wearing black running shorts, sneakers, and a white T-shirt with the slogan *Just Do It* as she backed the Honda CR-V up close to the front door.

She hopped out with a cheery wave. "You fixed your gates and put up security cameras."

He followed her to the back of the SUV. Her shirt rose up to expose the soft skin on her lower back as she lifted the tailgate and bent over to pull out material, wooden samples, and a heavy board with a bunch of pictures of furniture, sketches, and what looked like fabric swatches.

He pulled his gaze off her ass long enough to answer her question coherently. "The paparazzi are bloodhounds. I found one of the cheeky buggers climbing my tree last week. Can I give you a hand with that?"

"Sure." He obtained a teasing shot of cleavage as she dumped an armload of stuff into his hands before turning to grab the rest of her portfolio, hitching an over-stuffed tote up her arm, and following him through the front door.

She stopped short, assessing the new stainless steel monitor and intercom system built into the right foyer wall. The screen was broken up into four sections, revealing video from the security cameras outside. "Too bad." She tsked. "Not much I can do to make that more aesthetically pleasing. However, this is a time when function clearly outweighs form."

"Where do you want these?" Ian asked.

"Just put them on the kitchen island. It'll take me a few minutes to get set up."

"Would you like something to drink?" He crossed to the fridge. "Let's see. I've got beer … diet soda, orange juice …"

"Diet soda would be fine, thanks."

"Sophie, do you not drink, luv?"

"Sure I drink. I just don't care for beer."

"Do you drink wine?" He poured the drinks and watched her as she organized the materials, tapping on her iPad and laying out wooden pieces and materials.

"Yes, I like wine."

Ian came round with a beer and a hissing glass of dark soda. "What else do you drink?"

"What?" She looked up and digested the question. "Oh, I like a good margarita. In the summer, a cosmo always hits the spot."

"Hmm. I'll have to remember that." He tucked that information away in his mind for future reference.

She puttered away with all of her bits and parts, as he waited, holding the drink aloft. A V formed between her brows while her focus remained intense on the iPad. It was kind of cute, but he didn't understand how all of this was going to become his new living room.

"Can I ask you a question?"

"Yes?" Her blue eyes glanced up from the tablet, and she took the drink.

"What the hell is all this?"

She chuckled. "This, Ian O'Connor, is a multi-staged design proposal for your home. We have work to do in almost every room and outside as well. I'll go through it all room by room. We'll talk numbers then determine what you want done immediately and what can wait." With a few taps on the iPad, she pulled up a blue print of the great room; Ian had never seen anything like it.

They spent the next hour reviewing the materials she had prepped. Sophie recommended new hardwoods throughout the first floor, lighting changes in the kitchen and dining room, along with a tile backsplash, paint everywhere, built-ins for the TV, more lighting in the great room, a complete overhaul of the guest bath, new furniture inside and out, lamps, curtains, bedding and accessories. The bill was steep. More than he'd expected. However, her ideas were sound and delivered with such enthusiasm and excitement; he knew there was no way he could say no. Besides, it was only money. With the show taking off, there would be more where that came from.

Overall, her presentation blew him away. She must have spent hours and hours thinking about every detail for each room she designed. Details he never would have thought of. Moreover, the renderings on the tablet allowed him to see what the finished space would look like. As a matter of fact, the rooms reminded him of things he'd see in a magazine. Every time she brought up a rendering of a different room, he'd mutter, "Bloody brilliant."

They moved through the house as Sophie described the changes so he could see her vision.

As they headed upstairs, a loud buzzing noise halted them. "What was that?"

"Someone's at the gate. Probably the delivery kid. Go on up. I'll meet you up there in a tick." He took the stairs two at a time and jogged back down.

The security camera showed a beat-up, two-door sedan with a Chinese take-out box lit up on the roof of his car. After dealing with the delivery kid, Ian trotted back up the stairs to find Sophie measuring an empty guest room doorway, her body stretched high up on tip-toe and he took a moment to enjoy the view.

Her brow rose as she looked over her shoulder. "Everything okay?"

"Lovely. You fancy Chinese food?"

"Uh, sure. I like Chinese."

"Good. Now where were we?"

Her lips twisted into a smirk. "Let's start in here. This is the smallest of the three bedrooms, and I thought it would be an ideal place for your office." Pulling up the blueprint, she handed the tablet to Ian as she outlined a proposal to create a wall of built-in bookshelves while floating the desk in the center of the room. She moved about the room, gesturing with her hands as she explained each point. She also recommended the addition of a gas fireplace insert to give a cozy feeling to the room.

His eyes lit up at the idea of a fireplace. "Brilliant idea. I never would have thought to put a fireplace in here." Thoughts of snuggling up with her on the little sofa she described further sold him on the idea.

"That's what you're paying me for. To think of things you wouldn't." She grinned and tapped her noggin.

Their gazes connected and pheromones sparked. The room went silent. The only thing heard was their breathing as Ian's heart sped up. It was happening again, just like the first time in his bedroom. If he played his cards right, this time he'd get his kiss … maybe more. The smile slid from her face and her cheeks pinked. Ian speared her with his sultry gaze, holding her frozen in place. Her nipples hardened beneath her blouse

"Sophie." His whisper caressed her name.

His eyes followed her tongue as it passed across her lips, and his groin tightened. Just as before, he took a step toward Sophie. Her breath caught, and it was as if she were released from a spell. Her stormy, dark eyes fluttered closed, and she bowed her head, shielding her thoughts from him.

"Why don't we head into the master bedroom?" Turning away, she paced out of the room.

Damnit! Something spooked her again. Was there a boyfriend in the picture? Was she inexperienced? He discarded that thought immediately. He estimated her to be late twenties, and with a body like Venus, there was no way she'd be a virgin. Blokes at home would be lining up 'round the block to try and get in her knickers. He was sure men must have pursued her in the past. Maybe that was the problem; a blighter from the past had burned her. He'd have to chat her up a bit. Maybe he could finesse some answers out of her over dinner.

• • •

I was no fool. I was old enough to realize that, much to my surprise, Ian felt an attraction toward me. Whether or not he experienced the same sizzling friction was unknown. Ian seemed to be the type of man who liked all varieties of women, which wasn't surprising considering pheromones seemed to pour out of him like water from a fountain.

Even if I could get beyond the fact he had a girlfriend, what I couldn't get past was the fact I desperately needed the commission. There was an old saying about mixing business with pleasure. It was a bad idea. Moreover, it wasn't in my genetic makeup to have a one-night stand and pretend nothing happened the following day. Who was I kidding? I couldn't get past the girlfriend thing. Having been cheated on, there was no way in hell I'd play "the other woman." Whether or not I liked Tanqueray didn't matter. It was too hurtful to the third party, and it irritated me that Ian was trying to push limits and force me into that role, even if it was to just steal a kiss … I shook my head at the dirty thoughts scampering around in there. It would be wrong.

By the time Ian followed me into the master suite, I'd gotten a grip on my moment of insanity and was on the far side of the room tapping away at my iPad.

I looked up as Ian entered, but my eyes skittered past his gaze. "As we discussed last week, I've put together a Tuscan-inspired room. Using a faux plaster finish with golden tones on the walls out here, and terra cotta colors in the bathroom, it'll bring out the deep color of the countertops and cabinetry. I've found a bronze chandelier that would look fabulous over the Jacuzzi tub." I passed the tablet across the bed for him to see.

His fingers brushed mine. I pulled away as though I'd been burned and cleared my throat. "If you look to the fifth picture, you'll see I've chosen a heavy four poster bed, and luckily you have so much space in the room we can put a cream striped love seat at the foot of it with an antique trunk studded by brass nail heads. I've kept some of the clean, modern elements you like, and, I think, married them successfully with the Old World feel of the Tuscan design." I babbled, speaking much too fast. Normally, I stood next to a client and moved him about the room as I spoke, but I cautiously kept my distance with this one.

Ian eyed me inquisitively when I finally paused for a breath.

"Don't you want to see it on the computer?" I forced a smile, indicating the untouched tablet.

Finally, he looked down to review my plans. I waited as he tapped his way through the presentation. Fear gripped me and my confidence dropped as he remained silent. Not a flicker of interest passed over his face. *Crap, I should have gone with a more modern design. He hates it.* I fidgeted with the ring on my middle finger, a nervous habit.

"Listen, if you don't like the Tuscan theme, I can go back to the drawing board and create a modern design if you prefer."

Ian looked up. "Well, I don't know." He deadpanned for a moment.

I gulped and reached for the iPad. "Don't worry. I can start over."

He pulled the tablet away, then his wonderful dimples peeked out at me. "I love it. Don't change a thing."

The breath I'd been holding flowed out in relief and I shook a finger at him. "Whoa. You had me going there for a moment."

"Come on. Let's go downstairs. I'm feeling peckish and dinner's getting chilled."

I checked my watch. It was ten past eight, half an hour since the delivery kid arrived. "Right. I didn't realize how late it was. It'll just take me a few minutes to pack my things. I'll leave the design board with you, and if you want, I can e-mail the photos." I hustled past him down the stairs and started gathering my materials off the kitchen counter. I placed the design board on the mantle so Ian could look it over the next few days and see the colors and textures of the patterns in the daylight.

Ian hummed quietly while he pulled white Chinese takeout boxes from a paper bag and the combined scent of fried rice, salty soy, and spicy sauces filled the kitchen. My stomach rumbled. As I packed away materials, Ian laid dishes and silverware on the island for two.

Uh oh. A sense of trepidation came over me. He was expecting someone else for dinner, and I had an awful feeling that person was Tanqueray. If I didn't get a move on, the dreaded confrontation was about to happen. My comeuppance was at hand. The tote slipped from my fingers. Fabric and paint samples tumbled to the floor.

"Damn."

"Do you need some help with that?"

"No. I'm fine. I'm just all butterfingers." It was silly. My hands were actually shaking as I hurried to stuff everything willy-nilly into the bag.

"Would you like some more diet soda with dinner?"

"What?"

"What would you like to drink with dinner? Unfortunately, I don't have any wine, and as we've established, you don't drink beer. You're left with diet soda, orange juice, or vitamin water. Oh, and I could set the kettle on for tea if you'd like. Which would you prefer, luv?"

"Uh." I blinked. "Uh. Are you inviting me for dinner? Like now?"

"Better than tomorrow, don't you think? Then the food will be cold."

My anxiety about meeting Tanqueray deflated immediately as I realized he was setting a place for me. "I wouldn't want to impose. You can go ahead and eat while I finish packing." My hands fluttered in relief.

"Soph, there's no imposition. It's late. We're both hungry."

I shook my head.

"Don't deny it. I heard your stomach rumble all the way over here. I have all this food, and you did say you liked Chinese." He pointed a spoon at me.

"I did?" A small impish grin formed.

"Yes. Upstairs in the study. Now, put that Titanic tote aside and have a sit down."

I waffled for a moment. My stomach grumbled again. *What could it hurt?* "Okay." After laying the tote in the foyer, I returned to the kitchen.

Ian was spooning Szechuan beef over white rice.

"Ian, does Tanqueray mind if you have dinner with another woman?"

Ian's brows crunched together in a scowl. "Tanqueray? What the devil does she have to do with anything?"

I treaded lightly. "Well, as your girlfriend, she might not appreciate me eating dinner alone with you. She seemed rather possessive at the party … and we didn't exactly hit it off. You're not expecting her tonight, are you?"

His face cleared and he threw back his head in mirth. I stood puzzled, watching his reaction.

He shook his head. "You actually thought I fancied Tanqueray?"

I flushed. "Well, I, uh … "

He stared at me.

"What was I supposed to think?" I threw my hands in the air. "She was hanging all over you at that party. And she sent me possessive girlfriend vibes. And you went off with her to play pool."

"I went to play pool with her because you abandoned me." He waggled the spoon my way.

"I … but … I abandoned you?" I uttered in unbelieving accents.

He gave me a rascally grin. "You naffed off and left me. What do you have to say for yourself?"

I sighed in confusion. "I don't get it, Ian. She's tall and blonde. She's one of the beautiful people. I thought you were her boyfriend. You two looked like a couple."

His face became serious. "What do you mean 'one of the beautiful people'?"

"You know," I flapped a hand in his direction. "Like you. Hollywood is filled with beautiful people made for TV and movies. Tanqueray is airbrushed perfection. I don't fit into that group."

"What group do you fit into?"

"The average people group, I guess." I shrugged with discomfort.

"The average people group?" he mused and scrutinized me.

"Come on, Ian. You know what I mean." I waved a hand down my body and crossed my arms. "I'm not a size two. I don't compete with the Tanquerays of this world."

"You're right. You're not a size two, and you don't look like most of the starving models dashing around with Botox and silicone running out their ears. That's probably why I like you, Sophie.

You're real. You're not an ass-kisser trying to get a leg up. You say what you think. Besides, Tanqueray has a face like a bulldog licking piss off a nettle." Ian shook his head.

"I beg your pardon?"

"You know her face looks like a slapped arse. Poor girl."

I smacked a hand over my mouth, but the mirthful giggles spilled out anyway. "I've never heard of that. Your Irish sayings are quite colorful. Wait," I felt so relieved to have Tanqueray out of the picture, I decided to get in on the game. "I've got an American saying for you. She's got a butter face."

"What does that mean?"

"You know, she looks good, but her face."

His face lit with a smile. "Wait here's one you'll like, it's for a fellow. He's got a face like a welder's bench."

I doubled over in laughter.

"Oh, here's another: his face is like a bag of spanners."

"I don't even know what that means, but I'm totally stealing it for future use," I wheezed.

Ian's hilarity subsided, and he sent me a penetrating stare. "Let me assure you, Sophie, you don't have a butter face. And I would disagree with you."

"About what?"

"I don't think you fall into the average people group at all." Ian studied me and his eyes raked me up and down. What was going through his head? His arresting cerulean eyes held me mesmerized. I couldn't break free. My heartbeat picked up and the oxygen caught in my throat.

"No. I don't think there's anything about you I'd describe as average."

"Thank you, I guess." I self-consciously fiddled with my ring.

He finally broke the mounting tension. "Now that we've established a girlfriend isn't going to walk through the front door, can we eat? I'm as hungry as a pack of wolves."

I let out a croak that Ian took as an assent and pulled my stool up to the counter while he finished doling the sweet and sour chicken onto the plates.

"You never answered. What would you like to drink, Sophia, designer extraordinaire and troublemaker?" He placed a loaded plate in front of me.

"Just water, please."

He turned to fill my glass.

"And Ian … "

He glanced over his shoulder.

"Thanks for dinner. You're right, I *am* hungry."

Ian joined me at the counter and we both dug into the meal, enjoying the spicy Szechuan and fried noodles.

"I watched your show."

Ian paused with a fork halfway to his mouth. "And?"

"I'm hooked." I grinned. "I can see why everyone's talking about it. I absolutely adore Maria. She's my favorite character." I took a bite of rice.

Ian's fork clanked to his plate, and he gave me a hurt look. "Maria? What about Ryder?"

"Well, aside from you, of course. I mean everyone watches the show because of Ryder. He's all dark and intense, you know, and that opening shot of you coming out of the water makes all the women faint." I fanned my face.

"Of course they do." Ian waggled his eyebrows at me.

"Full of modesty, aren't you, O'Connor?" I shoved his shoulder, knocking him askew.

"Hey. Hey. Is this how you treat all your clients?" he teased.

He was right. I couldn't allow his playfulness to make me unprofessional. Even though we'd cleared the air about Tanqueray, I couldn't return his flirtation. I needed to maintain a professional distance and keep things on the up and up. Keep my eye on the ball. I forced my mien to become solemn. "No, Ian, I don't. I apologize."

"Ah, Soph, come on, luv. I'm just having a bit of a go at you. It's okay if you fancy Maria's character more than mine. Carmen Lopez is a brilliant actress. We're lucky to have her as part of the cast."

I nodded and folded my hands in my lap.

"Come on. Put serious Sophia away." He scowled then wiped his hand from top to bottom and changed his face to a mischievous look. "Can frisky Sophie come out to play?"

Rolling my eyes, I sighed. "Ian, you'd drive a saint crazy."

"All the more fun, eh?"

I shook my head and took another bite.

"So tell me, Sophie, why do you always try to be so severe, when I can clearly see the playful lass hiding in there?"

"It's important for my business. Clients respect my professionalism. Back when I was married, before I started my business, I didn't have so many responsibilities weighing on me, and I was probably more fun-loving." I shrugged. "When my ex and I divorced, things were … difficult for a while. As a matter of fact," I changed the tone of the conversation, "you're the first client to flirt so unmercifully with me. It's terrible. You throw me off kilter."

"You were married?"

I immediately wanted to bite my tongue. "Yup." I ducked my head and became very interested in my plate. I shifted food around, my appetite suddenly lost.

"For how long?"

"Three years."

"How long ago did you get divorced?"

"Five." I sighed.

"Any kids?"

I shook my head in the negative. "What about you? One of the rags at the grocery store said you're thirty-six. Have you been married?"

"Bloomin' tabloids don't get anything right. I'm only thirty-five."

I waited. Ian finished chewing.

"Nope. Never been married. My mum's an Irish Catholic and she takes marriage pretty seriously. Even though she divorced my father, she's been married for almost thirty years to Gabriel, her second husband. He raised me like his own; I call him Dad. It's tough in the acting business to find a real soul mate. So many of the women I work with are just trying to get a leg up, and they're willing to step over you to get there." He clicked his tongue. "I guess I haven't found the right girl to visit the vicar."

"Then it's a good thing you've stayed single. Divorce is a messy thing. Do you remember your parents' divorce?"

"Nah. I was only two."

"What happened, if you don't mind my asking?" Even though our conversation was turning incredibly personal, it felt so easy. I was surprised how Ian opened up to me.

"They were young and foolish. My father swooped me mum off her feet at the age of nineteen, and by the time she was twenty-three, it was all over. Mum left my father because he loved his money on Wall Street more than her, and she took me back home to Ireland." He looked into the middle distance, as if recalling a childhood memory.

"That's too bad. Did you see your father at all growing up?"

His eyes flicked back to me. "Oh, sure. Mum and Father are cordial enough with an ocean separating them. As a kid, I spent my summers in New York. When my mum married Gabe, he got a job in London, so we moved to Islington. Between the two cities, I caught the acting bug."

"I guess that explains your accent and dialect. You've got an Irish lilt, with English sayings, but when you're playing Ryder, you completely drop it to become an American."

"You have me there. My accent is a mishmash, but it has served me well. I can do a pretty good Welsh and Aussie accent, too. G'day mate."

"I was amazed with your Ryder change. Not only do you drop the accent, but your voice becomes ... I don't know, heavier ... rougher. You give it more intensity, enhancing the character."

He guffawed. "That's the only way I can speak American. Has nothing to do with my acting chops. I'm just imitating my father."

"Did your father remarry?"

"Yes. He married a very nice divorcée, Clarice. She runs her own travel agency. They've been married ten years."

"Do you like her?"

"Sure." He shrugged. "She's a good egg. She makes him think about other things besides making money. He travels more and they're happy."

Ian probably thought I was grilling him like a reporter on an interview, but I couldn't seem to help myself. His past fascinated me. "Do you have any siblings?"

He nodded, finishing his bite of food. "Mum and Dad gave me a half-brother, and I acquired a stepsister when my father remarried."

"You said your mom was Catholic. Are you a practicing Catholic?"

"Not really. I suppose I'm Christian, but right now I don't attend services. I have trouble buying some of the rhetoric that's coming out of the Vatican these days."

"Do you suffer from Catholic guilt?"

His laughter filled the room. "Don't we all m'girl? Don't we all?"

"Mmm, I wouldn't know. I'm kind of a lapsed Baptist. I haven't been inside a church for years."

"So, I just told you all my secrets. Tell me yours. What about Sophie Hartland?"

I slipped off my stool and carried my dish over to the sink to rinse it off. "Not much to tell."

"Come on, Sophie. Do you have any brothers or sisters?"

"I have a sister, Holly, who lives in Las Vegas with her husband and two-year-old daughter."

"Where did you grow up?"

"We lived on the East Coast, in Virginia, when I was young. When I was twelve, we moved out to Arizona." I pulled the dishwasher door open.

"What about your parents? What do they do? Divorced or still together?"

"My mom's a receptionist for a realty company. My parents were married for thirty-two years, then one day Dad had a massive brain aneurysm and keeled over, leaving my mom a widow at the age of fifty-five."

Ian's eyes widened in surprise by my bald statement. "That's a tough break. Sorry about your dad, luv."

Shrugging my shoulders, I concentrated on placing the plate into its slot in the dishwasher. I tried to swallow the unexpected lump in my throat. Tried to ignore it. Nevertheless, tears welled up. I rarely allowed myself to think about my dad's passing. Ian's sympathy brought up emotions I thought I'd packed up and closeted away, like an old suitcase.

I sniffed.

"Hell! Sophie, I'm sorry for pushing. I can be such a cock-up sometimes."

I placed my hands on the counter, turning my back to him, and worked to repress the unanticipated emotions overwhelming me. My body shook with the effort.

His warm hand cupped my shoulder. Reluctantly, I rotated and he gathered me close into his embrace. Embarrassment burned my cheeks, and I buried my head into his chest, curling my hands around his soft T-shirt. They weren't dramatic, uncontrollable sobs, merely silent tears that trickled down my cheeks.

Ian rubbed my back in slow, soothing strokes and made quiet shushing noises. "It's all right. Let it out."

We stood that way for a few minutes, Ian comforting me, while I fought to tamp down my feelings. Eventually, the tears subsided. I snuffled, and Ian slid a napkin into my fingers. With my head down, I subtly mopped up. When I was dry, I stepped back. Ian gave me space but didn't release me completely. Instead, he ran his hands down my arms, sending shivers through my system and maintaining me in his personal sphere. He smelled fresh and woodsy with the musky scent of man. His T-shirt was crumpled where my fists had clamped, holding on for dear life. Tentatively, I reached out to smooth the wrinkles. His sturdy hand clasped mine, pressing it to his chest. I could swear his heart-beat quickened under my touch, at the same time my own kicked up speed.

My lashes lifted to meet his searing gaze, his luminous eyes darkened to cobalt, and his muscle flexed under my fingers. Ian searched my face and I parted my lips, sucking in a soft breath. A flash of desire crossed his features. Without thought, I moved into his arms, plastering myself chest to breast. His soft lips were insistent, and with a moan, I caved, allowing his tongue to plunder the hot recess of my mouth. He tasted of oriental spices, and he wrapped one hand around my shoulders as the other gripped my hips, pulling me up on my toes even closer, so I felt his hard strength against the entirety of my body. I wrapped my arms around his neck, running my fingers through his thick, dark waves. My body took the lead, sensing and feeling.

Excitement and desire flowed through my veins, pooling low in my belly. I don't know what happened to my brain. It must have exited stage left. I'd never responded to a man as I was responding to Ian. Utterly uncontrolled.

Ian's hand slipped under my blouse and rubbed lightly against my belly, brushing further north until reaching its destination. A thumb flicked against my nipple through the silky bra. I hardened at the touch. My head dropped back, allowing Ian access to the soft skin on my neck, and taking advantage, his hot tongue laved the sensitive flesh. I think I moaned. My eyes fluttered open. Our distorted reflection on the silver toaster mirrored back at me, and to my deep regret, my brain entered stage right.

"Ian … " I moaned. Not a good move.

"Sophie," he whispered passionately, nipping at my neck.

"Ian. Ian." Gently I pressed against his hard muscles. "We have to stop."

He realized I was trying to extricate myself and reluctantly loosened his grip.

I stepped away, backing myself against the opposite counter. I pulled my top down. My breath was ragged. "I'm sorry, but I can't do this."

He watched me with a puzzled expression. "Why?"

I inhaled and exhaled to calm myself and unscramble my emotions. I needed to put together a cohesive argument as to why we couldn't just drop right down on the floor and go for it.

"Trust me, Ian, it's not because I don't want to. Look, I find you as sexy as hell, and for some reason completely unknown to me, you seem to feel the same way. Our chemistry is obviously explosive." My hand fluttered through the air. "But I can't allow it to interfere. I don't date clients … or sleep with them. I can't express to you how important this job is to me. If I allow you to have your way with me, after the one-night stand, it'll be … awkward," I struggled to put my thoughts into words, "between us, and possibly between me and my crew. I can't have that. It would be unprofessional and wrong."

"Who's to say it'll be a one-night stand?" He crossed his arms, clearly irritated.

My lips thinned. "Ian, come on. Nothing personal, but the tabloids paint you as a playboy."

"Lies—"

I stopped his denial with a hand. "At minimum, we both know you're a flirt."

Ian harrumphed.

"One day some girl will cross your path and knock your socks off, and you'll settle down into a relationship. You won't be able to help yourself."

"How do you know you're not that girl?" His eyes narrowed.

I smiled. "I think we both know I'm not that girl. I'm not exactly television star girlfriend material."

"Why do you keep saying that?" He stabbed a finger at me.

I shook my head and sighed. "I'm a realist. I am who I am. No matter what you say, I'm an average-looking, thirty-year-old divorcée with a moderately successful company. I can't compete with the twenty-somethings running around this town, throwing themselves at your feet."

"Sophie, Sophie, Sophie." He shook his head, tut-tutting. "What if I told you I thought you were the most attractive women I've met in LA? That I like how you don't bullshit me and your maturity is one of the things I find most alluring." He shifted closer, leaning in so I felt his soft breath brushed against my ear. "Besides, I fancy turbulent blue eyes and long, silky hair." His finger tucked an errant lock behind my ear. "The thought of wrapping myself around your naked, sexy curves keeps me up at night," he ended with a whisper. His eyes scorched me with their intensity.

It was far too easy for me visualize Ian's little fantasy.

"Uh." I cleared my throat. "Uh."

"Kitty-cat got your tongue?" He stepped back and winked.

I swallowed. "I would say you're making a valiant effort to get me into your bed."

"Maybe." His eyes smoldered. "Is it working?"

I coughed and looked away from his too-tempting, half-lidded come-hither expression. "Listen, Ian. Why don't we make a deal?"

His eyebrows shot up with interest. "What kind of deal?"

"You and I put the chemistry on the backburner while we work this job. And, if by the time we get to the end of it you haven't moved on to the next girl, we can go out … on a date or something and see where things lead. No strings."

"What happens if you've found another man?"

The question was so ludicrous I laughed. "Ian, you're too funny. Trust me. Guys aren't banging down my door. I'm not the one getting followed around by twenty year olds throwing their bras at me."

"That only happened once." He rubbed his reddened neck and glanced away.

The ticking of Ian's watch filled the room as I waited for his answer. He ran fingers through his hair.

"Okay. Here's what I'll agree to. If you hold me at arm's length, I'll respect that. But, I will take advantage if I see your resistance weakening."

I chewed my bottom lip at his counterproposal.

"Hey, that's the best I'm willing to do. Take it or leave it." He held up his hands.

"Crap."

"What? Am I so irresistible?" He smirked.

"You're like playing with fire. I'm afraid I'm going to go down in flames."

Ian's smirk turned into a full-on smile. He had me in a corner. "How long will the remodeling take?"

"Five to six weeks."

"Could be a long five to six weeks, luv."

"Tell me about it."

"Do we have a deal?"

I reached out to shake his hand. "Deal."

His thumb gently stroked the soft flesh. I had to make a physical effort to pull away. As I did so, he sent me a devilish grin. This was going to be a game for Ian, and he had nothing to lose. However, such a game, if I lost, could damage me and my company in many ways, not to mention the possible damage to my heart. I almost wished I had the chutzpah to walk away from the job and allow my sexual desire to take over. As luck would have it, my brain was still standing center stage and it made the decision for me.

Chapter 6

"The Forresters' touchup work is done, and I'll have the invoice to you by Monday, close of business. I can get my painters started on the O'Connor job as early as Friday. Why don't you and I meet at the house on Thursday early? Seven?" Jack scrolled through his laptop calendar.

The morning sun glimmered through the gauzy curtains, illuminating the buttery yellow walls of my home office where Jack, Michelle, and I were seated around a black painted wood table. The fabric whispered as I shifted on the padded chair, easing my foot out from beneath Sirius's sleeping head. The office space was originally a formal living room that I converted when I moved into my mid-century rambler.

"Seven works for me."

"Do you have a key to the O'Connor house?" he asked.

"Nuts. No, I don't, and I forgot he also has a gated driveway. I'll leave a message for him. We're going to have to work something out so you and your guys can get in. I think his schedule can be erratic, so I don't know he'll always be there to let you in." I held the cell phone to my ear, waiting for voice mail to pick up.

"Good morning, Sophie." Ian's voice rumbled over the phone lines right down my spine.

My mind went blank and it was a few seconds before I came back to earth.

"Uh, hi, Ian. I was expecting your voice mail." *Smooth, Soph, really smooth.*

"Would you prefer me to hang up and let you speak to the machine?"

Michelle gave me a strange look, and I made an effort to pull myself together. I didn't want to let my team see how much he affected me.

"No. Sorry, I don't want to interrupt you when you're on the job."

"We're on a break right now. Waiting for the lighting crew to set up this next shot so I have a few tics. What's on your mind?"

"It's your security system. Jack, my general contractor, can have his paint crew start as early as Friday. He and I need to stop by Thursday morning so I can go over the design plan with him. Will you be home? I'd like you two to meet."

"What time Thursday morning?"

"Seven."

"Hold on." He must have covered the phone with his hand because I heard mumbling in the background. "Can you make it six thirty?"

I looked over at Jack. "Can you do six thirty on Thursday?"

He nodded.

"Six thirty's fine. We need to talk about the rest of the job. I understand your schedule can be erratic. How do you want to work this out?"

"What do your other clients do?"

"Well, either there's a lady of the house who doesn't work, or some of my clients have housekeepers or onsite security to let us in, and others just give us a key to come and go at will."

"For a woman who won't go on a date with me, now you're asking for a key to my house. I don't know … it's a big step." He sighed. "I thought you said we had to wait five or six weeks."

My face burned with embarrassment, and I didn't answer.

"Sophie?"

I cleared my throat and put on my business demeanor. "What would you like to arrange, Ian?"

His chuckle rumbled through the phone. "So serious. Thursday morning I'll give you a key, and we'll program security codes in the gate for you and your foreman. Will that work?"

"That will be fine. Thanks. We'll see you bright and early Thursday morning."

"I look forward to it."

Grinning, I rolled my eyes and pressed *end*. I glanced up. Michelle and Jack stared at me. Jack's left eyebrow was raised and his mouth, crooked.

"What?"

Michelle giggled. "Sophie, you're as red as a beet right now. I think you like our Ian O'Connor."

I gave a nervous laugh. "Watch yourself with him, Michelle. He loves women and is a dreadful flirt. He says the most outrageous things."

"Was he flirting with you on the phone just now?"

"Yes." I couldn't hold back the huge grin that split my face.

"Hmm. This could be fun to watch."

"I don't know what you mean."

"You're always so self-possessed. With most guys you brush off their passes without breaking a sweat. This fellow flusters you, and he's a hunk."

"Men don't make passes at me. And, he doesn't fluster me."

"Oh, yes he does," Jack interrupted.

"I'm a thirty-year-old woman. I don't get crushes or flustered by pretty boys." I shook my head.

He laughed. "I'm with Michelle. This could be fun."

I giggled like a schoolgirl. "Cut that out. We need to get back to business."

•••

Jack's white Chevy truck idled noisily outside Ian's gate. I drove alongside and lowered the window. "Hey, you been waiting long?"

He shook his head. "Only a few minutes."

I pulled ahead and pressed the buzzer.

"Yes?"

"Morning, Ian."

"Soph, I'm still getting dressed. The door is open, so come on in."

A vision of Ian naked flashed through my mind. *Mm. Nice way to start the day.* Jack followed me through the gate and parked next to the CR-V. He held the front door as I juggled my tote and a cardboard tray of coffee.

"Christ on a crutch!" He exclaimed as he followed me into the kitchen and got a glimpse at the hideous blend of wall colors. "What on God's green earth are people thinking?!"

Placing the coffee on the island, I snorted then handed him an espresso. "Here. You'll probably need this. I know I do." I retrieved my skinny pumpkin spice latte and breathed in the coffee aroma.

Jack walked around inspecting the walls. "We'll need to put two coats of primer on the striped walls to keep it from bleeding through."

"There's black paint in the master. You might have to do the same thing there, too." We discussed the flooring plans and lighting design in the main living area, and then I took Jack outside.

He gave a low whistle as the dawning sun lit the natural vista of craggy hills and Stone Canyon Reservoir splayed before him. "I can see why O'Connor brought the property. The view alone sells it."

"My thoughts exactly."

My heart gave a quick jump at Ian's voice. Jack and I turned as one. Ian, drool-worthy as always, stood in a pair of dark jeans and a light blue button-down shirt.

I smiled. "Good morning. This is my main contractor, Jack Blumberg. Jack, Ian O'Connor."

They shook hands. "Fantastic place you have here, O'Connor."

"Think you and Sophie can fix it up?" Ian crossed his arms.

Jack nodded. "Sure, sure. It's mostly cosmetic. Knock down a wall, flooring, paint." He ticked off his fingers. "No problems. Just be glad the kitchen's already been reno'd. A kitchen reno is hell to live through."

I laughed at Jack. "You haven't seen the main floor guest bath. That's a gut job." Ian and I exchanged a knowing look. "Don't worry, Ian. I promise you're in good hands." I gently placed a reassuring hand on his forearm.

He gave a speculative look at my touch. "I have no doubt I'm in good hands."

I snatched my hand away then quickly took a drink of coffee to cover my discomfort. He gave me a wolfish grin.

"I brought you a cup of joe. Why don't we go in and get situated with the security codes?" I led the way back into the kitchen, the men following.

"You didn't get me a girly coffee, did you?" Ian took off the lid and sniffed.

I rolled my eyes and sighed. "It's just a dark Colombian roast cappuccino. No sugar. No cream. Is that manly enough for you?"

He took a sip and rocked his head back and forth in consideration. "Hmm … not bad. What's Jack drinking?"

"Jack drinks an espresso with a shot of vanilla, no cream, no sugar."

"Espresso. Now that's a man's drink."

Jack nodded in agreement and took a sip of his strong coffee.

I stuck my tongue out and scrunched my nose up. "Okay, so espresso is your thing. I'll keep that in mind for future reference."

"Glad to know you're keeping my preferences in mind."

"It's my job to keep your preferences in mind."

"All my preferences?" He leaned in closer.

My eyes skittered between Ian and Jack, who hid a grin behind his coffee cup. I could tell Ian enjoyed my discomfort. "Uh … don't you have to get to work?"

He gave a bark of laughter. "Come on, let's get you two set up."

We followed him into the foyer where Ian started punching numbers into the security keypad. After we were set up with our new codes, Jack headed down the hall to see the guest bathroom.

"I only have one spare. Can you get a copy made for Jack?" Ian gently placed the house key in my hand, allowing his warm fingers to linger on my palm as his thumb stroked the soft part of my wrist.

A zip of electricity ran up my arm at his touch, and my breath quickened. "Oh, you are so not playing fair."

He flashed me a deadly smile and his aqua gaze lingered on my lips. "Who said I was going to play fair?"

"Ian!" I stepped back. "I thought we came to an agreement."

"Our agreement was based on *your* resistance. I'm trying to weaken that." He nabbed the cup out of my hand and took a sip. His nose crinkled and a look of disgust crossed his face. "Yech! You call this coffee?"

The sexual tension broke, and I snatched my java back. "Hey! Don't pick on my girly coffee. It's pumpkin spice latte."

He snickered. Before I knew what was happening, he leaned in and gave me a quick kiss on the lips and a pat on the bottom. "Have a good day, luv. Don't forget to lock up when you leave." Then he was out the door.

My hands hung limply as I stood in shock and stared at the closed door, my mouth open. This was not at all what we'd agreed upon. How was I supposed to stay professional when my client flirted mercilessly and kissed and fondled me? I touched my lips where his had been a moment ago. My fingers came away with a trace of lipstick, and I grinned. Would Ian realize he was wearing Hot Lava Spice? *Served him right!* A horrible, screechy, ripping sound pulled me from my thoughts.

"You were planning to gut this entire bathroom, right?" Jack's voice called.

"Yes." I hurried toward the room. "Are you starting the renovation now?"

"No time like the present."

• • •

He licked his lips. Mmm ... she tasted like ripe peaches. With a light step, he sauntered to the car, flicking the keys around his forefinger. This was going to be fun. He grinned. Once he realized that her hang-ups came from the supposition that he and Tanqueray were an item, he'd planned to move full steam ahead. He couldn't believe it when she'd put a stop to that delightful kiss in the kitchen, just when he thought he was getting somewhere. However, after further consideration, it would be great fun pushing her buttons and taunting her into giving up on that silly pact they'd made.

The grin turned into an impish snicker as he recalled her discomfort while he flirted with her in front of her foreman. Since her divorce, he got the feeling she'd become very independent and there hadn't been many men in the picture. Well, he was just the man to break the dry spell. Besides, the conversation they had the other night made him want to know more. He hadn't talked about his childhood or religion with a woman since his days at university. It wasn't about bedding her ... well ... it wasn't *only* about getting her knickers off; she stimulated his brain. More than any woman had in recent history.

Chapter 7

I needn't have worried about keeping a professional relationship with Ian. We were finishing our second week of the renovation, and I had yet to see him again. Jack and his crew usually arrived by eight and left around four. I was at the house almost every day to check on the progress, take measurements, and drop off supplies. The painting was finished and the main floor bath had been gutted back to the studs. Jack planned to put it back together next week. The flooring had been delivered and sat in the dining room to acclimate before installation, also scheduled for next week.

I'd left Ian a few notes and texts to keep him in the loop and ask his opinion on modifications of the design plan.

His responses were succinct. *Looks great!* Or, *I'm in your hands, do what you think best* were pretty much what I had to work with. We had plans on Saturday to shop for the all-important "man sofa." The one thing Ian wanted to participate in purchasing.

On the outside, I kept my cool, professional façade. Although, I was loathe to admit, in reality, I was as excited as a child on Christmas morning to see Ian again. Even if his flirting made me uncomfortable, it also made me feel like an attractive, sexy woman. Something I hadn't felt since my divorce. I'd also noticed, since Ian hired me, he rarely showed up in any of the local tabloids. The two shots I saw were candids of him on the street. I didn't know if filming kept him too busy to be the playboy, or if he was keeping a lower profile since my previous accusations. Or, there was always the possibility Ian was surreptitiously dating other women and not making it into the press. A thought like that could circle in my head and drive me insane, so I did my best to push it out.

It was Friday, just past five. Jack and his crew finished cleaning for the weekend and left. I was alone at the house, holding two curtain fabrics against the new paint, debating which would look best when my phone interrupted the hush.

"Squawk! Pick up the phone!" Ugh. My mother. This was the third time she'd called this week, and I hadn't returned her previous calls. She wanted to talk about what was going on with my sister, but honestly Holly and I hadn't spoken since my birthday. I'd left a message for her the previous week, but no surprise, she didn't return my call.

"Squawk!"

I rubbed a thumb against my temple. "Hi, Mom."

"Hello, sweetie. I'm so glad I caught you. I've been trying all week."

"Sorry. We started two new jobs and it's been a little crazy. What do you need?" I wandered out to the back patio, leaving the door ajar, to allow the fresh air in and to clear out the paint smell. I flopped down onto one of the new, rattan lounge chairs.

"Well, I wanted to tell you I took your advice and joined Ourtime.com, and I have my first date tonight." She squealed.

"Wow, Mom. That's fantastic. What's the lucky fellow's name?"

"His name is Harvey, and he's only four years older than I am. He plays tennis and golf. He looks quite handsome in his photo."

"Well, that's good. You were worried you'd be stuck with some old coot with a saggy butt."

"Sophia Hartland! I said no such thing!" she said with a shocked voice, but I could hear a gurgle escape.

"Maybe not, but you were thinking it."

She giggled. "Maybe you're right."

"Where are you meeting him?"

"He's picking me up, and we're going to the golf club for dinner."

"Mom, you're not supposed to have them come to your home on the first date. Not even the second date. You're supposed to meet them on neutral ground and drive your own car."

"Oh, honey, I'm old-fashioned. I like a man to pick me up for a date."

I smacked my forehead, frustrated by her naiveté. "You don't know anything about this man. What if he's an obnoxious loudmouth and it's a horrible date and you can't leave because he drove?"

"I have my cell. I can call a cab."

"What if he gets handsy with you and forces unwanted attentions on you? What if he's a psycho killer who wants to take you to his backwoods house and chop you up in little pieces?"

Mom was quiet for a moment. "I'm sure the golf club wouldn't allow a murderer to join."

"Arrgh!" My eyeballs practically rolled to the back of my head. Dating had changed from when she and my dad did it; I'm sure she thought the endorsement of a country club made this man safe. My mother was far too trusting.

"I thought you'd be happy I'm going out."

"Oh, Mom. I am happy. I'm just worried you don't know the dating rules nowadays. You need to be more careful." The amber and golden hues of the setting sun streaked across the sky.

"What about you? I'm stepping out of my comfort zone. Are you dating anyone?"

I climbed out of the lounger and paced over to the pool. "Um … well there is this man I'm interested in."

"Is he handsome?"

"Oh, yeah."

"That sounded loaded."

"Handsome doesn't even cover it. He's gorgeous, and he's got these piercing blue eyes that make me weak in the knees, and he's smart and funny." I sighed. Slipping my sandals off, I dragged a toe across the cool liquid, disturbing the still water with little lapping waves.

"Umm, hmm."

"He's not my normal type. He's way out of my league."

"Oh, my darling girl, any man would be lucky to have you. So, when are you going out on a date?"

I let out a breathy whistle. "Hopefully, in about two or three weeks."

"Two or three *weeks*!" her voice cried so loudly I had to pull the phone away from my ear. "I don't understand you young people. Is this some sort of vetting process you put all your dates through? It's just a date, Sophie. You're not moving in with the man."

"I know, Mom. I know. It's a little more complicated than that." Blindly, I backed toward the lounger. When my heels hit the legs, I bent to sit, but instead of feeling the woody rattan, my backside came into contact with a warm body and a masculine hand slid across my hip.

"Aiieeee!" I screeched. My heart shot into high gear. I whirled around.

Ian beamed from ear to ear. His presence was so unexpected, it threw me off balance and I reeled back toward the pool. I tripped over one of my sandals, and before I realized what was happening, my foot met nothing but space.

Ian's face changed from a smug grin to surprise, and he lunged out of the chair to help, but it was too late.

My body tilted too far back to regain any balance, and I knew I was going in. "Not my phone." I hollered, and threw it at Ian in an effort to keep it from getting ruined.

Reflexively, his hand shot out and caught the cell as the chilly water enveloped my head.

I stood, spluttering.

He leaned over the pool. "Sophie? Are you okay, luv?"

Stringy, wet hair fell across my eye. I swiped the locks aside, spitting them from my mouth. "I'm fine. How long have you been sitting there?"

A shit-eating smile split his face. "A little while."

Long enough to hear me gushing over him to my mom, I'm sure. I was mortified.

"Sophie? Sophie? Are you there? Are you okay?" I barely heard my mom's voice coming from the phone in Ian's hand.

He passed the cell into my dripping digits.

"Mom, I'm fine. I have to go. I'll call you back." I cut her off before she could say another word and placed the phone on the side of the pool.

Ian leaned down toward me. "Here, let me give you a hand. I'm sorry, luv. I never thought you'd fall into the flippin' pool, and by the time I realized where you were headed, it was too late."

I ground my teeth, giving a noncommittal grunt, and took his hand.

"Here, give me your other hand and I can pull you directly up."

"No, just let me just get a foothold here." Placing my two feet on the side, I gave a hard yank and pulled Ian in. He sailed over my head and made a satisfying splash. I turned my back and pushed my way through the water toward the steps. Ian took his turn to come up sputtering.

"I suppose I deserved that."

"You deserve more than that." I muttered softly, not for his ears. I continued pushing my way through the water as I climbed the first step. There was a quick splash, and, fast as lightning, a band of iron wrapped around my ribcage, brushing against my cold-hardened nipples, and pulled me up against a solid, wet chest. All the air left my lungs.

"C'mon, Sophie. Don't be mad," he whispered. His humid breath danced across my hair.

My hands gripped Ian's arm and I dropped my head forward. "Ian, I'm not mad. I just feel really stupid for not noticing you were home and for falling in your pool. And it's a little cold, so do you think you can let me get out?"

His armed loosened immediately, and, with as much dignity as I could muster, I climbed out of the pool. There was a light breeze, and I wrapped my arms around my torso in an effort to warm up. Too humiliated to face him, I kept my eyes lowered.

"Come on. Let's get you dried off."

I grabbed my sandals and phone and followed him to the half bath on the main floor. He pulled two towels out from the under the sink cabinet, handed me one, and toweled his hair with the other. My mouth went dry as I took in the wet T-shirt plastered against his firm muscles. I wrapped my towel around my chest, too aware of my now see-through white silk blouse and manky back-of-the-drawer bra.

He placed a thumb on my chin and raised my face to meet his eyes. "I'm sorry. I shouldn't have eavesdropped."

I lowered my lids, shielding the ocean of uncertainty and attraction behind them. Thoughts tumbled through my brain; dirty thoughts that told me to rip Ian's shirt off and to hell with our deal. However, louder than my libido, my inner conscious screamed at me to get out, quickly, before I did something stupid. My conscious won. I took a small step away and opened my eyes.

"It's fine." I plastered on a smile and gave a laugh, which I didn't quite feel. "I'm sure it was kind of funny watching me pitch into the pool like that."

Ian scrutinized me with uncertain eyes. If he made any sort of move toward me, my resolve would crumble. The bathroom was tight with the two of us in it. Our breathing was the only sound. It surrounded us, and I waited in suspended animation to see which way the mood would shift. Even though I was soaking wet, my clothes plastered against me, his searing gaze warmed me.

Then the corners of his eyes crinkled. "It was kind of funny. I'm surprised the neighbors aren't banging on my door to find out what the screeching was all about."

Relief flooded me and a genuine giggle burst forth. "You like to keep me off balance, don't you?"

"It has its perks." He blatantly stared at my chest where I continued to hold the towel.

I rolled my eyes. "You are such a guy."

"No doubt about that. C'mon." His teeth flashed. "Let's get you a dry kit. I'll order up something for dinner, and you can tell me about all the brilliant things you're doing to the house."

I shook my head. "I should be going."

Ian crossed his arms and lowered his brows. "You're soaking wet. At least let me give you something dry to change into for the drive home." He stood immovable.

Arguing wouldn't get me out of the door any faster, so I gave in with a brief nod.

"Wait here."

Ian's damp feet padded across the living room as his hem left tiny droplets. The backside view of the clingy, sopping jeans was almost as yummy as the front. I sighed. He looked hot and sexy wet. A glance in the mirror told its own story. I looked like a drowned raccoon … with mascara running down my cheeks.

Oh, that's attractive.

By the time he returned, I'd removed the mascara, but a damp coldness had filtered into my bones. Goose bumps prickled and shivers quivered through my body. He handed me a small pile of clothes with a hair dryer on top.

Thankfully, I took his offering and quietly closed the door. It was a relief to peel off my drippy slacks and blouse. I vigorously towel dried warmth back into my body. The sweats were so large I had to roll them at the waist and ankles. My underthings were uncomfortably damp, even after squeezing excess water out, so I rolled them up with the rest of my soggy garments and went commando. Using his hair dryer, I finger combed the moist tendrils into some semblance of order. The mirror reflected my dry but disheveled state, and I was glad Ian had supplied me with a dark-colored hoodie to cover the white T-shirt. I was uber aware of my now braless state and the white T-shirt left little to imagination. When you're a skinny size two, like most of the wannabes flooding the streets, going braless is no big deal. When you're sporting full C cups, going without support is noticeable and uncomfortable. At least it was to me. The entire ensemble made a sort of ghetto chic statement when I finished it with my black wedge sandals.

Uh huh, sexy, Hartland. Real sexy.

The kitchen and family room were silent with emptiness. I dropped my clothes into a plastic bag left behind by Jack's crew. The crackling sack sounded loud to my ears as I crammed the mess into my ever-present tote.

"Ian?" My voice echoed in the stillness. I cocked an ear, listening for movement from the upper floor. Nothing. A quick getaway would be best, but I didn't want to be rude. Ripping a piece of paper out of a pad from my purse, I left a brief note thanking him for the loan and confirming our appointment on Saturday to look for the perfect sofa.

A soft whistle met my ears as I surreptitiously closed the front door.

"Planning to leave without saying good-bye?"

Caught.

I turned. Ian slipped out of the shadows of the garage.

"Of course not." I straightened my shoulders. "I called, but you didn't answer."

He gave me an indecipherable look.

I made an effort to create a semblance of poise. "By the way, I left a note on the kitchen counter for you about our meeting tomorrow. Are you still available to go couch shopping?"

"Sure. What time do you want me to pick you up?"

"You don't need to pick me up."

"Fine. You can pick me up. What time?"

"We can meet at the store. I'll text you the address."

"What if I don't know where it is?"

"GPS it."

"What if I don't have GPS?"

I raised an incredulous eyebrow. "Try Google Maps."

"What's Google Maps?"

"Are you pulling my leg?"

"Who me?" He gave me a wide-eyed look.

"Fine. I'll pick you up at nine thirty. The store opens at ten, and if we can't find what you're looking for there, I have a few more places we can check out."

"Is this place closer to my house or yours?"

"Mine. Why?"

"I'll pick you up. No need for you to go out of your way. Then you can direct me to the store, and I won't get lost."

"Oh, yeah?" It was my turn to smirk. "How are you going to find my house?"

"GPS," Ian deadpanned.

I couldn't hold back the chuckle that escaped. I had no idea verbally sparring with an actor could be so entertaining and frustrating at the same time. I tossed my tote into the CR-V and caved. "Fine, I'll text you my address. Pick me up at quarter to ten. It's only a few minutes from my house."

The hoodie's zipper got caught on my handbag as I slung it toward the passenger seat. I pulled it down to sternum level to try and unhook it, but the evening dusk had faded into darkness and the vehicle's interior light didn't shed enough illumination to see the problem properly. With my back to Ian, I hunched my shoulders, and tugged ineffectually at my purse in hopes it would release.

"Is something wrong?"

I grunted. "My purse is hooked on this zipper, and I can't get it to let go."

"Here, let me help." Ian placed a hand on my shoulder.

"No, no. I'll get it." I shrugged him off. I had no interest in letting him get close to my floppy, braless chest. I continued to tug, but my efforts were fruitless. Giving in, I turned around to face him with scrunched shoulders. "Okay. I need help."

He pulled a set of keys out of his pocket and flicked on a miniature LED flashlight. "Here, shine this at the zipper."

Ian took the purse and the zipper slid farther down to my waist. Thankful for the darkness, I directed the beam at the problem. His dark head bent over as he worked and a knuckle inadvertently brushed against my breast. My belly clenched with desire. It took a physical effort to breathe normally. I hoped Ian couldn't hear my heart hammering because I sure could. It pounded in my ears like a staccato drum. It felt like forever, but in a few seconds, he released the handbag.

"There you go." He took a step back and held it out.

"Thanks," I replied weakly and pulled the sweatshirt across my chest.

"So, we're on for tomorrow?" He seemed utterly relaxed. Apparently, I was the only one getting into a froth.

"Yes." I climbed into the SUV, turned over the engine, and rolled down my window. "Thanks for the dry clothes. I'll launder them and get them back to you tomorrow."

Ian's fingers curled over the window frame. "No rush. Besides, I like to think of you wearing my clothes without a bra and knickers."

Jeez, could this situation get any worse?

Ian wiggled his brows and flashed a cheeky grin. Taking advantage of my shock, he leaned in and gave me a hard kiss that sizzled all the neurons in my brain and headed south.

"Have a good night, luv," he whispered in the darkness. "See you tomorrow."

He sauntered into the house like he didn't have a care in the world.

I gave myself a shake. *Will I ever be on even ground around Ian? Why do I go from a cool, calm professional to an artless wreck every time he comes within a fifteen foot radius?*

"Squawk! Pick up the phone."

"Argh!"

Chapter 8

Ian arrived on time and I dashed through the light drizzle of rain, before he could get out of his truck. He handed me a cup of girlie coffee as I climbed into his midnight black Ford F150.

"Thanks for the coffee." I buckled up. "This is a very manly car."

"I thought we might need it if we found the sofa today. We can load it right into the back."

"Mmm hmm." I grinned into my coffee.

"What?" He glanced at me then back to the road.

"Well, the places we're going aren't likely to have your sofa in stock at the store. Generally, it'll be delivered from the warehouse."

"So, what you're trying to tell me is, I should have driven the Mustang."

"What kind of Mustang?"

"A classic, 1965 convertible."

"Aw, we could've been driving in a convertible Mustang. Is it red? Please don't tell me it's red."

He frowned. "Black. You want to scoot back and get it?"

I looked up at the lightening drizzle. "Not today. We've got shopping to do. The next time you pick me up, I will expect the 'Stang."

"Yes, ma'am."

"Squawk, pick up the phone," blasted through the cab. I scrambled into my bag, turned it off, and sent Ian an apologetic smile. "Sorry, it's my mom."

"Do you need to talk to her?"

"No, I'll call her back later."

The clouds cleared by the time we arrived at Maxim's Furniture, and I regretted my refusal to get the convertible.

We found the perfect sofa within fifteen minutes. Ian splayed across the velvety fabric, running his hand along the nap. A sneaker-clad foot rested on the wood coffee table, much to the hovering manager's chagrin.

"It's soft."

"That's because it's velvet. You like the feel?" I flipped through the fabric swatches, comparing them to the paint chips.

"Abso-bloody-lutely. I can think of a number of things I could do on a sofa like this." He shot me one of his wolfish grins.

I shifted, as heat flooded my downtown area, and pretended to ignore his *entendre*. A soft, heather grey swatch caught my eye, and I held it up for his perusal. "This would be an excellent color for the room, and I've got some fabric for the throw pillows."

"A set of aubergine pillows come with that material color." The manager supplied solicitously.

My nose scrunched up. "Won't fit our color scheme. Ian, what do you think?"

Ian glanced at the cloth, shrugged and continued to pet the couch. "You're the expert, luv. I'll go with whatever color you choose. You haven't steered me wrong yet."

"Can you get the pricing information and a brochure for us?" I smiled.

The manager scurried off to do my bidding.

• • •

The soft sofa would be perfect for lounging around watching the game, but they'd been in the store less than twenty minutes, and now that Ian had her all to himself, he had no plans to end their outing so quickly. After last night's unexpected wet T-shirt show, even the cold shower he'd had to take after she left didn't cool his desire for her. He'd dreamed about her and woken with a raging hard on. Maybe he could negotiate a shorter sentence with the deal they'd struck.

"I think I need to cop a squat on a few more before making a decision," he announced.

Her face displayed a flash of surprise, which she quickly masked. "No problem, if that's what you want. There are two or three more places on we can check out."

To the manager's disappointment, they headed to the next furniture store on Sophie's list. While traveling to the three shops, he pulled more family history out of her, and as he drove to the last store, Ian couldn't help sharing a hilarious incident at work just to see how she'd react.

"So, Jonathan—"

"Wait, which one's Jonathan?" Sophie asked.

"The one who plays Birk. Anyway, he's a real jokester. He worked with the special effects guy to rig these fake eyeballs to pop out when Gunnarson pulled back the sheet on the stiff. Scared the bloody piss out of the three of us. Carmen screeched and ran off set, while the rest of the crew rolled on the floor laughing their arses off. Carmen didn't speak to Jon the rest of the week."

Her tinkling laughter filled the cab. God, he loved the sound of it. It was a turn on as well as a boon to his ego that she appreciated his humor. As he spent more time with her, Ian was coming to find that he wanted to learn more about her to strengthen their connection.

"That's awful. Poor Carmen is probably scarred for life. I don't know how she puts up with all you boys," she scolded.

"Don't kid yourself. Carmen's a good egg. She knows how to put us tossers in our place. After Jonathan's little stunt, she guilted him in to buying her this green-grass juice slop she drinks every morning for the next two weeks. It smells like shite and makes him gag, but he does it."

"Excellent. I can see Carmen has you guys' number."

"That's the truth."

At the stores, Sophie made a clear effort to keep Ian at a distance. He decided to play it her way, and for once, he remained on task with only a few flirtatious quips aimed at her. Even so, every time he offered a helping hand, flashes of heat sparked between them, and he remained persistently aware of her position in relation to him. The way she moved and kept glancing at him under his lashes, he could tell was getting under her skin, but he pretended to remain unaware and nonchalant, although having her so close kept him at a constant low level of arousal. They struck out at the final store, and Ian could see that she was ready to return to the first place, but he had other plans to spin out the afternoon.

"I'm just not sure, luv. Let's think about it over some lunch, shall we?"

"Lunch? Are you sure you need to think about it? The size was perfect, you said it was comfortable and I can get it covered in a material which will work with the room decor. If we order it today, I can put a rush on it, and get it in a week, maybe two."

"Lunch first. What's a good place to eat around here?" He opened the passenger side door for her. The scent of strawberries wafted past as she flicked her hair and climbed into the cab. It took all his effort not to groan and bury his nose in her silky tresses. He thought he heard the click of a camera and his eyes darted around to find the culprit, but didn't see anything out of the ordinary. He shrugged; it may have just been a passerby. It wouldn't be the first time strangers snapped a quick pic. He'd been pleased they'd been left in peace on their outing, so far. It was something that was becoming less and less common as the show gained notoriety.

"We're not too far from my favorite spot, Trattoria Giovanni's." She said as Ian angled into the driver's seat. "I guess you could say I'm a regular there. It's a quaint little family run restaurant off the beaten path, about fifteen minutes away, and closer to Maxims. I'm assuming you want to go back and look at that sofa again."

"Brilliant." The car rumbled to life. "You can direct me."

"Just go to the end of the block and take a left. "

"Tell me about the food at this place."

"My favorite dish is the Portobello stuffed ravioli. I generally eat there a few times a month. They have this beautiful cherry wood and marble bar that the owner had shipped over direct from Italy."

When they arrived, the restaurant was half full, and a young waiter sat them at a table in an empty section. A few minutes after they were seated, a white-haired man came out from the kitchen to greet her. "Sophia! *Bella*! It's been a long time since you visit us."

"Too long." She stood and was enveloped by his embrace. His worn papery hands grasped her face, as she I leaned down so he could kiss her cheeks European style.

"Beppe, meet Ian O'Connor. Beppe Giovanni is the owner," she said with a delighted smile.

"It's good to meet you, sir." Ian rose and they shook hands.

Beppe made a grand gesture. "You finally come here with a man. Always the beautiful Sophia eats alone. Sometimes with the redheaded friend. It is good to see her with a handsome man." He shook his finger at Ian. "You take good care of our Sophia, or you will have to answer to Beppe."

Ian chewed his lip to keep from laughing at Beppe's paternal speech. Clearly, this man knew Sophie well.

Sophie's eyes danced. "Beppe, Ian is a client. We've been on the hunt for the perfect sofa today."

"Are you married?" Beppe asked Ian.

"No, sir."

More finger shaking. "What's wrong? Don't you want to date the beautiful Sophia?"

"With a straight face, he nodded. "Very much."

"Why don't you ask her out?"

"I did. She's making me wait."

Ian sat back and anticipated the reaction. He didn't have long to wait. Beppe's next statement made Sophie's cheeks turn a delightful pink, and if her facial expressions were anything to go by, she looked as if she wished the floor would swallow her whole. Ah, he loved watching her squirm. Her flawless face and sapphire eyes revealed so much.

Beppe turned to her, his silvery eyebrows feathered up, creasing his forehead. "What are you waiting for, *Bella?* This is a handsome man. No?"

"It's complicated." She grimaced.

Beppe threw up his hands in dramatic Italian style. "Young people today. Everything's complicated. Back in my day, you liked a girl, you asked her out. If she was a good Catholic, you married her and had lots of *bambinos.*"

Ian couldn't help chuckling at the simplicity of the old man's statement.

"What do you want to eat?" Beppe asked.

"What do you recommend?" he asked.

"Today?" Beppe's head tilted as he pondered the question. "Penne with marinara, peppers and sausage. *Buonissimo!*"

"I'll have that."

The little Italian turned to Sophie.

"I'll have the same. Thanks."

"You have a glass of Chianti with that. *Perfecto.*" He kissed his fingers and left.

"Look, I'm sorry about Beppe." Sophie rolled her eyes. "He and his wife Maria seem to think they're my personal matchmakers. Every time I come, they talk about setting me up with some man they know. Last time it was their accountant."

"He brings up a good question. Why no men in your life?" His crystal eyes pierced her; all remnants of funny flirtatious Ian vanished.

Sophie shrugged and shifted uncomfortably, but Ian continued to spear her with his eyes, not letting her off the hook.

"Gun-shy, I guess. My ex cheated on me and left my confidence in tatters after the divorce. I've had to work hard to build my company so it would flourish. I put men on the back burner. "

Irritation at her stupid ex flashed through him. "You're a lovely woman, and your ex was a blind prick." He reached across the table to play with her fingers. "Any husband who would cheat on a woman like you is a piss poor excuse for a man."

Her eyes shuttered, she disengaged their hands, and took a sip off water. "Maybe … but maybe we married too young. He never got a chance to sow his wild oats, as they say. Michael wasn't ready to be tied down with a wife and a mortgage."

Wild oats, indeed. What kind of cock up left a beautiful, ambitious, smart woman like Sophie? Ian just couldn't understand, and the fact that she sat across from him trying to justify his actions pissed him off. "That's *bollocks*. When a man finds the right woman, age doesn't matter. Admit it, Soph. He was a cheating arse."

The frown lines between her eyes disappeared and a burble of laughter escaped, going straight to his solar plexus. "You're right. He was an arse."

"That's better. Now, tell me how much longer this blasted renovation is going to take."

"If things keep running on time, then we could be finished in two and a half to three weeks at the most. Mid-November. Before Thanksgiving, in case you were thinking about having guests over."

That was the best news he'd heard all day. Although, it would have been even better had she said the renovations would end next week. "Brilliant. I want to have a party. Introduce you to all my friends and show off your work—"

"Excuse me."

They glanced up.

A college-aged brunette stood next to their table. "Are you Ryder McKay?" she whispered conspiratorially.

"Yes," Ian whispered back.

"Eeee!" She clapped her hands. "I'm your biggest fan. Can I get a picture with you?" The girl held up her phone.

Ian gave a slight grimace and looked at his tablemate in askance.

She shrugged. This was the first time today they'd been directly approached, although Ian was sure at least a few photos had been surreptitiously snapped while they'd been out and about. Really, it wasn't so bad, until the brunette practically fell into Ian's lap for the photo op, rubbing inappropriately against him. Sophie snapped the picture quickly and handed back the phone while Ian gently removed his "biggest fan."

"Thank you so much! You're the best actor, ever," she gushed.

Ian's pasted on a fake smile. "Thanks." He hoped the girl would leave soon.

"My girlfriends and I are going out to The Cellar tonight. You should join us." She giggled.

The Cellar was a sports bar that drew a lot of UCLA college kids and served greasy burgers and fries. The crowd was far too young for his taste, and with Sophie sitting across from him, no other women appealed to him at this time. "Unfortunately, I already have plans." He looked significantly at his tablemate.

Sophie's eyebrows rose to her hairline, and Ian winked at her.

The giggly twit glanced at her as if noticing her existence for the first time.

Sophie gave a smug smile and lifted her shoulders as if to say, "sorry, too late."

She giggled some more then trotted back to her table whispering, at top speed, to her friends. "I told you it was him. Can you believe it?"

"Does that happen often?" Sophie asked.

"Often enough. Don't get me wrong, the fans are great and the show would be nothing without them. I just hope her boldness doesn't encourage others to come over. It's such a rarity I get time with you."

She raised her eyebrows. "You're a busy man."

"You're a busy woman. And I must have been barkin' mad to have allowed you to talk me into this deal."

"I'm sure you can get any girl you want. Women line up around the block to date you."

"I don't want another woman. The only woman I want is you." His mien turned from playful to smoldering in a blink. His broad, callused hand dropped over hers. "I think Beppe's right."

Her face flamed and her jaw dropped. The afternoon's lightness fled with the sudden sexually charged tension. She caught her lower lip between her teeth, and he focused hungrily on her mouth.

"Here we are, penne with sausages and marinara." The server's appearance killed the mood. Beppe's tomato and cheese covered penne masterpiece arrived accompanied by a bowl of salad, garlic bread, and red wine.

While Sophie thanked the waiter, Ian slouched back in his chair. His expression turned enigmatic.

"I know you're going to love it. Beppe's Italian is the best." She gushed.

Leisurely, Ian sat forward and scooped a forkful of some of the most delicious marinara sauce he'd ever put into his mouth. Sophie waited on the edge of her seat for his reaction. You'd have thought she made the pasta herself. Nothing was more fun than pulling at Sophie; she always took the bait. He chewed and swallowed in an unhurried fashion and followed it with a swig of wine. His face showed no expression one way or another.

Finally, she cracked. "Well?"

He sipped the wine again and rolled his tongue around his mouth. "Not bad."

Poor Sophie, her shoulders sank dejectedly.

"You look like I stole your favorite puppy." Then he flashed a sexy smile. "I'm just having a go at you. It's excellent."

She perked up. "Do I have sucker written across my forehead?"

"Nah, I like messing with you. I never know what kind of reaction I'll get."

While they ate, she shifted the topic back to the reno. Unfortunately, there was little time to actually talk about it. Ian had been right. Three more people stopped by their table before they finished the meal. Sophie, being a good sport, snapped two more pictures, while he signed a bar napkin, a ratty piece of paper and declined an offer to sign a woman who thrust her chest at him. She settled for her arm. During the chest signing debacle, much to Ian's displeasure, Sophie paid the check.

He didn't say anything until they were back in his truck. "Damn it, Sophie. I was going to pay the check."

She waved his argument away with her hand. "You're my client. It was my treat. Besides, I can write it off as a business expense."

"Is that what I am to you? A business expense?" he said in a hurt voice.

"Absolutely not! You know you're more than that to me."

"I don't know anything!" he exploded. "You hold me at arm's length. You're always reserved, except for the few times your sassy side peeks out. I don't know where the devil I stand with you." *Where did that come from?* The angry outburst hung in the air between them, and she fidgeted with her hands.

"Come on, Ian. I'm a big girl. I'm used to taking care of things myself. Besides, we have a deal. I know it's hell waiting, but ... I can't go down that road with you until our business is finished," she answered in a quiet tone.

He sighed and wiped a hand down his face. "I know. You're right. I'm sorry. I'm just bloody irritated our lunch was buggered up by all those people. Fans are great, and it's the life actors sign up for. But … sometimes it's all rubbish."

She patted his shoulder. "I found it kinda funny."

He looked at her like she was insane.

"Oh, come on. You made that overweight housewife's day. By the way, some of her lipstick is still on your cheek." She pointed at her left cheek and handed him a tissue.

He wiped away the bright pink smudge in disgust.

"Now are you ready to buy a sofa?"

"I was ready hours ago. You kept dragging me from shop to shop."

"Urk. Why you! I was … you were the one … "

"Just having a go at you, Soph." He flashed a megawatt smile at her.

Her breath seemed to hitch. Hmm, perhaps he turned her on more than he'd originally thought.

"Let's go buy a sofa." He watched her swallow and nod.

• • •

"Damn it, Holly. I swear if you don't call me back, I'm hopping on the next plane to Vegas!" The cell phone clattered across the counter. It wasn't an idle threat. I was earnestly beginning to consider flying out next weekend to find out what the hell was going on with my sister.

It was Sunday, and my mother had called me three times during my shopping trip with Ian and once this morning to find out if I'd spoken with Holly. Neither one of us had heard from her, and Mom's paranoia wasn't only driving me nuts, it was starting to tentacle its way into my subconscious.

Sirius, sensing my sour mood, waffled at my heels. My fingers swept along his backbone and I crouched to eye level, taking his big head in my hands. "Who's my good boy? Who's a good dog?"

"Woof." He dropped a hank of rope at my feet, and a pink tongue zipped out, leaving a line of slobber along the side of my face. I tossed the rope down the hall. Nails scrabbled to find purchase on the tile as Sirius dashed away to retrieve his favorite toy.

My cell phone jingled out "Sweet Home Alabama," my sister's favorite song, and jerked me from my musings.

"Holly?"

"No need to come running out to Vegas, big sister. Everything's fine."

"What's going on, Holly? Why aren't you returning phone calls to Mom and me?"

"No reason. I'm just busy with Eva and taking care of the house and Omar." She sounded defensive. "Just because I don't have my own company doesn't mean I can't be busy too."

"Holly," I said dryly. "No one's saying your life isn't important and busy. But Mom's driving me nuts. What's going on? Did she make you mad? Is that why you're not calling her back?"

She sighed. "No, I'm not mad. It's just I don't really want her to come stay here again. I know she's angling to come out, but she irritates Omar. Then I pay the price."

"What the hell does that mean, you pay the price?"

"Oh, nothing. Omar just gets … you know … irritable. Didn't Mom do the same thing when you were married to Michael?"

"No. He loved Mom. He loved all women. That was his problem. Omar needs to get over himself. She's your mother. I mean, come on. His mom is no big prize either."

"Yes, but they live on the East Coast, so we barely ever see them."

I pinched the bridge of my nose between my forefinger and thumb. "Just call her. She's dating someone. I'm sure she wants to share her news. Tell her if it's inconvenient to visit right now, but the holidays are coming up. Omar's going to have to suck up some family time. You know Mom's going to want to see Eva for Christmas."

"Can you take her for Thanksgiving?"

Take her for Thanksgiving? She's not a pet! I rolled my eyes. "Yes, I suppose so. Do you want to come here for Thanksgiving?"

"Probably not. Omar's making plans to go skiing in Utah for the week."

For some unknown reason, that news irritated the hell out of me. "Fine. I'll deal with Mom for Thanksgiving, if you call her and work out Christmas."

"I'll see what I can do."

"You do that. And, Holly, you need to start returning our phone calls. Even if it's to say you got them and don't have time to talk. Otherwise, you'll end up with one of us unexpectedly standing on your doorstep. Got it?"

"Yes, yes. I've got it. Like I said, there's no need for you to come here. It's all fine," my sister replied sullenly. "Just don't call on Tuesday or Wednesday. Those are Omar's days off. Also, don't call before eleven. He gets in late and needs it quiet to sleep. I usually turn the ringer off."

"Tuesday and Wednesday, fine. Why don't you tell Mom? I'm sure she'd understand."

"Um-hm."

"Holly," some prickle of unease made me say, "if you ever need anything. Anything at all. You know you can count on me."

There was silence on the line.

Holly whispered, "Thanks, Soph." Then she hung up.

All of my sister's answers made sense, but in this equation, two and two didn't add up to four.

Frustrated, I whistled and Sirius scampered into the kitchen. He went into a delirious doggie dance when I hooked a leash to his collar. "Come on, boy. Let's go for a walk. Your aunt Holly is giving me a headache, and I need to get some fresh air."

Halloween was a few days away and my neighborhood was filled with ghosts and bats hanging from trees and jack-o-lanterns on porches. A few industrious souls turned their front lawns into moss and spiderweb-draped graveyards. Sirius set off at a scurrying pace, darting back and forth. He sniffed every tree, light post and fire hydrant in sight. I allowed him to set the direction and followed behind with my churning thoughts.

My woman's intuition sent up alarm bells, but my concerns were nebulous, and I couldn't put my finger on the exact problem. Holly's insistence no one come for a visit bothered me the most. Was my mother right about Holly taking drugs? Or was Omar just an overbearing jerk, turning my sister into a homemaker for his own needs and to hell with hers? Was he making her a *Stepford wife*? Or did Holly just need space? A child always added new stresses on a marriage. Maybe Holly and Omar were trying to work through the changes without the added pressure of extended family around. Perhaps they were fighting and she didn't want the family to see.

Sirius headed into the street, and I tugged the leash to reel him back onto the sidewalk. Maybe it was smart of Holly to put her marriage and family first. As she should. Was that one of the reasons my marriage fell apart? Did I allow my extended family too much access during our early years?

What was I thinking?

Mental head slap. Ian was right. My ex was a cheating arse.

So far, Ian was nothing like him. I enjoyed my time with him. Beyond his physical magnificence, he was a kind and funny man. A man who hadn't moved on to his next dalliance as I'd expected. Still, there were a few more weeks before the reno was finished, and Ian could prove me wrong. After all, he had women throwing themselves at him all the time, although I was impressed at his reaction to the stupid co-ed who fell into his lap. He didn't seem to appreciate it and removed her as quickly as he could.

Sirius jerked the leash, and I realized he was headed for a munchkin excitedly clapping her hands and hopping from foot to foot in the yard we were passing.

"A doggie, a doggie. Look, Daddy. Can I pet him?"

The father, who had grabbed his daughter's arm to keep her from running over to a large, strange dog, looked at me. "I don't know. We have to ask."

I nodded. "Sure you can. Sirius, sit."

Sirius plopped onto the cement, and his tongue lolled out of the side of his mouth. I gripped his collar as the curly brown-haired dervish flew toward us.

"Annie, slow down!" The father hurried after her.

Sirius tried to pop up, but I held him still. "Sit!"

I wasn't worried about Sirius biting the little girl. It was more likely he'd get overexcited and knock her down, all in the name of play.

When she got to the sidewalk, I knelt to her level. "Okay, okay." I halted her headlong rush. "First, you have to show Sirius you're a friend. Hold out your hand so he can smell it."

The child obeyed my instruction. Sirius gave a sniff then licked her hand. "What's his name?"

"Sirius."

"That's a funny name."

"It's the Dog Star. The brightest star in the sky," Annie's father replied and stuck out his hand. "Hi. I'm Gary Sumner, and this is my daughter, Annie."

"Sophie Hartland." I rose and we shook hands. "I live down the street, around the corner."

"It's nice to meet you. Sirius is a real beauty."

"Thanks."

"Annie's crazy about dogs, but my wife has allergies ... " He shrugged with a resigned smile.

I scrambled for small talk and fell back on an old reliable. "What kind of work do you do, Gary?"

"I'm a police detective with the LAPD."

"Then our meeting must be providence. I've been thinking about installing a new security system. What do you recommend?" We fell into conversation about the pros and cons of different systems while Annie petted Sirius.

"E-mail me and I'll send you a couple of contacts I trust." Gary dug a beat-up brown wallet out of the back pocket of his Levi's and handed me his business card. "

"That sounds good. Thanks, Gary. We'd better be on our way. Good-bye, Annie."

"Good-bye, Sirius. Come back and visit me again."

"Sure thing." I waved and as we continued our walk, my mind went back to Holly and her issues. Eventually, I decided Mom and I were being paranoid and to let it ride.

Chapter 9

I was bent over a piece of the headboard, spraying touch-ups, when Michelle stepped out onto the back patio. It was mid-week, and the house was a hive of activity.

"Hi, boss. Got the barbeque for the crew's lunch break."

The sun shone in my eyes when I looked up. I flinched and placed a hand on my forehead to shade the glare. "Glad you're back. The boys are getting hungry. I'm about finished with this headboard. Jack said he'd hang it after lunch."

"Sure thing. Is there … anything else?"

I straightened. "Javier's working on the tile in the bathroom. Why don't you take a moment to check it out?"

"Umm hmm. Annnyythiiiing else?" She wiggled her brows at me.

"What are you getting at, Michelle?"

"This." She slapped a magazine down on the granite outdoor bar.

"What's that?" My head tilted. I walked over to see what she was talking about.

A stubby pink fingernail stabbed at two photos on page three of a tabloid. I dug in my back pocket for my reading glasses so I could get a better look.

One was a grainy picture of Ian and me outside of the furniture store in Burbank. He held the car door and my eyes were locked on him. The headline read "Baby on Board." A short caption beneath the photo asked "Is handsome hunk Ian O'Connor off the market? He was spotted with an unidentified woman shopping for cribs. Are congratulations in order?" The second photo showed Ian's arm around my waist as he held the door while we entered Giovanni's.

Steam shot out of my ears. I held the tabloid closer. "What the hell? What the hell! Ian's right. The press just makes shit up.

They don't even sell baby furniture at that store." I threw the paper down.

"So, you're not pregnant?"

I gave her a squinty-eyed stare that could strip wallpaper off a wall.

"I guess that's a no."

"You're damn right that's a no."

"Hey." She put her hands up defensively. "What do I know? Ian's a hottie. I thought maybe you two were doing the knicky-knacky on the side, you know?"

"We are *not* doing the knicky-knacky. I don't do the knicky-knacky with clients." *At least not yet.*

"Okay. Okay. So, what are you going to do?"

I blew out a puff of air. "I suppose I should call him. I wonder if he knows."

"I'll just give you some privacy." Michelle tiptoed back into the house, and I pulled the cell out of my pocket.

"Hello? Is that you, Sophie?" Ian bellowed into the phone over the background sounds of wind and traffic.

"Ian?" I spoke loudly. "Um, I think we have a problem."

"What? I can't hear you. Let me call you back." Click.

My fingers drummed impatiently on the offensive piece of yellow journalism. The phone trilled the opening theme song to *LA Heat*. "Ian?"

"I stepped inside. What do you need?"

"Listen, I'm sorry to interrupt your work, but I think we have a problem."

"Okay. Something wrong at the house?"

"No. The house is fine. I'm holding a copy of the *Star* tabloid, and there's a photo of us from Saturday. It says you were shopping for a baby crib and indicates we're having a baby." I read the headline and caption for him.

The news met silence.

"Hello? Are you still there?"

"I am. I'm sorry about this—"

I cut him off. "There's nothing for *you* to be sorry about. You were right that these tabloids just make stuff up."

"They do indeed."

"What should we do about it? If my mom gets wind of this, I'm doomed." Thoughts of my mom's reaction made my voice pitch with panic.

"I'll phone my manager."

"He's going to say you should have hired a publicist to deal with this type of garbage." My shoes slapped against the concrete as I paced.

"You're probably right. If we ignore it, it might go away. If I stir things up, it might get worse."

"How can it get worse?" I whimpered. "They basically called me a fat cow. Do I look pregnant to you? Never mind, don't answer that."

"No, luv. You don't look preggers. If you do, the buggers probably Photoshopped it."

The picture showed me in profile and my jacket billowed in front. The wind must have kicked up at the exact moment the photo was taken.

"Do you want my manager to have them retract the statement?"

I blew out a sigh.

"Soph?"

"No. You're right. My name's not even mentioned. And they didn't actually make a statement, only conjecture. It'll probably get worse if we make a big deal about it."

A girl's voice called Ian's name in the background.

"You need to get back to work."

"Call me if you want me to do something about it. Okay?"

"Ian, they need you on set," the voice said closer.

"I'll be with you in two shakes." His voice faded out as he spoke to whoever called his name, then it came back full volume. "Are you going to be okay?"

"Yes, yes. I'll be fine. Get back to work. I'm sorry to have bothered you."

"You're never a bother. Call me if you change your mind."

The tantalizing scent of tangy barbeque danced across my olfactory senses when I entered the house. The conversation cut off. Jack, Javier, Michelle, and three other crew members huddled around the kitchen island harfing down pork sandwiches and fries, studiously ignoring me.

"All right. Out with it." I popped my left hip forward and crossed my arms.

"Out with what?" Michelle asked with wide-eyed innocence.

"Let's hear it. I know you were talking about the tabloid."

"So, boss, what color will we be painting the baby's room?" Jack deadpanned.

The crew broke up.

"Is that all you got?" I raised an eyebrow.

"Ian and Sophie sitting in a tree, K-I-S-S-I-N-G," Michelle sang. Jack joined in, and their voices rose together to sing the finale, "A baby in a *baby* carriage!"

Everyone clapped and made kissy noises.

I mashed my lips together. "Are you done now?"

"Lady, I'm just getting started." Jack guffawed then continued, "We'll be dining out on this for weeks. Maybe months."

"Okay, let's get this straight right now. There is no baby on the way." I pointed at Michelle's grinning face. "And there is no knicky-knacky going on."

"So, who's the hold out on the knicky-knacky?"

The crew's laughter scorched my ears. Michelle handed me a foil-wrapped sandwich.

"Here," Javier held out his half-eaten lunch toward me. "Do you want mine also, since you're eating for two, Missus Sophie?"

"Ha, ha. You guys are a laugh riot. I'm going to eat outside." I swept out with as much dignity as I could muster; their snickers followed me out the door.

• • •

Six hours later I steered out of Ian's driveway; the gate rolled closed behind me. Across the street stood a man next to a bright yellow crotch rocket, a camera held up to his eye. Luckily, I wore large sunglasses and my CR-V had tinted windows. Still, I shot into the street and whizzed down the road at a fast clip. At the first red light, I texted Ian.

BTW paparazzi vultures stationed outside your house.

My cell sing-songed "Let's Get this Party Started," by The Black Eyed Peas. I tapped my Bluetooth.

"Hey, Poppy," I chirped happily. Both our schedules had been so crazy, and Poppy had taken a ten-day vacation to Maui with Angel, so we hadn't seen each other in weeks. Except for the two phone calls pestering me to attend her Halloween party, we hadn't spoken recently either. Our communication had been limited to brief texts and comments via Facebook status.

"What's this I hear? You're having Ian's love child?"

"Did Michelle call you?"

"Michelle? No. My assistant, Cody, showed me the photo in *Star*. You're doing the nasty with Ian?"

"We're not. We were shopping for a sofa."

"So, you two aren't humping like rabbits?"

"Not right now."

"Oooo. That's a loaded response."

"Shesh. You're as bad as Michelle and Jack."

"What does Michelle know that I don't?"

"She knows nothing. Because there is *nothing* to tell," I enunciated. "I just spent the entire afternoon putting up with wisecracks from the crew. Don't you start."

The whine of a motorcycle made me check the rearview mirror, but I couldn't see where it was coming from.

"You didn't answer my question. Are you and Ian planning to do the dirty mambo soon?"

I realized, beyond texting Poppy that Ian and Tanqueray weren't an item, we hadn't spoken about him much at all. "We're not planning anything. Maybe we'll have a date after the reno is finished."

"Maybe you'll have a date?"

"Yes, if he hasn't started seeing someone else."

"Does he want to date you?"

"Um. Yes."

"Girl! What is wrong with you? Say yes! Go on a date with that fine man."

"I don't date clients."

"Have you lost your mind?"

"No. If I go out with him, I will totally sleep with him, and how would that look if I'm working for him? Think what would happen if he woke up the next morning and wanted to gnaw his arm off."

"Come off it. You're not coyote ugly."

"You know what I mean. What if, in the light of the morning, he sees my wiggly parts and totally regrets doing the nasty? Or worse, the sex sucks and he asks me to leave immediately afterward?"

"He's a man. I've told you before, men like boobs. They like something to grab on to. You're not a fat cow. You're shaped like a woman." This coming from a gorgeous redhead the size of a toothpick. "And with a man like that, the sex has got to be smokin'."

"If it's not, it would be awkward spending an entire month working on his house. We'd play the avoidance game. He could fire me. So, we made a deal—no dating, no hanky-panky until the reno is finished."

"Wait a minute. When did you make this deal?"

"Just before we started. The night I showed him the design board."

"So, something happened that night."

"Nothing. It wasn't a big deal."

"Spill."

"We kissed."

A shriek split my eardrum. "You kissed Ryder McKay! Omigod! Was it a good kiss?"

My cheeks dimpled. "Yup."

Poppy was silent. "Is that all you're going to say?"

"Yup."

"That's it. I'm coming over tonight. It's been forever and a day since we've seen each other, and clearly we have things to catch up on."

"Fine. Come on over around eight and bring a bottle of wine. I only have one."

"Do you want red or white?"

"How about a cab sauv?"

"I'll look. There were bottles left over from the Halloween blow-out you refused to attend. See you about eight."

I continued to glance at the mirror on my drive home. Nothing. Taking precautions, I drove by the house to see if there were any camera-wielding sharks before I pulled into the garage.

My sense of relief was short-lived. A whirr and clicking noise made me turn away from the mailbox at my front door.

"Do you know the sex of the baby?"

It was the same man I'd seen across from Ian's house. I scanned the street and located the yellow motorbike about four houses down. My eyes got squinty. "Did you follow me home? Are you stalking me? There are laws against that, you know."

The camera clicked three more times. "What's your name? How long have you and Ian O'Connor been dating? Are you living together?" He peppered me with questions.

The realization that this wasn't going to "go away" backhanded me like a tennis racket. I decided to meet the problem head on.

"Are you recording our conversation?"

"No, but I can." He whipped out a cell from his back pocket. "Shoot."

I pulled the phone up close to my mouth and deliberately enunciated each word. "There is no scoop. I am *not* having an affair with Mr. O'Connor. I am the proprietor of Hartland Designs, and I'm an interior decorator, working for Mr. O'Connor. We were *not* shopping for cribs, we were shopping for sofas. That store doesn't even carry baby furniture. If you're in the market for a decorator, look me up. I'm in the phone book. One more thing, if your paper prints any more lies, Mr. O'Connor and I will sue you." I flipped the mailbox shut. "Also, get off my porch. This is private property." I banged the front door in the stranger's face.

Sirius danced in from the backyard with his tail wagging and tongue licking to worship at my feet. Everyone should get a dog. They provided unconditional love and never cheated on you. I scratched behind his ears.

"Who's a good dog? Do you want your dinner?"

Sirius went into an ecstatic frenzy, huffing and snorting at the word dinner, and nosed his empty dish across the floor. While I poured kibble in his bowl, I debated whether or not to call Ian. Perhaps recording the conversation wasn't such a smart thing. The press was known for taking quotes out of context. Cripes, they could rearrange all my words and make it sound like I was the proprietor of a whorehouse providing services to Ian. The possibility of more lies being printed worried me, so I called him.

"Hello, luv. I got your text. It looks like we'll be working late tonight, so the vulture will probably have buggered off by the time I get home."

"Oh, I'm sure he will have buggered off by then."

"What happened?"

"He followed me home and snuck up on my front porch and hammered me with questions while I was getting the mail." It all came out in a rush.

"Fuckin' 'ell!" Ian spat out in a growly voice I'd never heard.

I was taken aback by his vehemence. There was silence on the other end. "Ian?" I said in a small voice.

"I'm still here," he ground out.

"Listen, I'm sorry. I checked my rearview mirror, but I didn't see him following me."

"Sophie."

"Yes?"

"I'm not angry with you. I'm angry those fucknuggets followed you home, and I'm trying not to blow a gasket here."

I'd never heard Ian curse like that, two fucks in the span of thirty seconds. He must be super pissed. "Oh. Well, there's really just one guy. I, uh, spoke to him. I think you may want to talk to your manager."

"What did you say?"

I explained our conversation and told him about the recording.

"Since they're following you, this is obviously not going to go away, luv."

"I know. It's not your fault. The media is voracious."

"Make sure to set your security system."

"Uh, riiight." I chewed a thumbnail.

"You don't have a security system, do you?"

"Sure I do."

I could hear him rub a disbelieving hand down his face through the phone lines.

"How can a single woman living in the LA area not have a security system?"

"I'm working on it. It just hasn't come to fruition yet. I'll call someone tomorrow to get it set up. Don't worry. I have Sirius, and Poppy's coming over tonight. There's safety in numbers."

"Sirius? Who the hell is Sirius?"

"My dog. He's a big dog. A black Lab. He's very protective."

"Hold on. I'll ring you back in ten." He clicked off.

That was abrupt. I pulled an open bottle of pinot grigio from the fridge and filled a wineglass to its brim. The glass was empty after three gulps, and I refilled it before heading into the family room to collapse on the couch. Sirius followed me and placed his big head on the cushion next to my left hand. This was Sirius's way of asking to be petted. I obliged. I could never refuse his sad doggie eyes.

By the time Ian called back, a warm jelly feeling floated through my limbs, my feet rested on the coffee table, and things didn't seem so bad.

"Hel-lo."

"A guy by the name of Hal is coming over. He's with Galveston Security. They're going to get you set up."

"When are they coming?"

"In about twenty minutes."

My feet thumped to the ground and I shot forward. "Tonight? No, no, no, no. Poppy's coming over. We're having a girl's evening. I plan to drink an entire bottle of wine. Call Hal back and tell him to come tomorrow."

"Either Hal's coming over or I am," he threatened.

I switched tactics and said in my best sex kitten voice, "Is that a promise, baby?"

Ian sighed. "You're killing me. You need a security system, and I don't know when I'll be able to get away from the studio. If I come over tonight, everything you told the paparazzi will become a lie. Do you really want that?"

Did I want that? Yes. "No."

"Please let Hal in when he shows up. Otherwise, I'm going to worry."

Guilt welled up for making him worry. "Okay. Hal can come in, but I'm still drinking a bottle of wine."

"Hey, feel free to get pissed. Just don't complain to me if you've got a foul head in the morning.

"Yeah, yeah."

"You're going to let Hal in to do his job. Right?"

"Whatever you say."

"Promise me, Sophia Hartland."

"Jeez. I promise."

"Don't worry, luv. This will all get sorted out."

My other line beeped. "I trust you. I've got to go. My mom's on the other line. I hope she's not calling about the tabloid. Bye."

"Keep your mobile close. I'll ring you later."

I clicked over to the other line. "Hi, Mom."

"Is it true?"

"I'm assuming you're speaking of the pregnancy rumors."

"Pregnancy? What? Are you pregnant?"

"Never mind. And no, I'm not pregnant. What are you calling about?"

"Holly left a message telling me she was going skiing at Thanksgiving."

"Don't worry, Mom. You can come visit me. We'll have a nice dinner here. I'll invite some friends over."

"I don't care what Holly says, I'm going to Vegas at Christmas. They can't keep me away from my granddaughter at Christmastime."

"I'm sure Holly will welcome you at Christmas."

The doorbell rang. Sirius popped up and stampeded to the door with a bark.

"I've got to go. Poppy just arrived. I'll call you this weekend to work out our Thanksgiving plans. Love you."

Poppy wasn't at my door. A cute, russet-haired guy with a baby face, wearing a blue polo and a Galveston Security logo stood on my front stoop. He took a step back when he caught sight of Sirius through the storm door. I grasped him by the collar, a precaution I always took with Sirius. Contrary to what I'd told Ian, he greeted everyone with a pink tongue lolling out of the side of his mouth and a flapping tail. If I allowed it, Sirius would most likely knock a visitor down and lick them silly rather than attack. Only on rare occasions did he take a dislike to someone, and I'm pretty sure he could be easily bribed with treats.

"Let me guess. Hal?"

"Yes, ma'am. That's me. Hal Pretsky at your service." He held out a set of credentials.

Sure enough, his credentials identified him as Hal Pretsky, Security Technician. I estimated his age to be mid-twenties.

"Come in. I assume you'll assess my needs tonight and we'll schedule the install after that."

"No, ma'am." He followed me into the hall. "Mr. O'Connor wants the system installed tonight. My partner's bringing another truck with the equipment."

"Tonight! How long will that take?"

"Depends. It normally takes half a day or more."

"Listen, tonight you can give me an estimate, and we'll get it installed tomorrow."

He tugged his ear. "Mr. O'Connor was pretty adamant. He wanted the system installed tonight."

"Uhn." I smacked my forehead. "Okay, Hal. I'm having company over, and it's too late to do a full install. Just tell me what I need, and you can come back bright and early tomorrow morning."

"But Mr. O'Connor … "

"Look, pal, what Mr. O'Connor doesn't know won't hurt him. I won't tell if you don't."

"I guess we could come back early tomorrow."

"Great. What time?"

"Seven."

"Make it eight. If you come at seven, I might have to kill you. Now, go call your buddy and tell him to get a good night's sleep."

"Yes, ma'am." He trotted out the front door, dialing along the way.

I was going to have to put an end to that. I hated when people ma'amed me. It made me feel like my grandmother. The guy couldn't be more than five years younger than me.

The doorbell chimed, again. Sirius barked, again. I grabbed his collar … again.

This time it was Poppy, dressed casually in jeans, sneakers, and a pumpkin wrap top.

"What's with the dude in your front yard?" She gave me a peck on the cheek and breezed past me down the hall to the kitchen. Sirius and I followed in her wake of Channel No. 5.

"He's my security system tech."

"Oh yeah? What kind of security system are you getting?"

"Whatever Hal says I need."

Poppy picked up the wine glass I'd left on the counter for her. "Mine?"

I nodded. "There's an open pinot in the fridge. Did you bring the cab sauv?"

She removed a bottle from a Trader Joe's paper bag and brandished it at me. "I also have Oreos, sweet potato chips, grapes, and Brie to heat up. I assume you have crackers."

The doorbell rang.

"Top shelf of the pantry." I left Poppy to warm up our dinner and trailed Sirius back to the front door. It was Hal.

"Did you call your buddy and tell him to come tomorrow?"

"Yes. It's all set for eight."

"Then come on in." I led Hal into the kitchen, where he instantly fell in love with Poppy. He might have drooled. Sometimes I forgot what her perfect figure, striking face, and flaming hair did to ordinary guys.

"So, Hal." I snapped him out of his trance. "Why don't you cruise around the house and figure out what needs to be done then get back to me."

"Yes, ma'am." He stuttered and backed out of the kitchen, taking his eyes off Poppy at the last minute

"Let's get comfy on the couch and we'll catch up." I scooped up the chips and cookie bag in one hand and the pinot grigio in the other. Poppy got the rest. We laid our bounty on the coffee table and dropped down on the couch. Sirius shoved himself past my legs, parked his butt between the two of us and proceeded to stare and drool at the coffee table fare.

"Here's to new men in our lives," Poppy toasted.

We clinked glasses.

"Wait. What new men?"

"Angel and I broke up."

"What? What do you mean you broke up? You just spent ten days on the beaches of Maui with him. What happened?"

"Correction. We spent four days."

"What happened? I'm out of the loop." I made a swirly motion with my forefinger.

Poppy gave a dramatic sigh. "He snuck out at one in the morning to screw the Australian surf instructor and thought I wouldn't notice. By the time he returned at five, his luggage was in the hallway and the front desk was kind enough to change the key card for me."

I snorted wine through my nose, and tears burned my eyes. "Where did he go?"

"I have no idea. Probably back to the surf instructor. I don't know. She didn't show up at the hotel after that."

"Does he have any of his stuff at your house?"

"Not anymore." She winked at me with sly nonchalance.

"What did you do?"

"Had a bonfire in the backyard."

My eyes popped wide. "Damn. When?"

"After the Halloween party. I thought it was a good time for a fire."

"I'm sorry I missed it. Did you have any stuff at his place?"

"Tsk. Puh-lease. That man-child rented a room in a fleabag townhome with four other smelly men. I went in the house only once."

"Weren't you heartbroken? Why didn't you call me?"

Poppy waved her wineglass. "Not really. He was starting to bore me. I mean, he had that sexy bad boy image going on, but …. Besides, when I showed up on the beach the next morning sans boyfriend, it was easy to meet men. As a matter of fact, I had my own little vacation fling with a dermatologist from Ohio."

"Ohio?"

"Just a sec. I have a picture on my phone." She headed to the kitchen to retrieve her purse.

Hal walked in. "I have a few recommendations for your security system."

"Have a seat, Hal. Would you like something to eat? Can I get you a soda or glass of water?"

He shook his head. "No thanks. I'm fine." He unfolded a brochure, handed it to me and sat in the club chair next to me. "As you can see, we offer both hard-wire and wireless security systems." Hal proceeded to outline the pros and cons of each system.

Poppy returned to her seat and waited patiently while Hal droned on.

I stopped him mid-spiel. "Hal, I'm gonna stop you there. Let's cut to the chase. Did you install Mr. O'Connor's system?"

"Yes. I was on the team that installed his system."

"So you're a trustworthy fellow. Right?"

"Yes, I'd consider myself trustworthy."

"Then just tell me what you'd recommend to, say … your sister or mother."

"Combo wireless and hard-wired. Touch pads at the front and back doors. Wire all your windows and doors. A couple of glass—"

I put my palm up and Hal stopped. "Whatever you say. It all sounds good."

"I can't believe you haven't done this already." Poppy said.

"There didn't seem to be an urgent need until today." I turned back to Hal. "What will this set me back?"

Hal tugged his ear. A habit he seemed to have when uncomfortable. "Um … Mr. O'Connor gave us his credit card and told us to put in a top of the line system."

Poppy squeaked.

I rolled my eyes. "I can pay for my own system."

More ear tugging. "My boss told me, under no circumstances were you to pay for the system … " His voice trailed off.

I huffed. "It's a conspiracy. So, what will this set Ian back?"

"I'm not sure I'm supposed to tell you."

"Cripes." I threw up my hands.

Hal's eyes ping-ponged back and forth between Poppy and me, but he remained mum.

My cell chimed Ian's ringtone. *Perfect!*

"Hello, Ian."

"Did Hal show up yet?"

"Yes, he did, as a matter of fact. I'm glad you called. It seems we're having a problem with the bill."

"What's the problem, luv?"

"They won't let me pay it. Hal's under the impression you're paying for my new security system."

Silence.

"Ian?"

"I feel responsible."

I didn't want to have this discussion in front of Hal and Poppy, so I moved to the kitchen. "This is so *not* your responsibility. It's *my* home. I can pay for my own security system."

"Look, we both know if I wasn't who I am, none of this paparazzi rubbish would be happening, and your dog would be all the security you'd need."

"Even so, it's not right having you pay for this. I don't rely on men to pay for my things." Michael had "paid" for things, too. Only as I found out later, he'd just piled it on a credit card. Whatever the case, I didn't need a *man* to pay for my stuff.

"I can afford it."

"So can *I*," I replied stubbornly.

"Soph, I need to go. We'll talk about this tomorrow. Bye." He hung up.

"Chicken!" I bellowed at the phone.

Fine. Two people can play this game. I marched back to the family room and stood in the doorway, hands on hips. "Hal, go ahead and charge Mr. O'Connor's credit card, but I expect to see a final reckoning. Clear?"

He jumped out of his seat. "Yes, ma'am. We'll be here at seven tomorrow."

"Eight!" I barked.

"Eight." Hal gathered his things and scurried out the door.

I flopped on the couch, stuffed a cookie in my pie hole and chased it with the rest of the wine in my glass. Poppy refilled me with the cabernet sauvignon.

"So, let's see this dentist from Ohio."

"Dermatologist." Poppy passed me her phone. The picture showed Poppy looking fabulous in a blue bikini, wrapped around a smiling dirty blond man wearing sunglasses and flowered board shorts with fabulous biceps. His skin was almost as fair as Poppy's. They looked adorable together.

"Mm. He's a cutie. I can see why you went for him. Did you exchange phone numbers?"

"Yes. But, it won't go anywhere. It was just a fling." She shrugged and popped a grape in her mouth.

"Hm … " I flipped through some more of the Maui photos. Poppy remained pale, the dermatologist darkened to a medium tan.

"So, what the hell's going on? Why is Ian O'Connor paying for your security system?"

"Uhn." I flopped my head back against the couch. "A paparazzi vulture followed me home from his house and pounced when I got the mail. Ian was pissed and concerned for my safety."

"That sucks."

"Tell me about it. He probably got some hideous photos of me giving him the evil eye."

"What are you going to do about the bill?"

"I'm going to take it out of my design fee."

"Smart thinking."

"That's me. Always using my noggin." I tapped my forehead.

"When are you going to let him into your pants?"

"Poppy!" I winged a chip at her head. "You're so crude."

"I don't know what you're waiting for." She plucked the chip out of her hair and crunched down.

I groaned. "The renovations will be finished in a few weeks. It'll happen soon. Then at least if it goes nowhere, I'm not working in his house every day."

"I think you're nuts. I would have shagged him seven ways from Sunday by now," she replied in her best English accent.

"Trust me. It's not easy. I keep making an ass of myself." I told her about the swimming pool accident and the phone conversation with my mom I was pretty sure Ian had heard. Poppy laughed hysterically.

We talked until we were hoarse and the wine bottles empty. She told me about the wicked things she did with her dermatologist in Hawaii, while I poured all of my doubts and uncertainties about Ian and my own insecurities into her ears. I wanted him, no doubt about it, but I my emotions were starting to play a role, and it worried me. I put her up in my guest room, and when I fell into bed, it was just past midnight.

Chapter 10

Like clockwork, Hal and his partner were on my doorstep at eight. If the doorbell didn't wake the house, Sirius made sure we were up with his barking. Fifteen minutes later, Poppy and I nursed hangovers with cups of coffee and aspirin, while the guys started their job. It was eight thirty when Ian called.

"Hello," I croaked.

"How's the hangover?"

"Bad."

"How's the security system?"

"Great."

"Mmm hmm." He paused. "You have anything to tell me, Miss Hartland?"

"Nope. It's all good."

"They're installing it now, aren't they?"

"That depends."

"Depends on what?"

"On whether or not you're going to blow a gasket, Mister O'Connor."

"You didn't let them install it last night, did you?"

"There wasn't time, and everything is just fine. It'll be up and running today, so don't get your knickers in a twist."

"Did you just tell me not to get my knickers in a twist?" he rumbled.

I sighed and put my head on the table. "Please, Ian, don't yell at me. I can't handle it this morning."

He snickered and softened his tone. "Poor baby. Do I need to get you a girlie coffee to make you feel better?"

"As much as I would adore a girlie coffee, I have to turn you down. In about ten minutes, I'm gonna pull my act together, shower, and head over to a prospective client's house. I won't get to your house until this afternoon, but thanks for the offer."

"How long will the install take?"

"Dunno. Let me check. *Hal!*" I immediately regretted raising my voice.

"What?" He came into the kitchen.

"Mr. O'Connor wants to know how long all this will take."

"Probably five or six hours."

"Five or six hours," I relayed.

"Put Hal on the phone."

I handed the phone over to Hal and laid my head back on the table.

"Yes, sir. Yes … of course, sir, by all means. Yes … Ok. Good-bye." Hal passed the phone back to me and disappeared.

"What was that all about?" I asked Ian.

"Just making sure he knows what's expected."

"Yes, sir," I snapped out.

"Smart arse."

"Good-bye, Ian. Have a good day at work."

"You too, luv," he whispered softly.

I hung up.

Poppy, who up until now sat silently watching the show, leaned in. "You've got it bad for that man."

A whimper slid out. "I know. It gets worse with every encounter. Except for our disagreement over the security system, and being stalked by the paparazzi, I swear, I'm already halfway in love with him before we've even had a real date." Although I planned to remain firm on the security system, it *was* kind of sweet that he'd offered to pay.

She patted my hand and gave a sympathetic nod.

I dragged myself down the hall to go stew in the shower.

An hour later, I backed out of the garage and a silver Prius pulled in, blocking my driveway.

What now?

A mousy, brown-haired girl hopped out and waddled up to my car, carrying a coffee cup. She adjusted an unattractive brown skirt and her square, black glasses and knocked on the window. She didn't seem to be the stalking paparazzi type, so I slid down the glass.

"Can I help you?"

"Are you Sophie?"

"Yes."

"Good. I was worried I might not make it here before you left."

I crunched my eyebrows.

"Mr. O'Connor said you needed a pumpkin spice latte." She thrust the Starbucks coffee through my open window.

I grasped the cup before the creamy liquid could splash all over my dress.

"I'm sorry. Who are you?"

"Oh, I'm Brittany." She let out an embarrassed snorting sound, but Brittany recovered quickly. "I'm Mr. O'Connor's new personal assistant."

Brittany looked like a recent college graduate who still needed to lose the freshman fifteen, or in her case the freshman forty.

"When did he hire a personal assistant?"

"Two days ago. Today's my first day," she said with pride.

"That's great, Brittany. Uh, thanks for the coffee. I'll make sure Ian never makes you do that again."

"It's no problem." She pushed her glasses up again. "You're much prettier than the magazine photo."

I fought hard not to roll my eyes. "Thank you. I'm sure Ian's told you the tabloid was a total lie."

Brittany winked and whispered, "Your secret's safe with me."

I whispered back, "There's no secret."

"Okay." She nodded and gave a thumbs-up. I could tell she still didn't believe me.

Whatever. "Brittany, I'm late for a meeting. Can you please move your car?"

Brittany scurried down to her car and the Prius silently backed out of my driveway and headed off.

Slipping my Bluetooth on, I told it to dial Ian as I motored my way toward San Marino. It went to voice mail.

. . .

"Thanks for the coffee. But really, it's demeaning to have Brittany fetch coffee for your interior designer. You'll be happy to know Hal's doing a bang-up job installing the system. All's well. Did you talk to your manager? There were no vultures at my house today." Sophie's message was delivered in a dry tone.

Ian could hear some of the frustration in her voice, probably left over from his overbearingness about the security system. But, really, what did she expect him to do? Leave her vulnerable and open to any paparazzi nut in the area? It really steamed him when he thought about some guy following her home, and if one could find her, so could more. He shuddered at the thought of Sophie pushing her way through a press phalanx outside her doors. At least he'd feel more comfortable knowing a state-of-the-art security system protected her.

After all, when he hired Sophie, he never figured she'd be put under the spotlight like that. It really wasn't nice that they said she was preggers, and he felt guilty that his celebrity status put her in an awkward situation.

He realized when they officially started dating, she might fall prey to the press, but he never expected it to happen beforehand. And really, what single woman in this area didn't have her own security system anyway? *Buggers. She should be thanking me for helping out, rather than arguing over the bill. Still . . .*

Ian called and left a return message.

"You're welcome for the girlie coffee. Consider it an apology for being pushy about the security system. Besides, Brittany didn't have anything else to do, so don't worry. I spoke to Tom. It's all taken care of. He told them to sod off."

Sophie. What was he going to do with her? She was worming her way into his daily thoughts, and not just sexually. Yesterday afternoon as he reviewed his lines during a break, he'd wished she could have been there to run them with him. And, on his way to work today he'd seen a Hulk-sized man out walking an unhappy cat on a leash. He'd been sorry Sophie hadn't been there to witness it so they could laugh about it together. She had such a wonderful sense of the ridiculous. That's part of what he enjoyed about being with her—when he cracked a joke she was sure to laugh. Not look at him strangely and say, "Huh?" like some of the other ladies he'd been with. She was smart, no doubt about it, and Ian admired her for it. Intelligent, funny, sexy. Sophie was turning out to be the whole package. Her independence, though, came with a stubborn streak the size of a football pitch.

Through all of this cat-and-mousing they'd done over their deal, he didn't really expect she'd get under his skin like this. It was brought home to him how important she'd become when that photographer stalked her to her house and upset her. It made him start to think about a relationship beyond his initial plans to get her in the sack.

Chapter 11

To my great relief, our shopping excursion garnered no further tabloid fodder. I assumed they moved on to concocting lies about other unsuspecting Hollywood stars and their fat employees.

We'd reached a point where the house no longer looked like a disaster area. The renovations were coming together to look more like the finished product. Jack and Javier completed the first floor bath, and the main floor guest room and study were completely furnished but needed accessorizing. Ian's weights had been moved into one of the rooms upstairs, and he could begin using it for workouts. It was Monday morning about nine. I keyed my way into Ian's house, lugging an armload of comforter. There were no contractors scheduled today, and I looked forward to the peace of working alone in the empty house.

I shoved the comforter into the foyer then left the front door open while I went back to my car to get another load of accessories. Four trips later, I carried a final armful of throw pillows and weaved my way through the pile in the foyer.

"Morning."

I nearly jumped out of my skin when Ian greeted me. "Shit!" Pillows flew in different directions.

He leaned against the kitchen counter, wearing a pair of plaid lounge pants, nothing on top, holding a yellow smiley face coffee mug. My eyes zeroed in on the light dusting of happy trail heading south, and I might have salivated over the naked chest.

"What are you doing here?"

"I live here."

I shot him a dry look. "I only meant, you're usually at work."

"I'm missing."

"I beg your pardon."

"Ryder is missing this week. I don't have call until Thursday."

"Uh-oh. Is your contract coming to an end? They aren't going to kill you off, are they?"

Ian laughed. "Not that I know of. Do you know something I don't?"

"Of course not."

I hadn't seen Ian in person since our shopping trip, and … with him standing in front of me, half naked, and … with the reno coming to a close, my mind started to spin. Maybe now was a good time to set a date.

"Soooo, the renovations are almost complete, and I was thinking … " I fidgeted with my rings.

"What were you thinking, luv?" He sipped his coffee.

"I was thinking about our agreement, and … well … I wondered … "

A female voice floated down the stairs. "Ian! Can you be a darling and bring up my handbag? I think my toothbrush's in there."

He looked over his shoulder to answer the voice. That's when I noticed the black Prada bag sitting on the center island and a pair of red pumps kicked off willy-nilly on the floor.

"Sure thing. Be up in two shakes, Kate." He turned back to me with a cheerful expression. "You were wondering … "

I couldn't see it, but I knew my face had fallen, and though I tried to hide it, I'm sure a stricken look gave me away. "I didn't know you had someone here. I'll come back another time."

His eyes widened in surprise.

Self-preservation kicked in. With unprecedented grace and a little luck, I hopped through the mess of bedding and bolted.

"Sophie, wait. It's not what you think."

I glanced back to see Ian trying valiantly to pursue me through the cushioned foyer.

"Ian? My purse, please?"

He didn't pause to answer the voice, but I had a head start, and I needed to get out of there before the tears started. I made it to my car, cranked the engine, and zipped down the drive, slowing for the gate to open.

Ian came into sight in the rearview mirror, shoeless and shirtless. "Sophie. Damn it! Wait!"

I didn't even look to see if there was a car coming as I whipped out onto the street. Luck was still with me. The roadway was empty. I drove on autopilot for some miles until I realized my breathing was out of control and pulled into a parking spot before I wrecked. My head thunked against the steering wheel.

"Damn, damn, damn." Thunk, thunk. *What was I thinking?*

I should have known I didn't really have a shot with Ian. I don't know if he couldn't wait any longer, or if he'd been hiding this chick on the side or what. But, obviously she'd slept there. Who could blame him? I couldn't compete with the women he came into contact with every day. Thank heavens he was in the kitchen when I arrived. The thought of walking in on him and his *amore* made me scrub my eyes in an effort to erase the mental image it conjured.

Get a grip.

Fanning my face, I inhaled and exhaled in an attempt to calm my thoughts. To gain inner peace. Anything to keep the waterworks at bay. After a bit, I calmed down and resigned myself to the reality of the situation.

Ian did nothing wrong. At the beginning of this deal, we both knew the other might find someone else. It wasn't like he cheated on me. Five to six weeks was a long time to expect someone like him to stay celibate. The man exuded sexuality, and women fell into his lap at the slightest provocation. Some with no provocation at all. Really, he owed me no explanations.

However, once again, I, Sophia Hartland, made an utter fool of myself fleeing the scene like my pants were on fire. Hindsight being twenty-twenty, I should have played it cool. Walking instead of running out the door. I should have said something nonchalant about entertaining a lady friend. Yeah, that would've been better.

Why oh why couldn't I be the calm and collected Grace Kelly type? What I couldn't figure was, why did we go through all that security system business? He'd seemed so protective of me. Maybe that was just Ian's way. He looked out for his friends … and people he hired.

The phone sang. Ian's name blinked at me. My brain told me I should speak to him; nevertheless, I chickened out and pressed ignore. Tomorrow would be soon enough.

I didn't want to go home and wallow in self-pity for blowing any chance I might have had with him. I also wasn't ready to cry on Poppy's shoulder, so I turned to woman's time-honored cheering up cure: retail therapy. It was time to spend Mom's birthday present, and Nordstrom's was located about twenty minutes away.

Two pairs of shoes, a pair of slacks, and a black dress later I sat in a café with an untouched Asian chicken salad and a half empty cosmo. My phone stared at me—two messages and a text from Ian. With a little liquid courage under my belt, I pressed the voice mail icon.

Message number one:

Soph, please ring me. It's not what you think.

Message number two:

Hartland, you can't ignore me. What am I supposed to do with all this shite in my foyer?

The text message was succinct.

Ring me!

The rest of the cosmo warmed my belly but did nothing to bolster my confidence. Continuing with today's theme, I took the chicken route. I texted him.

Ian, you owe me no explanations. I apologize for my abrupt departure. I'm working with another client this afternoon. I'll be back at your house tomorrow morning with my electrician. We can talk then.

There was no client this afternoon, and I was missing a full day of labor at Ian's. If he'd been going to the set, I probably would have snuck back to his house, tail between my legs. However, I just couldn't work up the nerve or the poise to face him. Tomorrow would be soon enough. Instead, I called Poppy for a little support.

"Hello, girlfriend. I'm glad you called. Can you work on Saturday? I need your decorating expertise for a last-minute party."

"Sure. What's it for?"

"An entertainment lawyer in Beverly Hills is having a schmooze fest in his backyard which is killing me because it's calling for a fifty percent chance of rain and now I'm scrambling to find rental tents because my regulars are already in use," Poppy ran her words together.

"Okay. Calm down. I'll meet you at the party supply warehouse Saturday morning, and we'll pull it all together."

"Thank you, thank you, thank you! I owe you one."

"It's no problem."

"I gotta run. See you Saturday." She hung up.

Well, so much for lamenting with Poppy. Then the cell phone rang with "Let's Get this Party Started."

"Yes, Poppy?"

"You called me. What did you need?"

"Nothing. It's no big deal. Never mind."

"I know that tone. What happened?"

My breath came out in a whoosh. "Ian slept with someone else."

"Oh, no. Sweetie, I'm so sorry."

"It's no big deal."

"It *is* a big deal. I know how much you were hoping it would come together with him."

I shrugged. "It's probably for the best. He would've broken my heart anyway. At least it happened before we did the deed."

"Who's the slut he slept with?"

"I don't know." I gave an abbreviated explanation of what happened at Ian's.

"So, you didn't see her?"

"No, I'm sure she'll show up in the tabloids any day now."

"I just can't believe he did it. What was all that about installing your security system? Then he sleeps with this ho. What the hell?"

"Maybe this chick was just a one-night stand. I don't know. Really, it's not like he's my boyfriend. Hell, we're not even dating. We don't have any sort of commitment."

"Just a sec." Poppy turned away from the phone to talk to her assistant in the background. "Listen, doll, I've got to go. I have a trophy wife in a frenzy over the color of tablecloths. We'll talk tonight. Damn, not tonight. I've got a mixer to attend. I'll call you soon. Keep your chin up. Remember, you did nothing wrong. Men are pigs who can't keep their wangs from wandering."

•••

With the dawn arrived a sense of clarity. Ian was free to date, kiss, or sleep with anyone he wanted. Like I told Poppy, we had no commitments to each other. However, I still liked Ian as a person, and he was the biggest and most famous client I'd ever worked for. Moreover, I was still hoping this job would turn into something bigger. As I drove over to Ian's, I resigned myself to the fact we'd be nothing more than friends. Besides, a friendship with Ian could last much longer than any sort fling we might have, and it reduced the likelihood I'd end up in any more tabloids. It was for the best. Really.

Ricky's van idled outside Ian's gate as he waited for me. I punched in the code and he followed me up the drive. This time I took the precaution of ringing the doorbell first. There wasn't a response to multiple rings, so I keyed in.

"Hello? Anyone home?" No answer. A minor reprieve.

The pillows and comforters I'd left in the front foyer were neatly stacked into a corner of the living room. Ian had left a note on the kitchen counter for me.

Have a radio interview this morning. Will be home by eleven. Please wait for me. -Ian

I took a few minutes to go through the electrical punch list with Ricky. Then while Ricky got things underway in the bathroom, I headed to the study.

An hour later, I'd just slid the last book into place when Ricky called. "Sophie, I'm ready to start the chandelier."

"Coming."

The chandelier was large and unwieldy, at minimum a two-man job. Thirty minutes later, I deeply regretted my choice of lighting. Nothing was going right with the beautiful chrome and glass monstrosity, and Ricky was on his third trip out to his van to look for a harness that would be strong enough to properly hold the heavy piece. I think he was punishing me for purchasing this beast by taking a smoke break while I stood atop one ladder balancing the chandelier on the other. My arms ached from holding it up for such a long time, and my back protested at the awkward way I had to lean forward to balance it. Finally, the door opened and closed.

"It's about time. This chandelier is killing me. Remind me never to order this piece again."

"I'll try to remember that," Ian's dry voice replied.

My head whipped around to look over my shoulder. The ladder wobbled and I leaned farther forward to compensate. Ian put his hand up to help steady me. Unfortunately, with my rear sticking out, basically the best handhold he could get was on that appendage. I cringed in mortification. Just when I'd resolved to be calm and collected the next time I saw him, he arrived when I was doing an impression of a demented cat in heat. As soon as Ian felt I was secure, he removed his hand, and to my horror, climbed the opposite ladder.

"This is perfect. I have you in a position where you can't run away." He shifted the chandelier slightly to relieve the load.

I ducked my head into my left bicep and moaned. "Why is it I'm perpetually thrown off balance around you? Literally and figuratively. It seems I can never get my feet under me when you're around, and I constantly look like an idiot."

"I don't know. Yesterday you hopped through the mess in the front hall with the agility of a gazelle being chased by a cheetah. Whereas, I wiped out on a pillow. Looking at it objectively, you fell into my pool as graceful as a ballet dancer."

"Good to know." My voice dripped sarcasm.

"Now about Kate—"

"Ian, you don't owe me any explanations. We have no commitment to each other. You're free to date whom you want. In the future, I'll make sure the crew and I ring the bell before entering. I should have done so yesterday. It won't happen again."

He watched me with a raised eyebrow and a smirk. "Are you finished?"

"Yes."

"Good, because I'd like you to meet Kate, my stepsister," he enunciated, "and if you don't have any plans tonight, please join us for dinner."

My mind went blank as soon as I heard the word stepsister. "Huh?" was my brilliant response.

His smirk turned into a wide grin. "Kate, my father's stepdaughter from New York, is in town for a couple of days. She'd like to meet you."

"Why does she want to meet me?" My brilliance continued.

"Perhaps because I've mentioned you."

"Me?"

"Yes, you."

"Why would you do that?"

"Because, besides my co-star Carmen, you're the sole woman in my life right now."

"I am?"

Ian gave me an arched look.

"So, Kate was the voice I heard yesterday?"

"Yes."

My face split into a wide smile. "You're not sleeping with some floozy."

"No. And for the record, I don't sleep with floozies."

"Good to know."

"So, you'll come?"

"What? Come where?"

He snapped a finger in my face. "Focus, Soph. Come to dinner with Kate and me tonight."

"Are you sure you want me to come?"

"I wouldn't have asked if I didn't."

"You should say yes. I'm making him take me to Nobu," a female voice said behind me.

Glancing over my shoulder, I spotted Ricky holding a long metal rod. He stood next to a willowy young woman with stick-straight, wheat-colored hair, dressed in a designer deep purple jumpsuit and sporting a cheeky grin.

"Sophie, this is my sister, Kate Dekker. Kate, meet Sophie Hartland."

"Um, hello." I nodded awkwardly at her from my perch.

"Hello."

"Are you two finished up there?" Ricky asked.

"I believe so."

"Not yet. She hasn't answered my question," Ian said.

"Are you planning to hold me hostage up here until I answer?" My eyes returned to his.

"Yes." His gaze tugged at my belly and left me speechless.

A subtle cough pulled me out of my libido-induced zone-out. "Okay then."

"Glad that's all worked out." Ricky's voice dripped sarcasm. "Hey, man, since you're up there, maybe you could give me a *mano*. Sophie's not strong enough hold this *bruto* at the angle I'm going to need to get this harness on."

"Sure, mate."

With some maneuvering and a heart-stopping moment when my foot slipped, I finally relinquished my place on the ladder to Ricky and joined Kate.

"It's a lovely chandelier," Kate complimented.

"Thanks. I'm never ordering it again. It's been a nightmare to hang, and if I bought it for another job, Ricky would probably chop me up into little pieces and leave me to the coyotes."

The whine of power tools split the air as Ricky screwed the harness into the studs. The boys grunted as they hefted the chandelier to the ceiling. I leapt forward to steady Ricky's ladder, and Kate moved around to spot her brother's. Ian's biceps strained under the weight when Ricky released his end to attach it to the harness. Finally, everything slid into place, and I clapped triumphantly.

The boys came down from their perches to admire the handiwork. We stood in a line: Ian, Kate, Ricky, and me gawking up at chrome and crystal like it was an original *Degas*.

Ricky stood on my right. "Sophie."

"Yes?" We continued to marvel at the chandelier.

"You know I love you, but if you ever order this *monstruosidad* again, I'm going to chop you up into *pequenos* pieces and throw you to *los perros*."

Laughter rent the air.

"I promise never, ever to use this again," I gurgled.

"You have to admit it's a beautiful piece," Kate defended.

Ricky just shook his head. "I'm going upstairs to hang fans." He folded one of the ladders, hefted it on to his squat but sturdy frame and exited the room.

Kate turned back to me.

"You've done a stunning job. If you lived out east, I'd snap you up in a New York minute." Kate looked to Ian. "I didn't see what this place looked like before, but from what Ian said it was a disaster. He's been singing your praises. I'd love to see some before pictures. I was thinking we should do a photo shoot here at the house."

"I don't believe I have any before pictures." He loosened a red tie and undid the top button of his blue shirt. His worn jeans and navy vest gave him a casual chic look.

"I have some. What photo shoot?"

Kate glanced at me. "Didn't my brother tell you?"

"Tell me what?"

"I'm a freelance writer. I'm doing a piece about blended families for *Redbook* magazine. It gives me an excuse to come out and visit sunny California and sponge off Ian." Her phone rang and she answered it, wandering away from us and out the back door.

He moved closer and I caught the scent of musky cologne. My emotions bing-banged all over the place with relief and joy. *Ian didn't sleep with someone else.* "So, what time should I pick you up?"

Ian's question didn't seem to filter in. "What?"

"Nobu. Tonight. What time shall I fetch you?"

"Oh." I finally slammed into the present. "I don't want to put you out. I can meet you there."

Ian sighed. "You're not putting me out. How about seven thirty?"

"Seven thirty would be fine." I bit my tongue in an effort to curb my enthusiasm.

"It looks like my house is almost done. When do you think you'll be finished?"

"Soon. I hope. I'll know more tonight. I'm expecting to hear back from some vendors on delivery dates."

We remained motionless, regarding each other. Very slowly, as if approaching a wild animal he didn't want to frighten, Ian cupped my cheek and bent his head toward me. The kiss was soft, just a light feathering touch, but even so, it set my blood on fire. I reached up, fervently running my fingers through his glossy locks, and pressed closer, allowing his silky tongue access. A low moan escaped. He ran his hand down to my hip. The back door slammed, jerking us both back to earth.

Kate's heels tip-tapped across the floor. "You two are going to need a fire extinguisher if you don't watch out. Ever hear of spontaneous combustion?" she drawled in the doorway, with a wary look.

"You'll have to forgive my sister," Ian said. "She was raised by a pack of wild baboons. We all make allowances for her." He leveled an icy stare at Kate.

"I'd better go up and see if Ricky needs my help. I'll see you two tonight." Ducking my head, I zipped past Kate and made good my escape, taking the stairs two at a time.

Chapter 12

I hopped on one foot over to the ringing phone, tugging at my new red Jimmy Choos. "Hello."

"Should I wear a royal blue dress or basic black on a second date?"

"I don't know, Mom. Where are you going?"

"Harvey's taking me out to dinner and dancing Friday night."

"Wear whatever you want."

"The blue looks really good on me."

"Then wear the blue." I slipped on the other shoe.

"But it has a low neckline, and I don't know if it's too sexy for a second date."

"Then wear the black." I flipped the bedside drawer open, shuffling the contents around until I spotted the lint roller.

"The shoes that go with the black are high, and I don't want to get sore feet while dancing."

"Then wear the black dress with the blue shoes." The lint roller wisped up and down my dress, removing Sirius's hairs.

"Is that allowed? Can I wear royal blue with black?"

"You can wear whatever you want. Step outside your comfort zone. Combine colors. Remove the neutral tones from your life."

The doorbell rang and Sirius set up barking.

"Mom, I've got to go. My ride's here."

"Wait a minute. Do you have a date?"

"Not exactly."

"Who's at your door?"

"My client and his stepsister."

"Are you going out to dinner?"

"Yes."

"With the guy you told me about? The one whose pool you fell into?"

"Yes, and it's not like that. His sister's in town and he asked me to join them for dinner. It's not really a date."

The doorbell chimed again. Sirius beelined into my room at full tilt to bark at me. Just in case I didn't hear him the first time. "Sirius, quiet!"

"Are you wearing a dress?"

"Yes." I trailed Sirius down the hall.

"And he wants you to eat with his sister?"

"I suppose."

"Then it's a date."

Ian stood at my door wearing black slacks, shoes, and a crisp white button-down. Heat pooled in my belly as I perused my delectable client. He eyed me from head to toe, taking in the flirty red and yellow scarf, little black dress, and red peep-toe platforms. A full-on smile gleamed at me and my breath hitched.

"Mom, wear the blue. I've got to go. Love you. Bye." I tossed the phone onto the hall table, grabbed Sirius's collar, and pushed open the storm door. The faint scent of fresh laundry and musky aftershave met my nose.

"Hi." I gave a shy smile.

"You look exquisite." He leaned in and bussed my cheek.

A flash of warm pleasure rushed through me.

"This must be Sirius. The other man in your life." Ian held his hand out for Sirius to sniff.

I was glad he knew dog protocol. One more mark in the good book for him. After a few snuffles, Sirius shoved his head under Ian's hand.

"I'm almost ready. I need to feed Sirius and check e-mail before we go. Do you and Kate want to come in and wait?" I glanced past his shoulder and gave a whoop of glee. "You brought the Mustang!"

"I promised you the last time we went out I'd bring it."

The passenger seat was empty. "Where's Kate?"

"She's meeting us at the restaurant. I hope you don't mind. She's bringing a friend from university to dinner." Ian followed me into the kitchen.

"No problem. The more the merrier." This was good news. Since Kate walked in on me slavering over Ian, I'd been wondering how the dinner would play out. A fourth person would keep awkward questions at bay. Sirius followed me around the kitchen as I prepared his dinner and shoved me out of the way when I laid it on the back patio.

"Would you like something to drink while I check my e-mail? Water, wine, diet soda?"

"Do you have any beer?"

With a cringe, I shook my head, and made a mental note to get some beer.

"Water will be fine."

I handed over a bottle from the fridge and invited him to sit at the counter while I slipped on reading glasses to sort through the e-mails on my iPad.

"Ooo, I like those glasses. They make you look like a naughty librarian."

My lips twitched. "Good news. The sofa we ordered will be delivered on Monday. That's three days earlier than I expected. We should be finished with your reno by next week." I held up my hand and Ian high-fived me.

"That's the best news I've heard all day."

"I know it's hard living through renovations, but you've been a real trooper. Just be glad we didn't have to rip up the entire kitchen."

"The mess hasn't been the problem. The problem has been waiting for you."

I flushed to the tips of my toes, pleased his interest hadn't waned over the weeks.

"So, you'll be finished by next Friday."

"Yup." I responded to an e-mail from Jack.

"Where would you like to have dinner?"

I lowered the iPad. "You mean next Friday."

"Once you toffs are done, all bets are off. It's time to pay the piper, luv."

My mouth went arid like the desert sun. Stalling, I scooped the water out of Ian's hand and drank deeply. "So, you're still in for … you know …"

His eyebrows lifted. "You couldn't tell from earlier today?"

My head bobbed. "Ok."

"Where would you like to go?"

"You pick."

"I pick my house."

That could be dangerous. I needed a public restaurant to provide a buffer. If we ate at Ian's, there'd be no way I could make it through the salad course, much less a full meal, before stripping him naked and trying out the new hardwoods, or possibly the sofa. Besides, I probably needed a full meal to provide energy before caving to his masculine charms.

"I'll think about it and get back to you."

• • •

Kate and her friend, Fletcher, walked into Nobu, a swanky Japanese restaurant Kate swore was "the absolute best," five minutes after our arrival. Kate's designer boots, skinny jeans, and flowy blouse looked like something straight from a New York fashion magazine shoot. Considering her job, it probably was. Fletcher's gregarious personality and rubber-like facial expressions loosened our group. However, I was still smarting from the post-kiss scene Kate had witnessed, and her behavior toward me was been a bit stand-off-ish. My defensive walls remained high.

Through the meal, I was placed in a tortuous situation of Ian's making. At the start of the meal, his knee "accidentally" brushed mine and sent little zingers up my spine. Then he moved on to gently drift a hand along my thigh. Frissons of heat hummed through my body. By the time dessert arrived, he scooted closer and comfortably slung his arm across the back of my chair, then proceeded to play with my hair. It took all my efforts to remain calm and unfazed by his touch on the outside, while my nether regions trembled with pleasure and anticipation. I tried to behave normally—laughing at Fletcher's jokes, glancing at Ian but not staring like an enraptured teenager.

Perhaps my hand reached too often for the wine because by the time dessert arrived, I couldn't stand it any longer and gave some sauce back to the gander. Ian ordered a chocolate concoction that arrived with whipped cream and a cherry on top. Before he could touch it, I stole the sweet, cream-covered fruit and popped it in my mouth. Making an O, I leisurely dragged it through my lips, laving the whipped cream with my tongue. His eyes widened and his nostrils flared. Once the cherry was clean, I sucked it back in and bit down with a snap. Ian sucked wind, and his blunt fingers reflexively gripped my neck.

"Gentlemen, I need to visit the ladies' room. Sophie?" Kate's eyes zeroed in on me.

In general, I wasn't one to go to the restroom *en masse* with the girls. Nonetheless, I acquiesced to Kate's silent request. I had a feeling a lecture or uncomfortable questions about my relationship with her brother were coming my way.

Kate stood in front of the long mirror putting on lipstick with the concentration of a heart surgeon, which was why I jumped when she spoke.

"So, what do you think of my brother?" Her eyes met mine in the mirror.

Here it comes. "I think he's smart, funny, and handsome. A talented actor."

"You're not his usual type." Her watery blue gaze widened innocently to look me up and down.

I narrowed my eyes at her scrutiny, well aware of my shortcomings. "What, intelligent?" I crossed my arms and leaned a hip against the counter.

A hoarse laugh rolled out. "That, too. But, no. Ian usually goes for the easy target and can capture the most stunning woman in the room by barely lifting a finger. Unfortunately, many of them are superficial flakes, hoping to hop the O'Connor gravy train. Nothing personal, but you're none of those things. You have a natural beauty, you don't seem to be interested in show biz, and there's nothing easy about you. When I walked in on you earlier today, I thought you two were just having hot monkey sex. However, my brother has mentioned your name in a dozen different conversations since I arrived. Tonight he can't stop watching or touching you. The two of you light up when you look at each other. The cherry almost made him fall out of his chair." Her guarded expression dropped, and she gave me an open, honest look. "I like you, Sophie. So, as a woman and his sister, I feel it's my job to provide a fair warning. Ian's a heartbreaker."

My smile dropped during Kate's offensive little narrative and my face burned. "No surprise there." Sarcasm dripped.

"But with you, I don't know. I think, maybe, you could break his heart." She tilted her head, and the lighting shadows accentuated her long, narrow nose.

"Not that it's any of your business, but we're not dating or having wild monkey sex. I don't date my clients. Nobody's getting heartbroken."

"You will when he's no longer a client," she said with certainty.

I remained silent and thinned my lips into a straight line, wondering what Ian had told his stepsister.

"You're a smart woman." She gave a throaty chuckle. "Making him wait. Most women jump in the sack with him right away. That's their downfall. He's had time to develop feelings for you. That hasn't happened to him in a while." Suddenly, her perfectly painted mouth split into a smile and she leaned in to impart her confidence. "I hope you catch my brother. It's time he settled down with a good woman."

Before I realized what was happening, she encompassed me in a peppery-scented and entirely unexpected hug. I remained stiff from shock during the brief embrace, but Kate didn't seem to notice.

"Just don't break my brother's heart, or you'll have to answer to me." She scooped up the lipstick, tossed it into her handbag, and strode out of the bathroom without a backward glance to see if I followed.

Chapter 13

The streetlights flashed by, alternately lightening and darkening the car. The sporadic illumination created mini prisms of the raindrops snaking their way across the window. The strange bathroom conversation with Kate buzzed around my head. All the insecurities I'd struggled with after the divorce came flooding back. In my head, I knew I was a fairly attractive woman with a successful business. However, I also knew Ian was way out of my league, and what Kate perceived as a "normal" girl simply highlighted for me how far apart our worlds were. I wasn't glamorous. I wasn't tall and skinny. I didn't speak Hollywoodese. He had invitations to be interviewed in magazines and talk shows. Ian's life revolved around glitzy, stylish show biz people. My life revolved around sweaty contractors.

"You're awfully quiet."

I gave a noncommittal murmur.

"What did my sister say to you in the loo?"

I continued to stare out the window. "What makes you think she said anything to me?"

"You didn't want to go dancing with her and Fletcher, and you clammed up once we got in the car. I had some choice words to say to her back at the house, after you fled upstairs."

"She warned me about your womanizing ways. Nothing I didn't already know." My gaze swept along his profile.

His jaw flexed. "Kate needs to learn to keep her bloody mouth shut."

"She's your sister. She just wants what's best for you."

His hand rested on the gear shift, and I patted it. He gave a grunt and flipped his hand over to curl around mine, which he continued to hold until the next shift change. "Did you decide where we're going for dinner Friday?"

"Spago." It was the first place that popped into my head. In all the years of living in LA, I'd never been to Wolfgang Puck's flagship restaurant.

"Done."

"Okay," I said with a skeptic eyebrow. I was pretty sure it'd be impossible to get a last-minute reservation at Spago for next Friday. I'd let him figure that out for himself.

The rain had slowed to a soft mist by the time we arrived home. Ian came around to open my door. His strong digits firmly gripped mine as he helped me rise from the car. He didn't release my hand but instead pulled me closer to hook it around his forearm. I don't know if I warmed up on my own, or if his body heat filtered through my coat, but my senses were in overdrive, and I focused on nothing else in the world except where our bodies touched. Once we stepped under the portico, he tugged me around, slipped his other hand around my waist and pulled me close. I searched his face, struggling to come to terms with the fact this painfully beautiful man was here. Holding me. Wanting me. Ian's forehead crinkled in a puzzled expression.

"Why?"

"Why what?" He glided a finger gently down my cheek to the soft underside of my chin.

Gentle tingles snaked down my back, slithering all the way to my toes.

"Why me?"

He inhaled and his lips curved into a half smile. "You mean beyond the fact that every time we're in the same room, we heat it up a hundred degrees?"

"Is that all? I'm just an itch that needs to be scratched."

"You're not an itch, Soph. You're quickly becoming an obsession. This waiting game is driving me batshit crazy."

I was too afraid to ask the real question praying on my mind. *Will it be over once we sleep together? Will the friendship come to an end? Can I be "just friends" with Ian after sleeping with him? Cripes! I need to get out of my head. Go with the flow. Stop worrying about the what ifs.*

With Ian's chiseled jaw and tasty lips hovering above me, it wasn't too hard to dismiss my worries. The man could make a nun toss her habit to the wind. In my high heels, I didn't have far to reach, and he met me halfway. His velvety tongue teased its way through my barriers. He tasted of wine, plumy rich and full, and the heat in my mouth went straight to my belly and headed south. I was sensitive of every juncture where our bodies met. Crushed material whispered around us. My hands wrapped around his neck, and I hung on as a drowning man holds on to a lifeline. He backed me up against the cold storm door and deepened the kiss. When we finally came up for air, our breaths heaved between us. I gripped Ian's shoulders, using the storm door for support as I searched for balance. My head thunked against the glass.

Unhurriedly, he disengaged my hands from his shoulders. He clasped them in his warm grip. His head tilted down to meet my forehead. "If I'm to stick to our agreement, I need to leave. Now."

"I thought all bets were off if you saw my defenses waver."

"Things have changed."

My eyes widened with fear.

His features softened. "It's no longer a game. It's more. I don't want to be some tosser trying to get into your pants. I understand why you don't want to compromise your professional standards, and I'm trying to be the gentleman."

I cocked my head. In that brief statement, Ian may not have answered all my insecure questions, but he answered the most important one. "There's something I want to show you. Can you wait here for just a minute?"

Ian gave a puzzled nod, and I slipped into the house. The alarm beeped, and I punched my code into the pad to turn it off. Sirius clicked up to me, his tail wagging. He followed me to the pantry where I found a large doggie bone, a treat I saved for special occasions, and chucked it out the back door. Sirius bolted after it like a homing beacon. It would keep him occupied for a few hours. I clattered down to my bedroom and zipped around the room, scooping up underthings, two outfits I'd tried on and discarded, three pairs of shoes, and a handful of scarves. I tossed everything into a heap on the floor of my walk-in closet and closed the door with a snap. I flicked open my lingerie drawer, and, with shaky fingers, searched for the lacy panties that matched the bra I wore. Slipping out of the suck-you-in-iron-Spandex I sported to improve my figure's silhouette, I pulled up the wisps of silky triangles and tossed the torture device into the hamper. Being a decorator, I was obsessed with candles. They littered my bedroom and living areas, and, a few matches later, their soft glow flickered through the house like lightning bugs on a summer night.

When I opened the door, Ian slouched casually against the front porch railing, talking quietly on his phone. "Sure, if they can work around the shooting schedule, set me up. That Monday would probably be fine. Text Brittany and have her put it on my calendar." He glanced at me. "Listen, mate, I've got to go. We'll hash out the details tomorrow."

I crooked a finger at him and pulled him into the house by the lapels of his coat. I relieved him of his outerwear. His eyes widened as they took in the wavering candles.

"I think we've waited long enough. No more games."

Ian clutched my shoulders and his hands slid down to my elbows. "Sophie, I can only take so much. You're serious?

My head bobbed, and I unbuttoned the top two buttons of his shirt.

"If you're sure?"

I gave a mysterious Cheshire cat smile, took his left hand in my right, and led him down the hall to my bedroom.

• • •

Ian didn't need any further encouragement. As soon as they entered the room, he closed the door, reversed their positions, and plastered Sophie up against it.

"Thank the lord, you've come to your senses." He removed her silky scarf and replaced it with his lips, raining fiery kisses down her sweet-smelling neck. His hands tugged her dress up past her thighs, above her waistline, until he could splay his fingers across her silky belly. "It's been hell waiting to touch you like this."

Her stomach quivered beneath his touch and her breath came out in panting puffs, as his nose delved into the V of her décolletage. He felt the scrape of her nails as she ran her hands through his hair. The slippery material of her dress slid easily up the rest of her body, and she lifted her arms to help him. He tossed the fabric aside and took in the sheer beauty of her body.

Her hair tumbled down around her shoulders in sexy disarray; cobalt eyes, darkened with passion, gazed at him; and her pouty lips were swollen from his kisses. A red, lacy bra covered her full breasts, and he reached out with both hands, flicking a thumb across each perky nipple.

A mewling sound from deep in her throat escaped, and she chewed her bottom lip. She lifted her hands across her belly, as if to shield it from his gaze, but he pulled her hands away.

"Let me see you," he whispered and ran a finger from her sternum up, above her bra line, all the way to her collarbone. Then he slipped the straps off her shoulders and unhooked the bra. She wore nothing but a tiny triangle that covered her vagina, and red pumps. Her hips flared out from a small waist, and her perfect skin glowed in the soft candlelight. Desire flooded him, and he had to remind himself to go slow, and fight the animal instinct clawing at him to throw her down and ravage her.

"God, you're beautiful." He cupped her full, warm breasts in his hands.

Her lids swept down as if to deny him the truth, but he lifted her chin with his finger.

"Sophie, look at me."

She met his hungry gaze.

"You are beautiful, from the tips of your toes to the top your head. Your sexy figure's been driving me bonkers for weeks."

She blinked and his lips descended on hers. Searching with his tongue, he moaned when she opened for him. As their mouths danced, he fondled her breasts. Rolling the nipples with his thumb and forefinger, he swallowed her whimper then moved to taste her neck.

Her fingers were suddenly in a frenzy, tugging and pulling at the buttons on his shirt. As he nibbled her jawline, he heard her mutter, "To hell with it." There was a popping sound as buttons flew in every direction.

"You're over-dressed," Sophie mumbled tugging the oxford over his head. Finally released from the shirt, her dainty fingers trailed across his chest, followed by her lips that nibbled a path from left to right. His cock, already stiff, turned rock hard at her touch. Her hands lazily explored his chest, running along his hard abs, then, heading south, they danced along the skin just above his belt line. He sucked wind as she played with his belly button then slipped three fingers under the waistband, tickling the sensitive skin.

She grinned as though she knew exactly how it tortured him.

That is enough. In a quick movement, he spun her around, backing her up against the bed. Her knees bumped against the edge and she fell backward with a squeal. He toed off his loafers, released his belt, unzipped and dropped his pants, kicking them aside.

Her eyes grew wide at the sight of his erection, reaching out to tentatively touch it through his boxer briefs. Slipping her thumbs beneath the waistband, she pulled the last bit of clothing off, and his shaft sprung forward.

"My, my," she whispered, dancing her fingers across the turgid flesh.

"My turn to play, lassie." He growled and dove into her buffet of naked skin. Licking and kissing every inch of her, he made her writhe beneath him, moaning and sweeping her hands through his hair and along his back.

When he couldn't wait any longer, his fingers ripped aside the tiny piece of material hiding her womanhood and slid between her slick folds. She gripped his shoulders and his thumb flicked the engorged bud as he buried two fingers inside her.

Jesus, she was dripping. "Ah, luv, you're so wet."

She moaned and he stroked her until she panted from need.

"Ian, Ian," she whimpered, tugging his hardened cock in her hand.

He didn't wait for further invitation. Rising above her, he submerged himself with one swift stroke. She felt like electric velvet, smooth and soft and exhilarating all at once. Her breath hitched. And he pulled back, afraid he'd hurt her.

"Okay?" He asked.

"Mmm hmm." She gave a sexy smile while peering at him half-lidded. "Don't stop."

Slowly closing over his shaft, she pushed up with her hips and met him halfway.

"Christ, you're so tight."

"You feel so good.." She sighed and pushed him in deeper.

He made a hissing sound as he sucked wind through his teeth. "We have to go slow, luv, or I'll never last. You feel so good."

Effortlessly, their bodies worked into a timeless rhythm as he gripped her hips, thrusting slowly into her. But Sophie seemed to have other ideas. Thrusting her hips faster, her fingers dug into his backside and their tempo increased. Breaths mingled. Hands caressed and flesh stroked. Sophie's eyes squeezed shut and her breath gasped as she reached for the peak.

"Open your eyes, luv. I want to see you come," Ian demanded.

Her tempestuous eyes popped open, and with a sweep of his thumb across her clit, she yelled his name, contracting around him. Milking him, she sent him over the edge of the cliff and he collapsed atop her.

As their breaths slowed to normal, he rolled over and draped her across his chest.

Oh yeah, I could do that again. All night long, if I have my way.

• • •

"I've got to let him in. He's going to wake the entire block."

Ian trailed a delicate fingertip down my collarbone and headed south along the top of my breast, giving me shivery goose bumps. Sirius whined and scratched at the back door, pulling my attention away from the shivery yummies. The bone had kept him busy for about two hours. However, he'd been whining and giving short barks for twenty minutes, and I knew it wouldn't take too much longer before it turned into a full-scale Armageddon-like cacophony. I rolled out, snagging a soft velvet throw that had slid off the bed sometime during our passionate antics, and wrapped it around myself.

"You know I've already seen you naked." Ian tugged at the blanket.

"Yes, but you were in a passion-induced haze. Wouldn't want to ruin the mystery." I grinned.

He turned onto his back, and I enjoyed the view as his hard abs rolled gently with laughter. Most of the candles still glowed, but I wasn't ready to walk around Ian with all my jiggly bits hanging about, even in the flickering light.

The rain stopped a while ago, but the backyard was still damp and mucky so I snatched a towel before opening the door. Sirius tried to scuttle past, except I was used to this routine. I dropped the towel, grabbed his collar, and gripped the throw at my breast. Unfortunately, there is absolutely no way to wipe a dog's feet without using both hands, so I gave up on my modesty and allowed the blanket to drop to my waist while I wrestled with Sirius. It wouldn't be the first time he saw me in my all together. Finally wiped down, I petted him and told him to go to his bed. He trotted down to my office where his dog bed lay. My knees cracked stiffly as I stood, and the blanket fell to the ground. It would, of course, be at this moment when Ian walked in, flicking on the overhead light full blast.

"Yeeks!" I crouched down and scrambled to retrieve my mantle of modesty before he could spot the imperfections and cellulite dimples in the bright light.

"Have you got any tea? I'm parched."

It was a pleasant sight to view his muscles and magnificence in dark blue boxer briefs. The show must have him shave or wax his chest because he was clean up top, but my eyes were drawn to the short softies heading down the happy trail. My grip slackened, allowing the blanket to drop to my shoulders, and my mouth went dry.

"Luv, if you keep looking at me like I'm a tasty tiramisu, we're going to end up trying that last thing we did right here on your countertops."

"Okay."

Ian's gaze turned to blue fire, and he was on me within three strides. Everything became a flurry of hands flying and tongues licking and tasting. The afghan dropped, Ian's boxers disappeared, and I only vaguely remember the coldness of the granite countertop beneath my bare bottom. You would have thought we hadn't had sex in months rather than twenty minutes, the way we went at each other.

Afterward, we took turns sharing a carton of orange juice, drinking straight from the container. Ian stood between my legs as I remained perched on the counter. He retrieved the blanket and wrapped it around my shoulders. My fingernails played along his upper bicep, outlining the intricate lines of a tattoo.

"What is this? It looks Irish."

"It's a four-cornered Celtic knot."

"What does it mean?"

"Earth, fire, water, and air. They intertwine to create balance. It can also be interpreted as a symbol of protection."

"It's beautiful." I blew lightly against the black ink. "I'm too much of a chicken to get a tattoo. The needles freak me out." My lips grazed the complex design.

His finger raised my chin, and his mouth nibbled along my jawline. A gentle breath whispered through my lips.

"You know, I'm never going to look at this counter the same way again. Every time I walk into the kitchen, I'm going to think about what we just did."

"Lucky you." He smirked. "Maybe we can try it in my kitchen next time."

A delicious glow filled my belly. Ian spoke about next time. Once we finished the orange juice, he scooped me up and carried me down the hall back to bed. Another first for me. No man had ever hefted me around.

Chapter 14

I woke up burning hot, on the edge of the bed. Ian's body heat wrapped around me from behind, and Sirius's cold nose nudged me from the front. I reached out to shove Sirius back and slid out from underneath Ian's heavy arm and leg. He rolled over, flopping spread eagle on his back. His long limbs took up most of the bed. I slipped into the bathroom to relieve my bladder and have a quick wash before wrapping myself in a soft, flowy, green silk robe I'd worn maybe three times. Usually I opted for a snuggly blue terry cloth robe, but this was a special occasion. There was an outstanding specimen of man in my bed, and the morning called for a little glamour. It was too bad I didn't have a pair of feathery high-heeled slippers like Liz Taylor wore in old movies. Ian would have to settle for beige bedroom shoes. I caught my hair up in a ponytail and headed to the kitchen to feed the dog and start the morning routine.

I had planned to be at Ian's most of the day to work with Ricky, but I didn't feel the need to rush this morning. Instead, I texted him and told him I wouldn't be at Ian's until ten. I got caught up responding to e-mails. At some point, the shower sound filtered into the back of my brain, and before I realized it, three quarters of an hour had passed.

Ian wandered into the kitchen, hair wet and slicked back, smelling of my lavender bath soap. I slid the reading glasses down my nose to observe him. He wore the black slacks and shirt hanging open and had bare feet. I'd never noticed before how sexy men in pants and bare feet were. Or maybe it was just that everything about Ian turned me on. I was still marveling at the fact he was here. In the morning. He didn't sneak out in the middle of the night and didn't seem to be in a hurry to leave now.

"Is that coffee I smell?"

I pointed to the back corner where the coffeepot sat on its warming plate. Ian poured himself a cup.

"That's a pretty get up." He nodded my way. "You're wearing those saucy specs again. They really turn me on." He gave a leer. "What are you working on?"

"Just cleaning out e-mail. A pair of chairs I ordered for another client is in limbo because the fabric is on back order."

The doorbell rang. Since Sirius was still outside, it wasn't followed by a crazy barking dog.

"That's for you," Ian said.

My brows knit. *Who the heck can that be?* I opened the door. Ian's assistant, Brittany, stood on my porch. She wore straight leg jeans, a black raincoat tied at the waist, and dark green flats. The outfit was a hundred times better than the first time we met.

She held a Panera bag toward me. "Here you go. Mr. O'Connor phoned and said you needed breakfast. He said he didn't know what you'd like, so he had me pick up one of each. That's a very pretty robe." She winked. "Anyway, I hope you find something you like. Bye."

My thanks died quietly as she cruised up the street in her silent Prius. I stalked, there was no other way to describe it, down the hall to the kitchen. "Did you tell her you were here?" I squealed, flapping my hand.

"Hell, no. I just told her I wanted to buy you breakfast this morning."

"Ian! Your Mustang's in my drive." I hooked a thumb over my shoulder. "Plus, I answered the door in a silk robe. How stupid do you think she is?"

His cheeks reddened, and he had the decency to look sheepish. "Sorry. I forgot about the car."

"So much for keeping this quiet," I huffed.

"Is it a secret?" His voice was gruff and low. He wouldn't meet my eyes and instead looked out into the backyard.

This surprised me. I walked over to him and softened my tone. My hand brushed his forearm. "Don't you want to keep it quiet? You know, away from the paparazzi? Especially considering the fiasco the last time we were in public?"

Ian put his mug down. Palms warm from the coffee cupped my face. "Yes, the paparazzi blokes are arseholes. Sophie, I know you've got some crackbrained idea that you're not in my 'league.'"

My breath caught somewhere in my chest. His intense cobalt gaze bore into me.

"You far surpass it. You're beautiful, smart, sexy as hell. You're well beyond this limey git's 'league.'"

His lips were featherlight at first, then they hardened into a searing kiss, as though staking his claim with a brand. My mind went blank, and I goggled when Ian came up for air.

A little half-smile lurked. "I'm hungry. Let's eat."

I gulped and nodded and felt bereft when he stepped away.

We sat at my small bistro-style table next to the sliding door.

"What would you like?"

"Whatever," I replied absently. My mind whirled in a dozen different directions at once. Not being overly familiar with the "awkward" next-morning business, things were going fairly well. The good news—my makeup-less face and grungy ponytail didn't seem to be driving him away. Instead, he'd phoned his personal assistant to deliver breakfast and was staying to savor a cup of coffee and morning coze. It'd been a long time since I'd breakfasted with a man I'd recently had wanton sex with.

I bit into the flaky croissant while Ian regarded me with a serious mien. Actually, upon closer inspection, he seemed ill at ease.

Uh oh.

"Sophie."

Here it comes. "Yeess?"

"Um, this may not be the best time to bring this up."

Do I have something on my face? Surreptitiously, I wiped my nose and mouth.

"I, uh … " He stroked a hand through his damp locks and a curl fell across his forehead. "We didn't use rubbers. You kind of surprised me last night. I thought we should talk about it."

I released the breath I'd been holding. "I'm on the pill."

Relief played across his features and the tension released from his shoulders.

"To regulate my cycle." I took a bite of eggy goodness, chewed, and swallowed. "However, how do I know you don't have some skeevy STD or God forbid, HIV?"

Ian choked on his coffee. "I've been tested, and, unless I'm in a long-term relationship, I always use condoms."

"Always?" I raised an eyebrow.

"Always. You seem to be an exception to the rule. When I'm with you, it appears I lose my mind." He reached under the table. His hand slid up my silk-covered thigh. "What about you?"

I gave him a wry look. "It's called abstinence. Or more like unintentional celibacy."

He took a bite of food and shook his head. "I don't know what's wrong with the chaps around here."

"Too much competition."

He muttered something that sounded like "bloody fools" and gulped his coffee.

"You know, I do have food. I could've made us something."

"Soph, I saw your refrigerator last night. There's a bottle of wine, two takeout cartons, and some condiments. Also, some dodgy fruit."

He was right. I needed to get to the grocery store and start stocking my house like an adult. Not a college kid.

"I'm sure I have some cereal," I said in a small voice.

"Forget it. This hit the spot." He took a bite out of his second egg sandwich. "Besides, it gives Brittany something to do. That's what a personal assistant's for. Right?"

"Sure. I guess so." I had no idea. I considered Michelle a coworker. Never in my wildest dreams would it occur to me to ask her to deliver coffee or breakfast to my boyfriend. "Why did you hire her?"

"Tom, my manager, suggested it. He felt I needed someone to keep my calendar straight, field calls, and run errands. Brittany's actually been a big help, fetching coffee or lunch for me. Picking up my laundry. Taking phone messages. She's arranged my interviews and such." He ticked each item off on his fingers. "And Clara, the show's costume designer, took Brittany under her wing, so she's improved her kit." That would explain the decent outfit. "The popularity of the show is increasing my schedule. Tom's call last night, he hooked me up for a spot on *Good Morning America*. They're rotating the bumpers and promos through the cast. Brittany's keeping it all right and tight for me."

"So, should I call her when I want to make a date with you?" I smirked.

"No," he said with abrupt firmness.

I gave a feline smile and ate my breakfast.

Chapter 14

"I'll take six of those rattan love seats, a dozen armchairs, three coffee tables, four end tables, that Tiki statue, and we'll need three bars." We walked at a crisp pace as I rambled off the list, pointing at each item along the way. Priya, the efficient assistant helping me, marked each piece on her clipboard. It was T-minus eight hours for Poppy's last-minute party, and she'd left me in charge of the rental furniture, props, and décor. Fortunately, the exec throwing the party wasn't very imaginative and had requested a Hawaiian-themed party. Throw around some Tiki torches and palm leaves, and we were good to go. Poor Poppy left an hour ago, after receiving a panicked call from her own assistant. The lead singer of the band the hostess booked was ill from some bad oysters, and he wasn't likely to be straying far from the bathroom tonight.

My phone buzzed with a text from Poppy:

Arranged the tents with lighting. They're lackluster white. Can you do something about them? All the freakin' bands are booked! Am flipping out! I think I still have my violin from high school. You play an instrument?

"Priya, do you have any overhead fans with big leafish paddles?"

Her shiny diamond piercing flashed as she scrunched her nose in thought. "No, I don't think so. We've got some large brown fans over here." I followed her to a different part of the warehouse that contained lighting fixtures.

"Okay. These could work. I'll get some palm leaves to attach to the paddles. We'll take four."

I texted back:

I played a mean recorder in fourth grade. Don't worry about tents. I've got it covered. Have you looked into Caribbean steel bands, since we're going island? Find a pianist or guitarist who can play in the house. Check with the college music programs.

I tucked the phone into my back pocket when Ian's ringtone chimed. "Hello."

"Morning, beautiful."

My cheeks warmed. I turned away from Priya and tucked a stray lock behind my ear. "Hello, Ian. How are you?"

"Lonely. It's been too long since I've seen you."

Ian left my house Wednesday morning following our breakfast. By the time I showered and got to his house, he'd left to spend the day with Kate. Around seven, he phoned to invite me to join the two of them for dinner and a movie. I declined. Since Kate was leaving the next morning, I figured the two of them should spend her last hours together without a third wheel. It might also have had to do with the fact I was still disturbed by Kate's powder room pow wow and the fact I'd denied an intimate relationship with her brother, which was no longer the case. Ian had to work late both Thursday and Friday. We spoke on the phone, and he sent me funny, flirty texts. Friday evening I arrived home to a bouquet of summer, sky-blue orchids waiting on my front stoop and a reminder to set my alarm.

"Me, too." I sighed.

"Brittany says I've been invited to a party tonight. Would you like to join me?"

"I'm sorry. Poppy's got a last-minute gig she needs me to work tonight." Considering all the help Poppy had given me to make contacts when I first started my design company, pitching in when she was in a crunch was the least I could do.

"What about lunch?"

I grimaced. "I'm at the furniture rental warehouse right now, and I've got three more stops before heading to the party venue to set up."

"Bollocks. What time will you be done? We can meet afterward."

"I have no idea. I stay until Poppy doesn't need me anymore. Sometimes that's eleven, sometimes it's two."

"Text me when you're done, then come to my house. No matter what time."

"Really?"

"Tom says I should make an appearance at this party. I'll leave when you do."

I shrugged. "Okay. If you're sure."

"It'll be boring as hell without you. I wish you could come and step out in that sexy, black dress."

"I have a red dress you might like … " My lips split into a sly smile.

He groaned. "Saucy minx, get back to work."

"See you later."

"Not soon enough."

I turned. Priya stood no more than six feet away, trying to look busy with her clipboard. Her shiny dark hair fell across her face, but she was so close there was no way she couldn't have overheard the conversation.

"Sorry about that."

"Your boyfriend?" Her ebony eyes shined.

"No! I mean, yes. I mean … I don't know. I think it's too early to put on the boyfriend title."

She gave a knowing nod. "Is he cute?"

I laughed. "I don't think Ian runs in the cute range. More like smokin' hot."

"Those can be the hardest to tie down."

She had no idea. "Where were we?"

Half an hour later, I motored over to Fabric Planet, my favorite warehouse for finding eclectic materials in downtown Los Angeles. My phone rang an unknown number.

"Hello, Hartland Designs."

"Sophie?"

"Holly?"

"Yeah, it's me."

"Is everything all right? Whose phone are you using?"

"That's why I'm calling. I have a new cell. Use this number when you need to call or text me from now on. Okay?"

"Sure. Is everything else okay? I've been meaning to call you. After Thanksgiving I'll have a little time to breathe. Why don't I fly out for a few days?"

Silence.

"Holly?"

"Um, maybe. Let me check with Omar." Her voice wasn't the rich, full-of-fun Holly I knew. It sounded reedy and thin.

I pulled into the parking lot. "Holly, talk to me. What's going on?"

"Nothing. Insomnia. I didn't get much sleep last night. That's all."

"Oh, hon, insomnia sucks." I'd suffered from countless sleepless nights stewing about Michael's extra-marital activities. The day after we split, the relief was undeniable. I slept like a baby. "Is there something preying on your mind?"

"I … was just … thinking about going back to work, but I don't want to put Eva into daycare."

"Well, that can definitely be a stressful decision for you. Maybe you can go back part-time. I'm sure it'd be good for both you and Eva to have some time apart."

"I suppose," my sister said faintly. "What's happening with you? Are you going to Mom's for Thanksgiving?"

"She's coming here. Originally, she wanted me to come out and meet Harvey, her new beau, but apparently Harvey's heading to Ohio to visit his grandkids."

Holly giggled. The first sign of humor I'd heard out of her in months. "Mom has a beau. I can't believe it. But if she's busy with Harvey, she won't be bugging us so much. Right?"

"I suppose. Don't forget to give Mom this new number."

"I gave it to her last night. I called while she was getting ready for her date. She was as giddy as a teenager going to her first Homecoming dance."

My other line clicked, and Poppy's number flashed at me. "I've got to run. I'm working a gig for Poppy today and everything is at sixes and sevens."

"Sure. Call me on this phone. Only this phone. Okay?" she stressed.

Uneasiness prickled my scalp. "Holly … I'm here for you. If you need me to come to you, I can. Anytime."

"I know. I love you." She disconnected.

Poppy's call went to voice mail, while I sat in the half-empty parking lot and stared at Holly's new phone number. Why was my sister so adamant I only use this number? My woman's intuition was on high alert, pinging like active sonar. I needed to do something, only I didn't know what. Was Holly really doing drugs? Ian's renovation should be finished by midweek. I needed to get out there to find out what was happening. My voice mail icon blinked, but I ignored it. Instead, I got online and thanks to modern technology, twenty minutes later I was booked on a Southwest flight the Monday after Thanksgiving. Come hell or high water, I was heading to Sin City to get to the bottom of this, whether Holly liked it or not.

...

T-minus one hour until party time, and Poppy's capable assistant, Cody, buzzed around talking into her headset, putting out fires, and coordinating last minute details in her skinny jeans and silver ballet flats. Poppy was at an over-the-top children's birthday party for some agent's kid, and she planned to arrive at the Hawaiian extravaganza around nine. Until that time, Cody was in charge.

As I decorated the tents, ominous clouds rolled in from the coast and the evening became progressively humid. The tents would be filled with guests taking shelter from the storm before the night was out. Fifteen minutes later, Cody's blue butterfly top flagged me down as I walked into the bustling hive of catering staff in the kitchen.

"Did you get your uniform yet?"

"No. I brought a flowered shirt, black shorts, and flip-flops. I thought that was the attire for the wait staff. Are we supposed to wear something different?" I glanced at the chefs preparing the food for tonight. They wore flowered shirts, black pants and black waiter shoes.

Cody's russet eyes darted past mine. "Didn't Poppy tell you?"

My arms crossed, and a bad feeling crept over me. "Tell me what?"

She chewed her lip.

"Tell me what, Cody?"

Two girls in their early twenties entered the kitchen. They wore small triangle bikini tops, carnation flower leis around their necks, a carnation tucked behind one ear and green grass skirts hanging at their hips. Each one picked up a tray of food and headed back out to the dining room to set the buffet.

I goggled at them. "You're joking, right?"

Cody shook her head.

"Do you have to wear one?"

Cody shook her head again. "Just the wait staff. The bartenders are wearing board shorts and leis."

"Poppy must be out of her mind if she thinks I'll wear a bikini and grass skirt. There's no way I'll fit into those little triangles!" I pointed an accusing finger at the retreating girls.

"Um ... "

"Cody ... " I growled.

She blanched. "She bought a special bikini in your size."

"I'll kill her. What the hell is she thinking?"

"Sorry," Cody squeaked.

I gnashed my teeth. It wasn't her fault. "Where?"

"The van is around the side of the garage. Deirdre should be out there. Just tell her your name."

I rearranged "the girls" one more time and looked in the mirror again, hoping for a different outcome. However, no amount of adjustment could change the result. Poppy had at least purchased a sturdy bikini top for a C cup. The twit also purchased a push-up style that generated an obscene amount of cleavage and created a boob shelf. My lei did nothing to hide the situation. Instead, it perched like a display on the boob shelf.

I sent another text to Poppy, the third since discovering her treachery.

You are dead meat. Do you hear me? This thing makes my chest look like a pair of overripe cantaloupes.

Poppy replied. LOL.

This isn't funny! You're not a nice friend.

I'm sure you look fabulous. Quit whining and get out there. We need you.

I brushed my hair out until it hung in waves down my back, tucked a yellow carnation behind my ear, and flip-flopped out of the bathroom ready to do battle.

Half an hour into the party, and two lewd propositions later, I returned from my car, wearing my flowered shirt tied at the waist with the buttons open partway down. The boobs still stood at attention, but the baggy shirt did a reasonable job downplaying the state of affairs.

Cody bustled up to me, her mouth open. I shot her a "don't mess with me look." She turned on her heel and marched away. Smart girl.

"Excuse me. Those look interesting. What are they?" A voice above the din of conversation and soft piano music halted me.

I turned and held the tray of hors d'oeuvres out to a roguish, six-foot blond. "Bacon wrapped scallops."

"Don't mind if I do." His golden brown eyes scrutinized the delicacies, then he flashed a schoolboy smile and scooped a skewer off the platter. He had a fresh-faced, wholesome appeal that would have interested me had Ian not been in my life.

I started to move off.

"Wait." His hand curled around my arm. "I'm not done yet. These are delicious. Did you make them?" The stranger took another skewer and popped the delicacy in his mouth.

"No. There's a catering staff."

"This is a real nice party. I'm surprised old Rueben shelled out for it." He leaned in and lowered his voice. "Fellow's pretty tight with a buck, if you know what I mean." He winked.

I whispered back, "I don't know what you mean. I've never met Rueben, only his wife."

"That would explain things. Sheila can get him to pony up for a good show." Another scallop went down the hatch.

"So, how do you know Sheila and Rueben?"

"I'm a casting director. Entertainment lawyers come with the job. Rueben and I go back a few years. Are you an actress?"

I looked cross-eyed at him. "No. Why would you ask that?"

"Lots of waitresses are." He shrugged and brandished a skewer in my face. "You've got a real exotic look about you." He zeroed in on the cleavage. "I might have something for you."

I made a mental eye roll and jolted to attention as a warm hand snaked up underneath my shirt and lips brushed my temple. My elbow jerked back and met hard abs. An "oof" whispered across my ear.

"Hitting on my girl, Rich?" a heart-stopping voice rumbled.

My head whipped around. "Ian! What are you doing here?"

"I told you I had a party to attend. What are you doing here?"

"This is Poppy's party."

"So my party and your party are one and the same."

"Yeah, and Poppy's going to owe me big time after making me wear this getup."

Ian leaned in to get a closer look at the goods. "I kind of like it. Maybe even better than the black dress." He gave a naughty grin and snatched the last scallop off my tray.

"O'Connor, introduce me."

Ian eyed the blond and drew me in closer, staking his claim. "Rich Kline, meet Sophia Hartland. My interior designer."

"So this is the pretty decorator you've been keeping all to yourself. I can see why." Rich's eyes narrowed, appraising the hand at my back.

Tension radiated off Ian and his hackles rose like a wary dog.

"How do you two know each other?" I tried to play mediator.

"We roomed together in New York right after university," Ian said.

"It took me three years to convince this nodcock to come out here. I got him cast in his first commercial."

Ian grunted. His animosity surprised me. Normally he had such an easygoing personality. I never expected this type of territorial behavior. Obviously, there was more between these two than met the eye.

"There you are." Poppy stepped to my other side, creating a quartet out of our trio. She flashed her teeth. She wore a simple black sheath dress and black pumps. I ground my teeth, still stung by her perfidy. I was the only woman older than twenty-two toddling around the party in a ridiculous grass skirt and bikini.

She leaned around me. "Hello, Ian. It's nice to see you again. Doesn't Soph look great tonight?"

He acknowledged her with a nod.

Her eyes bounced with impish delight between the two of us. Though I'd explained the innocent mix-up with Kate, I had yet to tell her about my night of passion with Ian. As a matter of fact, I hadn't told anyone. I'd hoarded our coupling like a delicious secret.

"Well, hello, beautiful. Who are you?" Rich oozed.

"Poppy Reagan." She shook hands with him and turned on flirt mode. "And you are?"

"Poppy, this is Rich Kline. He's a casting director. Rich, Poppy owns the party planning company that made this happen." I said.

"So, I have you to thank for the delightful outfits the waitresses are wearing." He slyly eyed my cleavage then swung his attention back to Poppy. She gave a throaty laugh and Rich's eyes lit up. Ian's hand flexed against my waist.

Poppy reached into her bra and pulled out a business card. Rich's Adam's apple bobbed. "Here, hon, be sure to call if you need an event organized."

Not to be outdone, Rich dug in his coat pocket and pulled out a card of his own. "Let me know if you're ever interested in getting into acting. I'm sure I can find you something." Pulling out a second one, he turned to me. "Here, Sophie, you too."

I made no move to accept the small blue cardstock. Instead, I held out the tray, and he dropped it. My lips curved into a sickly smile. "Thanks."

Cody hurried up to Poppy and whispered frantically in her ear. She excused herself and, as cool as a cucumber, strode toward the back of the house.

Frankly, I'd had enough of Rich. I disengaged Ian's hand and stepped away. "I'd better refill my tray and see if Poppy needs my help. Rich, it was nice meeting you. Ian, we'll catch up later."

As I retreated, I barely heard Ian's grumbly undertones.

"Leave her alone. She's not an empty-headed actress you can screw for a laugh."

"Which one?"

"Both!" he barked.

Chapter 15

I strode into chaos. In an alcove leading to the laundry area, a grass skirted waitress—Jennifer, I think—sobbed uncontrollably onto the shoulder of the head of the catering staff. Four of the catering staff stood on the opposite side of the kitchen, grouped together like Cheerios, watching the soap opera unfold. Cody, looking stricken, towered half a foot above a tiny, spiky-haired woman, who shook a finger and berated her. I identified the speaker as Sheila, our purse-loosening hostess and Poppy's client.

"You hired her. You should have known better. Your website says you do background checks on all the people you hire!" Her hand flailed about, encompassing the room of staff members.

"Well, ma'am, our background checks generally don't provide us with information about who our employees recently slept with," Cody responded.

"Well maybe they should!"

Cody's shot me a panicked glance. Thawacka, thawacka, I flopped into the fray to provide reinforcements.

"Ladies, what's the problem? Maybe I can be of some assistance." I placed a hand on Sheila's back.

"Who are you?"

"I'm Sophie Hartland, the decorator and a friend of Poppy's. What can I help with?"

"That waitress over there had the gall to accuse one of my guests, Frank Speck, yes, that's right, *the* Frank Speck, of sleeping with her in exchange for a role. She had the nerve to throw these accusations in front of his wife. Then she pushed him in the pool." Her voice rose above the din of Jennifer's wails.

Uh oh. Frank Speck was a big shot Hollywood director. Tittle tattle in the tabloids hinted he'd had romances with at least two of his leading actresses.

"I can see that would, indeed, be a little problem." I said.

"A little problem? Julianna Speck is incensed!"

"I'm sure this is all a big misunderstanding. We'll get it straightened out. Don't you worry."

"How on earth do you propose to do that?"

I had no idea, but right now I just needed the hostess to take a chill pill and return to her party guests, so I could go out back and help Poppy diffuse the situation with the director and his wife.

The kitchen door popped open. Ian strolled in, observed the hubbub and immediately retreated onto Rich Kline's foot. Rich's expletive was covered up as one of the catering staff dropped an empty pot, its jarring clang only added to the cacophony of the melee.

Cody blanched and I shot a dirty look at the staffer.

She reddened, "Sorry." And bent down to pick up the offending pot.

"Omigod, is that Ian O'Connor?" Sheila whispered.

My head whipped back to her. "Why yes, it is. Have you met?"

She shook her head.

"Let me introduce you. Ian, could you come over?" I crooked a finger at him.

Ian looked as though he'd rather do anything but continue farther into the hullabaloo, but he could probably see the pleading in my eyes, so he stepped forward.

"Ian, this is our hostess, Sheila Schwartzman," I bellowed over Jennifer's lament.

"It's lovely to meet you," Ian drawled.

"Thank you so much for coming. How do you know Sophie?"

"Sophie's my interior designer."

Jennifer's sobs quieted to a soft snuffling, which allowed all of us to drop our tones down to normal voices.

"I was thinking of redoing our basement rec room. What do you think of Sophie's work?"

"Frankly, Sheila, they don't come any better."

Sheila gave me a considering look and I decided to take advantage of the distraction.

"Ian, why don't you and Sheila get a drink from the bar in the front room and become better acquainted?"

Sheila looked thrilled to get to spend time with my Irish cutie. Ian, less so. Still, he stepped up to the plate and took one for the team.

"Brilliant idea, luv."

I'm pretty sure I was the only one who heard the sarcasm in his response.

"Why don't we get ourselves martinis?" She hooked her arm through Ian's.

Rich, who'd hovered in the doorway during the exchange, held the door open for the pair.

Once they exited, I pointed a finger at him, "You, come here."

Rich pointed to his chest. "Who, me?"

"Yes, you."

Rich stuffed his hands in his pockets and ambled over to Cody and me. "I was just looking for some more of those bacon scallop thingies."

"In a minute." I turned to Cody. "Send Jennifer home. Her being here will only make things worse." Then I turned to the hovering Cheerios. "Okay, folks, show's over. Get back to work."

"If we send Jennifer home, we're down a waitress," Cody uttered.

"You," I pointed to the pot-dropper, "take a tray out and bus the empties. Help the other waitresses anyway you can." Back to Cody. "Where's Poppy?"

"She's out back trying to calm Julianna Speck down. She threatened to sue the company."

"Cripes." I sighed and rolled my eyes. Just then, a strobe of light lit up the kitchen and a crack of thunder shook the house.

"Rich, what do you know about Frank's peccadilloes?"

"I've cast a couple of his movies. I know that he bought Nadia Badesha's silence with a yellow Porsche."

"Do you think he slept with the waitress?"

"Undoubtedly."

"Cody, tell Jennifer there's an extra five hundred if she'll go quietly." Cody efficiently bustled to the alcove to deal with the watering pot.

"Listen up. You want a date with Poppy?"

"The glorious redhead? You bet." He rubbed his hands together. "What do I have to do?"

"Okay, forget the scallops. You're about to become useful. Follow my lead."

I grabbed his hand and pulled him behind me into the backyard. A hoard of party guests, retreating from the downpour, advanced on us like stampeding bulls at Pamplona. Rich and I pushed our way upstream, and I finally found Poppy in a far corner of the tented alcove. She and Frank Speck hovered over an irate, petite, honey blonde flapping her hands and speaking in a low but angry voice.

"Stop telling me to calm down, Frank," Julianna hissed and shook her finger at him while leaning over a coffee table.

"Hello, Frank." Rich and I broke into their little trio.

Frank, a balding forty-something year old, gulped and pulled it together. "Rich. It's nice to see you." They shook hands. A towel was thrown over his right shoulder and his comb-over floated in the breeze.

"Julianna, you're looking lovely tonight." Rich gave her the socially acceptable air kiss.

Julianna, dressed in a too-tight, hot pink tube dress that ended just below her butt cheeks, had an angry, pinched face that looked less than lovely. However, Rich's engaging smile and smarmy line took some of the wind out of her sails.

"Thank you, Richard. It's kind of you to say so." She flashed a too-white smile. "Who's your little friend?" She eyed my getup.

I was seriously going to kill Poppy before this night was over.

"She's a friend of Ian O'Connor's. Sophie, meet Frank and Julianna Speck."

I shook hands, with a still-damp Frank Speck. "Nice to meet you."

"How do you know Ian?"

"I'm his decorator." I handed Frank my card. "Tonight I'm working with Poppy. I wanted to assure you the situation has been taken care of. The waitress, who had the temerity to push your husband in the pool, has been fired and is being escorted off the premises."

Poppy frowned at me. Frank looked positively relieved.

Julianna looked anything but relieved. "Well, I'm not sure that's enough."

Rich slung his arm over Julianna's shoulder. "Come, come, my dear. Vindictiveness is *not* in your nature. You know poor Frank here brings out all the crazies just because he's such an important man in Hollywood. We don't want to give credence to this little tramp's accusations by causing more of a ruckus. The poor girl's lost her job, without a reference tonight. Do we really need to torture her more? She's probably got one of those syndromes like bipolar or ADHD. She needs medication."

"Maaaybeee … " Julianna seemed to be swayed by Rich's argument.

Frank ran a hand along his wife's back. "Lamb chop, come now. Let's not allow this uproar to ruin our night."

"Frank's right. Why don't you join me for a drink, darling?" Rich offered.

Julianna gave in and shrugged. "Fine. Lead the way."

Rich winked at me then glanced significantly at Poppy, as he and Julianna walked away.

"Mr. Speck," Poppy said, "I'm sorry you were pushed in the pool. If there's been any damage to your clothes, you can send the bill to me."

Frank wore dripping khakis and a black polo. I doubted there was any damage to the clothes. However, throw in a ruined phone or Rolex watch, and the bill might get pricey, but I wasn't about to allow Poppy to pay for any of it.

"Don't worry, Poppy, I'm sure Mr. Speck can take care of any damage." I gave him a stern look and crossed my arms. "Jennifer's silence, however, will cost you five hundred, and you'll be calling in a favor. Contact one of your director friends and get her a bit part. Understood?"

Frank looked at his shoes.

"Sophie!" Poppy hissed. "I'm sorry, Mr. Speck, I have no idea what she's talking about. Please ignore her."

"Trust me. It's a lot cheaper than a new Porsche."

Frank's head whipped up and his bulgy eyes met mine.

"Isn't it, Frank?" *Geez, I sound like a mafia thug. When did it come to this?*

His cheeks turned red and he had the decency to look ashamed.

Silently, he pulled a damp leather wallet out of his back pocket and handed me five soggy hundred dollar bills. "Thanks," he mumbled.

"No problem."

With the situation taken care of, Frank made a scurried exit.

Poppy threw her arm over my shoulders. "I owe you one, girl. That woman was talking about suing me."

"I know. Cody told me. Your payment may come sooner that you think."

"Oh, yeah?"

"I promised Rich Kline you'd go out on a date with him if he helped us out of this jam."

"The cutie who just walked off with Julianna?"

"Yes. So, when he calls, it'll be time to ante up."

"No heartbreak there. I think he's adorable. Did Jennifer really sleep with Frank?"

I stuck my tongue out with a cringe. "Probably."

"Eww. He may be a big shot director, but he reminds me of George Costanza from Seinfeld. I bet he has a hairy back too. What do you think?"

"I think … I don't want to think about that. By the way, you are in the doghouse for making me wear this ridiculous outfit. I can't believe Ian saw me wearing it."

"What do you mean? He couldn't take his eyes off you."

"Who *can*?! I have a boob shelf! They're practically floating in my face."

"So?"

"So! I look like an idiot."

"Don't be silly. Ian ate it up."

Suddenly, I had a very bad feeling. I shrugged her arm off and planted myself in front of her. "Did you know Ian would be here?"

Poppy grinned unrepentantly. "I might have seen his name on the invite list."

"Please tell me you didn't change the outfits at the last minute just so I could strut a boob shelf in front of Ian."

Poppy's grin widened to a full-on smile. "Well … "

"I'm going to kill you slowly with a dull grapefruit knife."

"Oh come on. I thought I'd move things along. After all, I thought everything got straightened out once you found out the woman at his house was his sister. Right? What are you holding out for? Just sleep with the man already. Good golly, Miss Molly! Seriously, the reno's almost done what are you waiting for?"

My face burned and I looked away from Poppy's dancing eyes. "Um."

"Wait a minute. What's that look for? Did you sleep with him?" She gave a conspiratorial whisper, shifting back into my line of sight.

"I … um … he … " I rubbed my temple. "This is not the time or place to discuss my personal life." I turned on my flip-flopped heel and thawacka'd away.

Poppy laughed gleefully. "You can't hide from me. I know where you live, Hartland!"

•••

It was almost two hours later, Ian found Sophie relaxing in an empty tent, feet kicked up on a coffee table, grass skirt hanging willy-nilly. She looked worn down. The party had become boring, and he was ready to go home and spend more time with her. He'd been searching for Sophie for half an hour and was afraid she'd already bolted, so he was relieved to find her still here.

"I've been searching for you for twenty minutes." He dropped onto the love seat next to her and rubbed a hand up her supple thigh. A soft breeze blew the newly clean air, and the tent gently flapped.

"I'm hiding out from Poppy. My feet are killing me. Flip-flops aren't supportive enough for five hours of waitressing. Or maybe I'm just getting too old for this shit."

Ian pulled the nearest foot onto his lap. The purple flowered flip-flop plopped to the floor, and his thumb stroked the instep.

"Ahh … " Her lids dropped closed. "If you continue to do this, some dork is going to post a picture online, and all our baby daddy denials will be in the toilet."

"Do you care?" *Did he care?*

She threw an arm over her eyes and sighed. "I probably should, but right now your magic fingers are making me feel so good, I just can't work up the energy to make you stop."

His stomach rolled as a breath of laughter glided over her toes. She could be such a contradiction.

"How's the show coming? Any spoiler alerts I should know about?"

His hands froze. She pulled her arm away and opened her eyes. Ian gave her a hard stare.

"What? What did I say?"

"I didn't think you watched the show."

"Don't be silly. Of course I watch the show, it's important to you. It's your career. Besides, I told you Carmen is my favorite actress. I think I have a girl crush on her." She nudged his abs with a red polished toe and grinned.

This was welcome news. He'd gotten the vibe that she didn't watch much TV and wasn't really into his show. "Would you like to come to the set sometime? I can introduce you."

"Do you want me to?"

He'd love to introduce her to his cast mates and show her around. They'd enjoy her dry wit, and he'd pretty much do anything that allowed them more time together. "Sure. Lots of the production crew bring their girlfriends. Or, if you want, you can come the next time we're filming on location."

That brought a lovely smile to her face. "I'd love to visit the set, if that would be okay. It sounds like great fun."

"Absolutely. Let me know and I'll arrange it. I never thought you'd be interested. You always seem so aloof about show biz." Ian pulled her other foot onto his lap and rubbed his thumb along the instep.

Her body became relaxed and floppy like a bowl of Jell-O beneath his ministrations. "Of course I'm interested in your work.

I'm sorry if you've gotten the wrong impression. I think you're a talented actor. If I seem aloof, it's because I've lived in the area so long, I've become immune to it and tune it out. I don't think about you as Ian, the big television actor. I'm more focused on our business together. You know, one-track mind. For the most part, I've wanted to create a luxurious, functional living space for you to enjoy in your off time, while trying not to throw you down on the closest hard surface and drag my tongue from your neck to navel."

Ian's hands froze, his shaft hardened, and his aquatic-blue gaze washed over her, spearing her like a fish.

She gulped and her eyes widened in surprise and disbelief. It was as though her expression said, *"Did I speak those words out loud?"*

"Um." She pulled her leg away.

He released her foot and in a swift movement curled a hand around her neck. "Not so fast." Their lips met in a demanding kiss, and her hands snaked around his head. Her fingers glided through his hair and desire slithered into his gut.

"Here you are."

They broke apart.

"I hope I'm not interrupting." Poppy folded herself into an accompanying chair. She crossed her legs and watched them with a sly, catlike gaze.

Sophie collapsed against the cushion, and Ian picked up her foot and continued rubbing.

"Poppy, I'm done in. Do you still need me?" She asked.

"Pfft. We're doing fine. It's the bartenders who are still going strong. The catering staff is cleaning up. You can head out when you're ready."

"Thank God."

"Here are my favorite people, all gathered together. It must be destiny." Rich flung himself down in a chair opposite Poppy. "What are you plotting out here? Hmm? Deciding where to go for the after-party? I know this wonderful little club down on the strip."

"Aren't you getting a little too old for the club scene, mate?" Ian drawled looking him up and down.

"You're never too old for the club scene. What about you, Red?"

"I'm afraid I'll be here until the bitter end. It's my job, you know," Poppy replied.

"Sophie, you owe me one. Convince your stick-in-the-mud, limey boyfriend to come out to the clubs," Rich cajoled.

"Frankly, my feet are protesting at the thought of walking from here to the car, much less dancing at a club all night," Sophie replied.

"Sorry, buddy, looks like you're on your own tonight." Ian eyed his former roommate, relieved by Sophie's rebuff. He trusted Rich about as far as he could pitch him and really had no interest in allowing him to be around Sophie any longer than necessary.

"Well then, I'd better get another drink before they wrap up." Rich stood and held his hand out to Poppy. "Buy you a drink, m'dear?"

Poppy's eyes darted back and forth between the three of us, but whatever *tête-à-tête* she had planned with her girlfriend wasn't going to work out. Ian didn't feel in an obliging mood tonight, and now that he had Sophie in his sights, he wasn't going to let her get away again. Poppy bowed out gracefully, rising, she placed her arm through Rich's, and they headed back to the house.

Ian rolled his head along the back cushion, and Sophie reached over to brush an errant curl off his forehead.

"Where are you headed after this?" Ian asked.

"I don't know. Where should I be headed?"

"My flat is closer."

"Indeed it is."

He reached over and played with a lock of her hair. "Can you give me a ride home?"

"Didn't you drive?"

"Nope. Caught a lift."

She sighed. "I'd give you a million dollars if you drove me home."

"I'd like that in tens and twenties, if you please."

"Mmm. I bet I can think of other ways of paying you." Her tongue slowly glided along her upper lip.

The taunting playfulness went straight to his nether regions. She was so adorable and sexy all at the same time. Ian growled and pulled her into a horizontal position. "You know vat happens to little girls who don't pay their dues? Ve haf vays of making you pay," he said in a terrible Russian accent then proceeded to smother her with kisses.

She fell into a giggling fit. "Stop. Stop." She laughed breathlessly. "I'll pay up."

"So, you're coming over?"

"I'll go wherever you drive us." She ruffled through the skirt and reached into her shorts pocket to pull out the car keys. Ian's hand curled around the metal as she dropped them in his palm.

Thirty minutes later, the gate rolled closed behind the CR-V as Ian motored them up the drive and came to a quiet halt. Ian opened his door and the overhead lights came on, but she didn't move.

"You're coming in, right?"

"This feels strange."

He closed the door and the car went dark. "What's strange about it?"

"I've been working for weeks in your home. It feels strange knowing I'm going to do … *it* … with you. In there." She pointed at the house.

"We can do *it* right here in the car if you prefer."

She shot him a "get real" look.

"What's the difference whether we're here or at your place?"

"I guess I'm still struggling with the fact you're my client, and I'm about to cross a line that can't be uncrossed." She shrugged.

He could see she still grappled with the newness of their sexual relationship as well as the client-contractor connection that had not yet come to an end. To her, his house still represented that professional relationship, while her home seemed to be neutral territory. "Do you want me to take you back your house?"

"You'd do that?" She sounded surprised.

"If it makes you feel better."

Expressions flitted across her lovely face and he waited patiently as she waged an internal debate. Suddenly, the overhead lights popped on, and she stepped out.

"What's up? Are we staying?"

Her blue eyes wide, she leaned across the console, grabbed him by the shirt, and pressed a hard kiss against his lips. "We're staying."

He grinned. "Then that's settled."

He carried her enormous tote to the front door as she rustled behind him in her grass skirt into the foyer. After he turned the alarm off, he whirled around and scooped her up into his arms.

She giggled. "Ian, what are you doing?"

"Taking you up to my lair, where I plan to do naughty things to you." He leaned down and their lips met, slow and simmering. She quivered in his arms.

"What kind of naughty things?" She whispered along his jawline, nipping at his bristled chin.

"The kinds of things that make you cry out my name and beg for more." He climbed the stairs two at a time.

"What if I'm not in a begging mood?" She teased.

"Trust me, I'll put you in a begging mood."

"I'd like to see you try." She glided her hands through his silky locks.

"That sounds like a challenge." He tossed her into the middle of his king-sized bed; her grass skirt splayed everywhere.

"Now, how do we get rid of this lawn you're wearing?"

She reached behind and seemed to struggle. "I think it's got a knot."

In a swift movement, Ian flipped her over and tackled the stupid thing. As he wrestled with the knot, he leaned over, brushed her hair aside and placed soft kisses along the lower part of her neck. Her breath hitched and she shivered.

"I can't seem to get it loose." His breath whispered across her earlobe just before he lapped at the cute little freckle he saw there.

"Scissors. Knife. Cut the damned thing off. I don't care!" she said in a frenzied voice.

"That sounds a little bit like begging."

"Ian," she pleaded.

"All right, all right. Give me a moment." He chuckled and pulled out a pocket knife.

"That's useful."

He slid the knife under the skirt releasing it. Ian folded the knife closed and tossed the mess over his shoulder.

"Now, where were we?" She tittered.

"I believe we'd arrived at the point where you beg."

She collapsed his elbow, shoved him onto his back and straddled him. "No, I think *you're* about to beg *me*." Her fingers unbuttoned the top three buttons, and she leaned down to lick his collar bone. It was a toss-up who did the most begging.

Chapter 16

The scent of coffee wafted across my nose. My body lay in the state between wakefulness and sleep—at that point where you began to feel your limbs and became aware of your surroundings. The point where, with a little push, you could either doze back into the dream world or come to full cognizance and greet the day. Sunshine played along my eyelids and the coffee smell pulled me fully awake. Ian sat on the side of the bed holding a black mug. I yawned and stretched; my stiff muscles protested.

"Morning, luv." He placed a kiss upon my forehead.

"Is that coffee, perchance, for me?"

I wrestled myself into a sitting position and pulled the sheet up to my armpits for the sake of modesty and he handed me the mug. I took a sip of the warm brew pushing back a hank of hair.

He laughed, and, with one finger, tugged the sheet down past my naked breasts.

"Ian." I slapped at his hand.

"It's not as though I haven't seen them."

"But not in the light of day. Breasts are a nighttime thing." My cheeks burned.

"In my house, breasts are an all-the-time thing."

His lips swooped in to suckle the hardening nipple. Wind whistled through my teeth and I struggled not to spill my coffee. Ian removed the mug from my hand and placed it on the bedside table. He moved to the other breast, and soon I no longer cared about the coffee … or anything else for that matter.

Forty-five minutes later I lay spent across Ian's hard chest. My fingers tingled and I was seriously considering remaining in bed with Ian, Zen master of sex, for the rest of my life.

"I think your coffee went cold." His chest rumbled under my ear.

"I don't care."

"I was going to offer to make you some breakfast before you tempted me with your naked breasts." His fingers played with my hair.

I slapped at his belly. "Don't put that on me. I was trying to be modest. You were the one who started it."

He chortled. "I admit, I can't resist you. You're a wanton sex goddess, calling to me like a Siren."

Let's Get this Party Started, sang out from my left.

"And there's your mobile."

"I thought I left it downstairs with my handbag."

"It's been ringing all morning, so I brought it up with the coffee."

I rolled off Ian, found the cell on the bedside table, and pressed ignore. I had half a dozen missed calls and three messages.

Ian climbed out of bed and pulled on a pair of cotton, plaid lounge pants. "You like omelets?"

"I love omelets."

"I'll get started while you check your messages."

The messages were from Poppy, Mom, and a hang-up from Holly's new cell.

I called Holly first. She didn't answer. I decided Poppy could wait. It was likely she just wanted to grill me about my relationship with Ian, and we'd need a few hours and a bottle of wine.

Ian busily chopped mushrooms as I entered the kitchen and I allowed my fingers to drift lightly across his naked shoulder blades. Goose bumps rose along his back, and he winked. Ian moved on to chopping up green and red peppers, and as I watched the small muscles in his hands shift and flex, my body unexpectedly reacted, as thoughts of what he did with those hands last night jacked up my libido. I sighed. This was nuts. All he had to do was cut vegetables, and it got me hot and bothered. I poured a cup of coffee in an effort to distract myself from the wicked thoughts running through my head. I didn't know how long this fling would last, but today I rode high on the wave, reveling in my new title as wonton sex goddess.

"Can I help?"

"Nope. Have a seat and watch the master."

I padded around to one of the stools at the breakfast bar to enjoy the novelty. My ex never cooked for me. Michael's idea of cooking was to pull a frozen dinner out of the freezer and pop it in the microwave.

"Poppy has a date with Rich tomorrow. They're going to a Lakers game."

"Put a warning in your friend's ear. Poppy seems like a nice girl, and Rich is a bit of a drive-by dater."

I nodded. "So, the love 'em and leave 'em type."

"Yes."

"I thought that might be the case. He's quite the charmer—comes on a bit strong, though. What's the deal between you two?"

"We were flat mates in New York after university." Ian stood with a spatula in his hand. "He was in marketing at the time. He had a bad habit of dating girls from whatever production I was rehearsing. He'd screw them once or twice then move on to the next. Invariably, the next being the girl's best friend. It was a mess. I had some poor sap crying on my shoulder and blaming me for introducing them. He also wasn't above stealing girlfriends."

"Ouch. That explains your circling dog impression last night."

Ian shot me a frown.

I dialed Poppy.

"Who are you calling?"

I held up a finger.

"Sophie! Where have you been? I've called three times this morning."

"I'm having brunch with Ian. Listen, he told me to warn you about Rich. Apparently, he's a man whore. So, whatever you do, don't sleep with him. Sounds like he's a two-ply guy. Don't get attached. He'll be moving on soon enough."

"Really? He seemed pretty cool, and he's got a nice tushie."

"Great butt, not withstanding, Ian called him a drive-by dater. So beware.

She sighed. "Where are you having brunch?"

"At this great little omelet place. I'll tell you all about it later." Ian slid a mouthwatering omelet in front of me. Egg lightly browned, with mushrooms, peppers and cheese squishing out the side. "I'd better go. My breakfast just arrived."

"Sophie, wait!"

I hung up and shut my ringer off. Poppy was probably frothing to hear the details, but after the dirty trick she pulled with the bikini grass skirt yesterday, she'd have to wait a bit longer.

"This looks delectable."

"Two-ply?" Ian raised his eyebrows.

"Yeah, double up on the condoms." My phone vibrated, but I ignored it.

He snorted. "I'll have to remember that."

"Yes, you should. From what the tabloids say, you're not much different from Rich."

"You and I both know the rags often get it wrong."

"So, you haven't slept with all those women they attach to you."

"Not even half."

My left eyebrow rose disbelievingly.

"Look, I'm not a monk. I've slept with my fair share of women."

"Mm-hm. What exactly is a fair share?"

"I don't know. More than five, less than a hundred."

I choked on the coffee. Ian handed me a napkin. "Less than a hundred!"

"It's never a good idea to talk about past affairs."

He was right. My past wasn't up for discussion either, not that it even compared to his colorful one, but there were always relationship skeletons. "You're right. Let's not talk about the past." I took a bite of the warm egg confection. "Mm … Aren't you eating?"

He shook his head. "I ate over an hour ago." He grinned unrepentant. "Sorry. You were sleeping like the dead and I didn't want to wake you. I was hungry."

"It was a wearying day."

"So it seems. Your friend Poppy is quite something."

My eyes flew up to meet his clear gaze. "You're not tempted to take a page out of Rich's playbook are you?" I'd never been threatened by Poppy's beauty. On the other hand, I'd also stayed out of the dating pool for the most part, and I'd never dated someone in Ian's league. My past with Michael still gnawed at my confidence and made me wary of the possibility of cheating.

His eyebrows crunched together and he glowered at me. "I'm not Michael, Sophie. Don't compare me to him. I've never cheated, and I sure as hell wouldn't do it with your best friend."

Justly chastised, I looked at my plate. My fingers fidgeted with the fork. "Sorry," I mumbled.

Ian came around the island, and, with a firm finger, lifted my chin. I kept my eyes down.

"Look at me," he demanded.

Giving in to his command, I met his angry scrutiny.

"Right now, you're the only woman in my life. No matter what the tabloids might portray, I don't have multiple women waiting in the wings. I'm not a cheater, and it makes me bloody furious when you talk like that. What's in your past is just that—your past. Not mine. Understand?"

I gulped and nodded. *Crap. Were my insecurities going to mess this up with Ian?* I needed to stop allowing Michael's infidelity to taint my perception of the male species as a whole, and specifically Ian.

"You're right. I'm sorry, that was out of line. Michael's unfaithfulness has nothing to do with you. It's something I need to get past."

His eyes still held irritation but his shoulders relaxed. "I understand it's hard for you to let go of what Michael did. But, you need to, if we're going to move forward." He wrapped his fingers around my neck and pulled me in for a hard kiss. "Now, eat up before your omelet gets cold."

Chapter 17

My keys jingled against the counter as I plunked my overflowing tote on the granite and tossed my phone into my purse. I flipped through the mail, sorting the junk from the bills. Out of my periphery, I spotted movement at the back door, but it didn't register until a knock sounded; my stomach dropped and with wide eyes, I zeroed in. Holly, barely recognizable, stood with her knuckles pressed against the plate glass. Little Eva clutched my sister's other hand, and she sucked her thumb, her brown eyes watchfully wary of Sirius, who sat complacently leaning against my sister's left leg.

The lock snapped under my fingers and I whipped open the sliding door to let them in. My heart continued to pound. Something was very wrong.

"Holly!" I hugged my too-thin sister then squatted down to Eva's level. "Hi, sweetheart, do you remember your aunt Sophie?"

She crowded closer to Holly's leg, her mouth sucking faster as she pulled a dirty pink blanket against her cheek, her soft, baby curl ringlets sticking out in a variety of directions. Sirius followed them in and went directly to his bowl. Slurping sounds filled the kitchen. I waited for Holly to say something; instead, she removed her sunglasses. The movement spoke volumes, and, in an instant, I realized how far off base Mom was with her drug theory. Holly's eye was purpled and swollen, and the cheekbone held a recent cut, made by a ring if I had to guess. The air whistled through my teeth. She shook her head and glanced down at Eva.

"I bet you guys are hungry." I smiled at the little tike. "Would you like some milk and a snack?"

Slowly Eva nodded then glanced at her mother for confirmation. With tenderness in her eyes, "Evie, why don't you sit down at the table and Aunt Sophie will get you something to eat."

My sister led her daughter to the table and got her situated. Sirius's nails clicked along the tile to lie down under the table. Eva eyed the dog warily and lifted her legs but remained silent.

I whistled. Sirius popped up. "Go to your bed." He trotted off to my office, and Eva visibly relaxed.

The refrigerator revealed an opened bottle of Chenin Blanc, from which I poured two glasses, along with Eva's milk, and dug out graham crackers from the pantry. They were unopened, so I figured they weren't stale. Holly didn't hesitate, drinking half her glass in a single gulp. I sat across from my sister, observing the destruction. Her normally high-styled toffee hair hung limp at her shoulders; the brown eye that wasn't injured was dark with sleepless circles and bloodshot. The weight loss had hollowed her cheeks, making it look like her ears stuck out more than normal, and she wore a loose T-shirt with baggy denims that had seen better days. The only thing that reminded me of the old Holly was the perfect French manicure; her hands were unadorned except for the stark white outline on the left ring finger.

"How long have you been waiting for me?"

"We got in about two thirty."

I nodded. It was almost five now. "Did you fly or drive?"

"Bus."

Eva finished her snack and sat quietly, picking at her blanket.

Holly looked down. "Sweetie, would you like to watch *Sesame Street*?"

She nodded, her eyes droopy.

"Why don't you put her in my room? She can take a nap there if she wants. Use the blue remote, and PBS is channel twenty-six."

Holly led Eva down the hall. I opened the back door to see if there was any luggage. Tucked in a shaded corner of the brick patio stood a pink Barbie backpack, a car seat, and an oversized black duffel on wheels. I pulled them into the kitchen and left them by the door. Holly returned to her seat at the table.

"Thanks for bringing our stuff in. She'll fall asleep soon. She was too excited to take a nap on the bus."

I gave a wan smile. "How long has it been going on?"

Holly didn't flinch or pretend she didn't know what I was talking about. "Since before Eva's first birthday."

"He never hit you before that? You never saw it coming?"

Holly looked away, unable to meet my eyes. "He hit me once while we were engaged, but he was so apologetic and swore it'd never happen again; he bought me flowers and a diamond necklace. For a while, it didn't."

"After you got married?"

"Things were fine for the first six months. Then work got really stressful for him and we were fighting more." Her shoulders lifted. "I figured it was what all couples went through, adjusting to married life. He wanted me to be a housewife, at home when he was, dinner on the table, and run his errands for him during the week. I cut my work back to part-time at the gallery so I could be there for him. I wanted to make him happy, and I thought it was important to our marriage."

Needless to say, I was appalled. Granted, my own marriage wasn't perfect, but even during the worst of times, Michael never raised a hand to me or expected me to give up my job to cater to him. As humiliating as the cheating was, it had to be better than the type of abuse Holly was undergoing.

My sister continued, "When I got pregnant with Eva, things improved. He was always checking on me and solicitous of my feelings. He was so excited."

"What about after Eva was born?"

"Things were rough here and there. We fought, but I chalked it up to the lack of sleep."

"Then what happened?"

She shrugged. "He started drinking more and having evenings out with the guys. He'd come home and start accusing me of cheating on him. He became really possessive. He began calling me at home and checking up on me. I had to quit the gallery because he thought the owner and I were sleeping together." Holly snorted and shook her head. "The owner's gay, but Omar didn't believe me when I told him. I always have to keep my cell phone on in case he calls, because if he can't get in touch with me, he goes nuts."

"Why didn't you talk to Mom at Easter?"

"I couldn't. I was afraid of what he might do to her, or Eva. That's why I wouldn't allow her to take Eva over to the hotel. He's threatened to take Eva away from me if I don't do what he says, so I don't let her out of my sight. I never, ever allow him to take her anywhere on his own. I always make sure we go as a family."

"What made you finally leave?"

She pointed to her eye. "He did this in front of her. He's always waited until Eva's in bed." She shook her head. "Sunday night he just lost it. I hadn't ironed his favorite shirt, and he flipped out. He wanted to take it on his trip."

Realization dawned. "So he's away? Does he know you're gone yet?"

Holly shook her head. "He's at a conference in Fort Lauderdale. I have the home phone forwarding to my cell, so he doesn't know we're gone. He keeps an eye on the credit cards and bank accounts, so I sold my engagement ring and diamond necklace for money."

I chewed the inside of my lip, trying to work out the next steps to help Holly. "How long before he finds out you're gone?"

"Hopefully, not until he returns to Vegas on Thursday. I'm not sure that he won't have one of his buddies at the casino check on me while he's gone."

Today was Tuesday. Our time was limited.

"I have a friend on the police force. I think we need to call him."

Holly's eyes widened in panic, and she started shaking her head. "No. He has friends on the force in Vegas. He'll figure out where I am. He'll kill me and anyone that stands in his way."

I grabbed her hands. "Holly! This is exactly why we need to call the police. This is California. We're not in Vegas."

She vehemently shook her head.

"Listen, you came to me for help. Right?"

"Yes."

"Then I'm going to help you, but we're going to do it the right way. Do you understand?"

Holly gnawed on one of her perfectly manicured nails.

"Do it for Eva." I pushed.

"You know this police officer personally? Do you trust him?" She eyed me.

I nodded. "He's my neighbor, a block away. We can trust him, and it's especially important we call the police if Omar threatened your life. How long do you think it'll be before he comes looking for you here, or, God forbid, at Mom's?"

"That's why I came here. I didn't want to put her in danger," she whispered.

"Okay. There are things we need to do. Taking out a restraining order should probably be a priority. The second would be talking to a divorce lawyer. Stay here, I'll be right back."

In my office, I shuffled through an old-fashioned Rolodex, searching for the business card. I found it under D for detective. My fingers dialed as I walked back to the kitchen.

"Detective Sumner."

"Gary? This is Sophie Hartland, your neighbor, with the black Lab named Sirius. Remember?"

"I sure do, Sophie. What can I do for you?"

"I was wondering if you could come by the house. My sister's here and … she's having some trouble with her husband."

His voice turned serious. "I'll come right over."

Fifteen minutes later I opened my front door to LAPD Detective Gary Sumner. I held onto Sirius's collar and motioned for Gary to enter. Some of my anxiety must have shown on my face, because his hand went to the gun on his hip and his eyes darted around.

"Is everything okay, Sophie?"

I expelled a breath. "Yes, yes. Come in, Gary. Thanks for getting here so quickly."

My sister stood when we entered the kitchen.

"Holly, this is Detective Gary Sumner, my neighbor."

Gary took in her bruised eye and ragged appearance as they shook hands. "It's nice to meet you, Holly."

"You too, detective," Holly responded weakly.

"Gary, can I get you a drink? We're having wine, but I've also got soda and water."

"I'll have water, please." Gary took a seat across from Holly. He removed a small pad and pen from his pocket and flipped to an empty page. "I assume I'm here because your husband did that to you." Gary indicated the black eye.

She bowed her head.

Lowering myself next to my sister, I answered for her. "Holly arrived this afternoon. She lives in Las Vegas with her husband, Omar, and daughter, Eva. He's currently in Fort Lauderdale at a conference."

"Is your daughter okay?" He continued to address Holly.

"Yes. She's fine. Omar has never laid a hand on her."

"Where is Eva now?"

"She's napping in the bedroom."

"Okay. There are a couple of avenues we can take here. First, if you're willing to press charges, you can have your husband arrested."

She started shaking her head.

"Second, and this is important, we need to take out a restraining order against him. Has any of his abuse landed you in the ER?"

My sister's ears burned a deep red as she stared intently at the woodgrain on the table. She spoke so softly I could barely hear her. "About nine months ago, when he hit me, I fell and cracked my wrist against the coffee table so hard I got a hairline fracture. I had to wear a brace for six weeks."

The air whooshed out of my lungs. Excusing myself, I stomped out back, slamming the door behind me. I was already furious at myself for waiting too long to go out to her and at Omar for doing this to her to begin with. My emotions were riding high, but right now I was livid with my sister for remaining for so long in the relationship. *He broke her wrist! And she stayed! And never called me!* The soft grass hushed my steps as I paced the yard, taking deep breaths, and worked to get a grip on my anger. I knew Holly needed my support and not more people yelling at her, but I had difficulty comprehending her decisions. It wasn't as though she had no family to run to. Granted, she did eventually come to me, but how many times had he slapped her around before she decided to go? Five, ten, twenty? I closed my eyes and turned my face to the sky, allowing nature's warm rays to calm my fury.

I returned to the kitchen where Gary was photographing Holly's face and a nasty bruise around her thin wrist.

"What I'd like to do is have someone from the California Alliance Against Domestic Violence come out to meet with you. She can get you and Eva entered into the program and situated into an undisclosed abuse shelter."

"It's all right, Gary. Holly and Eva can stay here with me," I interrupted.

Gary's sharp hazel eyes pegged me. "I'm sorry, Sophie, but it's not all right for her to stay here with you. From what your sister's told me, Omar is a danger not only to Holly and Eva, but to anyone who stands in his way. That includes you. There are only a few places Holly would run, and he knows that."

We were interrupted by the doorbell. Sirius set up barking. Holly jerked and her eyes turned wild and panicky; she got up and sprinted down the hall to where Eva slept.

Gary looked at me. "Are you expecting someone?"

I shook my head and started to stand, whistling for the dog. Sirius obeyed and scurried into the kitchen.

Gary motioned for me to stay where I was. With a gesture so smooth it was probably ingrained, his hand moved to the gun on his hip as he stalked through the hall to the door. I remained poised, my hands on the table, half-standing, with the chair pressed against the back of my knees.

He opened the door. "May I help you?"

I didn't hear the response, but Gary blocked the door and asked his name.

This time the voice made it to my ears. "Ian O'Conner, and who the bloody hell are you?"

My heart leap with relief.

"Detective Sumner." Gary flashed his badge.

"What's wrong? Is Sophie okay?" His voice pitched. "Soph, are you in there?"

I vaulted into action. My chair crashed to the floor, and I skittered down the hall. "It's okay, Gary. He's all right. Let him in. He's my ... ah ... friend of mine." Sirius followed, galloping and whuffling at my heels.

Gary stood back to allow Ian to enter. Ian brushed past him, and I threw myself, drama queen style, into his arms. Sirius circled us, whining and pawing at our legs.

Ian's arms wrapped around me like a wool sweater. Their strength provided a sense of security. I buried my head into his neck and breathed in his delicious musky scent. Even though I wasn't the one who'd been abused, my sister's fear and stress had spilled over and Ian's presence helped dispel some of the anxiety.

His sturdy hand rubbed along my back comfortingly. "Steady on, old fella." Ian acknowledged Sirius and gave him a reassuring stroke. "Soph, what's wrong?"

I wrapped my arms tighter around his neck and tried to calm my hammering heart.

"It's okay, luv. It'll be okay, whatever it is. I'm here, sweetheart. I'm here," he whispered in hushed tones.

There was movement behind me. Ian looked up and froze. I loosened my grip and glanced over my shoulder. Holly stood in the kitchen entry with Eva wrapped tightly around her neck, still half-asleep.

"It's okay, Holly. This is my friend, Ian O'Connor. Why don't you and Gary move into the family room, while I have a moment with Ian?"

The actor? Holly mouthed as she passed me.

I nodded.

Ian followed me into the kitchen and paused by the island as I righted the overturned chair and headed to the fridge.

"Can I get you something to drink?"

"What's going on?" His voice was solemn.

My hand dropped away from the handle and I sighed. "Holly is my sister."

"The one who lives in Vegas?"

"Yes."

"What happened?"

"Her husband."

The warmth in his eyes evaporated, turning to ice. "How can I help?"

I shook my head. Most men, at this juncture, would offer to leave. Not Ian. He offered help. "Just … stay with me. That's all."

"I can do that."

I took his hand and we headed back into the family room. Holly sat on an overstuffed cream chair with a dozing Eva snuggled under her chin. Gary had pulled up an ottoman across from her and was talking on his cell phone.

I introduced Ian and Holly, and we took seats on the couch while Gary finished his call. "Okay, that was someone from domestic abuse. They're sending a counselor over. We'll get the paperwork started for a temporary restraining order and to move you into a shelter."

Holly nodded in resignation.

"Wait a minute, Gary. I told you Holly can stay here. I have a security system. I'm sure if we keep it set, everything will be okay."

Gary shook his head. "It can take up to ten minutes for the police to get here. That's a lot of time for an angry man to do damage. You or Holly could get hurt, or, as your sister's indicated, he could kidnap Eva. Unless you can afford private security, it's best for Holly to go into the program."

"What about a hotel? Can't we book her in a hotel under an assumed name?" I was grasping at straws. "There are a million hotels in the LA area. He'd never find her."

"Unfortunately, from what Holly tells me, he has contacts in the Las Vegas police force. It's likely he can trace not only her credit cards but yours as well. Unless you were planning to put her in a fleabag motel that will take only cash?" Gary looked significantly at Eva.

Holly sat silent, clasping Eva to her breast. Her eyes bounced between Gary and me as we talked.

I turned my full attention to her. "Honey, are you going to be okay with this?"

She shrugged noncommittally.

Ian cleared his throat. "She could stay at my place."

All three of our stunned pairs of eyes turned to gape at him.

"What?" He shrugged. "My home is fenced with a gated entry, I've got a security system with cameras and, as far as Omar knows, I have no connection to your sister."

Gary was temporarily thrown off his game as he considered Ian's suggestion. I stared slack-jawed, taken aback by his generosity. Not many single men would offer to take in a stranger and her small child to avoid a crazy abusive husband.

"It's not what I would recommend," Gary stated.

"Are you serious?" I asked Ian.

"Deadly. I don't take kindly to men who beat their wives," he ground out through a clenched jaw. "Sophie can back me up. My security system is top of the line. If need be, we can hire a bodyguard for the girls."

Considering Ian's masterful approach to my security system, I had no doubt he'd hire a bodyguard for me or my sister in a heartbeat. "I'm not sure we need a bodyguard."

"It's still risky." Gary shook his head.

"Holly, what do you want to do?"

Eva snuggled close, sucking her thumb. Holly stroked her curls as she considered the possibilities. "I'd rather not go into a group home, but I don't want to impose on Ian."

"It's not an imposition. Your sister is finishing up the renovations this week, so she'll be there. I have to be at the studio all week, so you'll have the run of the place during the day."

"If you're sure."

"Then it's settled. After you finish up here with the detective, Sophie can bring you over." Ian stood.

"You're going?" I asked.

"I think it's best. I need to run a couple of errands. I'll see you at the house tonight."

I walked him to the door, followed by the intrepid Sirius. "Thank you for doing this. We'll try to figure something more permanent out soon."

"Don't worry." He brushed a thumb across my cheek. "Holly is welcome to stay as long as she needs. Which room should I put them in?"

"The main floor guest room and bath is finished. Let's put them there."

"Does Eva need a crib or something?"

I shook my head.

"Why did you stop by?"

"I got off early and wanted to see you." He leaned down. His soft lips met mine in a tender kiss. "Take care," he whispered and then was out the door.

Chapter 18

"Hello, lovelies. Come on in." Ian welcomed us into his home.

I followed Holly, who held an alert but hesitant Eva. My niece's dark eyes darted around as she sucked her thumb, taking in the new surroundings. All of the living room furniture had arrived. Michelle and I'd completed the final touches earlier today, and I'd taken photos for my portfolio. Originally, I'd told Ian I'd stop by around seven so we could toast the finished product. Sadly, the ice blue with black lace corset and garter set I'd bought to celebrate the occasion remained folded away in my lingerie drawer. It would have to come out at a happier time, when my sister's situation was behind us.

Eva caught sight of a brand new Minnie Mouse kitchen sitting in the center of the great room entryway and pushed against her mother to be let down. Holly let her loose. She removed the thumb and toddled over. She opened the pink oven door filled with plastic pots and pulled at a handle. The pile fell out on the floor, and her legs crouched down to inspect the bounty.

Ian stood to the side, hands on hips, watching with delight as Eva handled fake fruits and vegetables. He turned his grin and twinkly eyes my way. I might as well have ripped out my heart and placed it in his hands then and there. Who could not, absolutely, fall tops over tails for a man who offered his home to a stranger and her daughter and then bought the little girl a Disney kitchenette? I walked over and he slid an arm around my waist.

"Did you just buy this?"

He nodded.

I reached up on tiptoe to kiss his cheek. The stubble tickled my lips.

"Did you eat yet?" he asked.

"Yes. We picked up fast food on the way over. I'll stop by the store tomorrow morning to get some groceries for the girls."

Holly knelt next to Eva and pretended to eat soup from a pint-sized pot.

"I had Brittany pick up a few things. She got milk, cereal, oatmeal, fruits and veggies, deli meats and some toddler snacks she found in the organic foods section. I didn't know if she was potty trained. Do we need to get some diapers?"

Holly answered without looking up. "Eva's potty trained, but she still sleeps with a Pull-up at night. I have about a dozen in my luggage."

That was a relief. "Did you have Brittany pick up the kitchen?"

"Nah. She did the boring stuff. I went to the Toys R Us in Century City. You should see what I got for the pool." He rubbed his hands together.

I raised an eyebrow.

With a little boy look, he trotted down to the guest room where Holly and Eva would be sleeping. He returned with a bag the size of a small elephant and proceeded to pull out a pink Dora the Explorer life vest and dropped it on the floor. Then he reached in and pulled out a handful of Dr. Seuss books; a soft, gray stuffed Horton elephant; and two purple toddler one-piece bathing suits. "I didn't know if you brought your swim kit." Some blocks and a turquoise princess dress with matching shoes and a star-tipped wand followed the swimsuits, and finally he pulled out a box with a picture of a giant, blow-up hobby horse with a squirter that shot water through its mouth.

Holly and I stared at the bounty of toys littering the floor. Her eyes went from me back to Ian.

"What? Is she too young for it?"

"Not at all," I answered for Holly. "Did you pick all this up after you left?"

"Yes."

Holly got off the floor, hugged Ian, and kissed his other cheek. "Thank you," she whispered with tears in her eyes.

Ian cleared his throat. "Uh, no problem."

Then Holly threw her arms around me. "I don't know how I can ever repay you two."

"Hey, we're sisters." I returned her constricting, desperate embrace.

"I've a few calls to make. Why don't you girls get settled? I'll be in the office." Ian retreated.

"Mommy, el-phant."

Eva had moved over to the stash of toys and held the Horton by an ear. They were the first words I'd heard her speak since their arrival.

"That's right, baby. His name is Horton."

"Fred." She tucked the plush animal under her arm then produced a dainty yawn.

"Why don't I show you to your room?"

We scooped up the books and Holly's duffel bag, and the girls followed me down the hall to the Art Deco bedroom.

"This is beautiful, Soph. Did you decorate it?"

"Sure did."

"It's gorgeous. I love that painting. Where did you find it?"

Eva parked herself on the floor with her pink Barbie backpack and proceeded to pull out all her worldly goods.

"I painted it." An abstract canvas of shapes and lines in soft purple and honey colors complemented the headboard and wall color.

"You're very talented." She couldn't keep the surprise out of her voice.

"Gee, thanks." My sarcasm dripped.

"I'm serious. Did you ever think of painting more artwork?"

"I tend to make a piece for each client if my style fits in their décor."

"How come I never knew that?" She tilted her head and her tired, somber eyes regarded me, as though seeing me through new lenses.

"I started doing it about three years ago. I don't really think of it as high art." I shrugged. I touched a long, thin box with a picture of a white plastic bedrail lying across the end of the bed. Ian thought of everything. I hoped his generosity meant he'd forgiven my thoughtless comments over breakfast on Sunday.

Eva finished her inventory and sat in the center of a pile of clothes and small toys, her ratty blanket, and Horton gripped tightly in one hand while sucking away on the thumb of her other hand.

"Why don't you get Eva cleaned up and ready for bed? I'll unpack your things."

Holly dug toiletries and pajamas out of her luggage and took Eva into the bathroom to wash off the funky bus smell and get her ready for bed. Meanwhile, I unpacked the limited luggage, organizing their clothes into the closet and dresser. Eva's high-pitched giggle echoed through the bathroom walls. Luckily, her disposition was sweet and flexible, but her quietness troubled me. Her wide, brown eyes seemed to comprehend her life was changing. Hopefully, for the better. I prayed Holly left early enough in Eva's development that the little girl wouldn't remember the violence.

The bedrail slid easily between the mattress and box spring, and I snapped it into the upright safety position. The girls came in, their hair damp, smelling of strawberry shampoo. Eva wore a Little Mermaid nightgown, her tiny pink toes peeping out from the bottom. Holly sported pink, polka-dotted shorts and a blue tank top. The purple-black bruise on her wrist stood out against her golden skin.

"C'mon, sweetie, hop into bed." I patted the side nearest the bedrail. With Holly sleeping on the opposite flank, there'd be little risk of Eva falling out of bed onto the hard floor.

The imp snatched up her scruffy blanket and stuffed elephant and crawled under the covers. "Aunt Sophie read?" Doe eyes implored.

My heart constricted, and I kissed her forehead. "Sure, sweetie." I picked *Horton Hears a Who* out of the stack and climbed in next to her.

"I'm going to get something to drink, if that's okay." Holly watched us snuggle on the bed.

"We'll be fine." I waved her off.

She kissed Eva. "Night, night, my sweet baby. I love you."

"Love you, Mommy." Eva gave her mother a sloppy smack on the cheek.

• • •

An exhausted Holly sat at the counter, beer in hand, speaking quietly about her daughter who she clearly loved to death, while Ian stood across from her, eating a banana. Sophie wandered down the hall turning off lights as she went.

"Is she sleeping?" Holly asked.

"Like a log."

Holly gave a relieved sigh. "Thank heavens."

"Would you like something to drink?" Ian could see the strain around Sophie's eyes and in the tightness of her jaw. "Beer? Wine?"

"Just water. I'm driving."

"You're not staying?" Ian and Holly chimed together.

She shook her head. "Not tonight. You'll be okay, Holly. I need to get some things in order for the morning."

Ian frowned and his brows knit, but Sophie avoided his intent stare as, she climbed onto the stool next to her sister.

"Tomorrow morning we're going to the courthouse to file a restraining order and get things rolling. I need to know you're committed," she said. "I'll stand by your sided to fight this bastard, but I won't fight you, too."

Holly shuddered. "I have no energy left to love him. Not only do I want him out of my life, I want him out of Eva's."

"Good. Then we start tomorrow."

She gulped the last dregs of her beer. "I'm pooped. Good night, Ian. Thanks again for letting us stay."

"Any time." He waited until Holly had shuffled down the hall to her room before confronting Sophie. "You can't stay?"

"Sorry, no." Her ponytail danced as she shook her head. "I don't have any of my stuff, and I need to prepare for tomorrow. Sirius needs me, and I need to talk to Michelle to see if she can babysit Eva while I take my sister to meet with an attorney."

"I can go pick up Sirius and you can call Michelle from here," he argued. There was no reason for her to return home. He had a bad feeling about this tosser, Omar. He didn't like Holly's fear of him, and had no doubts that he meant what he said about killing her. This wasn't the first abuser he'd come across. The thought of any man slapping a woman around disgusted him, and he didn't want Sophie anywhere near this arsehole.

"Ian, I have business to take care of. Besides, I'm not the one in danger."

"That's not what the detective thinks."

"What time will you leave tomorrow?" Her mouth was set in a stubborn line and her body language made it clear, Ian wasn't going to win this argument tonight, but it didn't mean he wouldn't revisit it again tomorrow. And again, if need be, until she came to her senses.

"About five thirty. I'll try to be quiet so I don't wake the girls. They look exhausted." He came around to sit on the stool Holly had abandoned. "Do you want me to ask around for a good divorce attorney tomorrow? You know they grow on trees here in LA."

The quip produced a slight lift to the corner of her mouth. "No. I already have one."

Ian let out a grim sigh. "I keep forgetting."

She tilted her head. Emotions Ian couldn't understand rippled across her face. "Thank you for this. You've gone above and beyond the call of duty here. I don't know why you'd go through so much trouble, but I appreciate it all the same."

He trailed a callused thumb along her jawline. "I'd do it for any friend in need. She's your sister, a *ghra mo chroi*."

Her brow knit. "What language is that?"

"It's Gaelic."

"What does it mean?"

Instead of answering, he leaned in and his lips drifted along hers. Her fingers rubbed against his stubbly cheek. The kiss turned hard and needy. She broke it off and buried her head in his neck, breathing hard. She tightened the embrace, as if to draw strength from him.

To his regret, she released him and sat back. "I have to go."

He took her hand as they sauntered to the door. "Keep me informed about what's going on. Put your cop friend's phone number on speed dial, in case her husband shows up."

"I'll do that."

"I don't like the idea of you being alone. If he shows his face, you'll move in here until this gets cleared up and we know what we're dealing with."

She didn't acknowledge the demand, just opened the front door. Loathe to let her go, Ian walked Sophie to her car and reluctantly closed the door behind her. She started the engine and the window slid down silently. Ian stuck his head in and laid a perfunctory kiss on her lips.

"Be careful."

"I will. I promise."

Chapter 19

Wham! Wham! Wham! "Open the door, Holly! I know you're in there."

Sirius added his frantic barks to the beating noise at my door and in my chest. It was a few minutes past five in the evening on Thursday. I'd returned home from Ian's about an hour ago and had just hung up with him after a lengthy debate over my returning there to spend the night, when the banging began. With trembling fingers, I fished the phone out of my purse and told it to call Gary Sumner. Thank God for modern technology, because I'm not sure I could have actually dialed the phone.

"Detective Sumner."

"Gary? It's Sophie Hartland."

Bing-bong. Bing-bong. Wham! I jumped. Jesus. He'd break the glass on the storm door if he kept up like that. Sirius' barking subsided to a low, eerie growl. His hackles rose, and goose bumps slithered down my backbone.

"What's going on, Sophie?"

"My sister's husband is here. And he sounds pissed."

"I'm sending a cruiser over now. Stay away from the windows and keep the door locked."

We'd hired a process server in Las Vegas to deliver the temporary restraining order to Omar upon his return from the conference. The process server was supposed to contact us when he delivered the package. Apparently, he forgot that part. Omar must have returned home and immediately set out for LA.

"Holly! You can't hide from me!" Bing-bong. "It was very foolish of you to run. You know I can find you."

He paused for a moment. "Holly? Come on, baby. Come out and talk to me." His voice wheedled. Silence.

Wham! "Holly, get out here now!" No more wheedling. "You're mine! Remember our wedding vows. I own you!"

I own you? Rage short-circuited my brain. Ignoring Detective Sumner's advice, I snatched the Louisville Slugger from beneath my bed and stomped down the hall. In a red haze of fury, I whipped open the front door.

My face must have reflected the anger coursing through my body, or perhaps it was the sight of my large, black Lab baring his fangs. Whatever the case, Omar stepped back.

"This isn't the seventeenth century, you cretin. You don't *own* my sister. Get the fuck off my porch, you piece of shit," I snarled through gritted teeth and snapped the storm door lock.

"Holly's my wife. It's not your place to interfere." He puffed up his chest and shook his fist at me.

"You like to hit women? C'mon, pal, why don't you try taking a swing at me? I've got a friend here who'd like to tap dance on your face." I bounced the Slugger in my left hand. The wrath pumped adrenaline through my body, and my fingers no longer shook.

"I don't know what sort of tales she's been telling you, but she fell down. That's how she hurt herself."

"I don't know what prehistoric cave you crawled out of, but you need to go back there. You lying turd." I hissed and slit my eyes at him.

"Holly!" he hollered, looking in the front window of my office. "I know you're here. You can't keep Eva from me. She's my daughter too."

"They're not here."

"Where else would they be? Arizona, perhaps?"

I couldn't risk him going to my mother's. "Neither. She's in a safe house. Where *you* can't get to her."

"Then let me come in and see for myself."

"Piss off."

He balled his fists and his nostrils flared.

"You do understand what the restraining order means? You may not get within a hundred yards, and if Holly was here, you'd be in violation."

"I suppose you helped her get that useless piece of paper."

"Her lawyer helped her get that *useful* piece of paper."

"Lawyers." He spit out.

"You need to leave. Now."

"I'm not leaving until I've seen my wife!"

Behind Omar, a black and white police cruiser pulled up. A brunette officer climbed out of the car. "Is there a problem?"

She approached Omar with a hand, resting on the service weapon attached at her hip. He glanced over his shoulder at the cop, and then his narrowed black eyes swooped back to me.

"This man is trespassing on my property. He needs to leave," I spoke up.

"Sir, do you live here?"

He didn't answer; he stood, seething. I gave back, glare for glare.

"Is this your home?"

"No," he ground out.

"I've told him to leave. He needs to get off my property." I stared him down.

"Sir, it would be best if you leave now."

"*I'll kill you! Bitch!*" He punched his fist against the storm door so hard a crack in the glass formed and split from top to bottom.

I jumped back, pulling a teeth-baring, frantically barking Sirius with me.

"Put your hands on your head and get down on the ground. *Now!*" The police officer had her gun pointed dead center of Omar's back.

Slowly, he laced his hands behind his head and dropped down to his knees. If looks could kill, I'd have exploded where I stood. Evil hatred spewed forth from his obsidian hard eyes. I had no doubt, if there hadn't been a police officer pointing a gun at him, we would've gone head to head. Shame really. I'd been looking forward to trying out the bat.

"Put your face to the ground," she ordered.

Omar's forehead touched the porch. A black, unmarked police vehicle careened into my driveway and squealed to a stop. The female officer snapped her gaze away for a second to see what was coming from behind. Gary jumped out of the vehicle with his gun drawn.

"Detective Sumner. I called in the drive-by." He flashed his badge. "What happened?"

The cop holstered her gun and cuffed Omar. "Officer Kettlewell. This man is trespassing, and he just broke the lady's plate glass window."

Gary looked up. "You okay, Sophie?"

Sirius emitted a low growl. "Yes, I'm fine."

Gary helped Officer Kettlewell get Omar to his feet. She reeled off his Miranda Rights as they escorted him to the black and white's backseat. Then Kettlewell sat in the front with the door open, tapping on the cruiser's computer. The two had a brief conversation before Gary returned, shaking his head.

"I want to press charges for destruction of private property and trespassing." I tapped the split glass.

"May I come in?"

"Just a minute. Let me put Sirius away. He's in a bit of a mood." I led Sirius to the office. "Go to your bed."

His brown doggie eyes stared at me. "Go on." I stepped over to his bed and patted it. "Come to bed."

He trotted over and stood on his bed but didn't lie down. A reedy, pathetic whine stopped me short. I knelt and hugged him, scratching behind his ears.

"Who's a good boy? Hm? You want to stay with Mommy, don't you?"

His wet tongue slurped my face and Sirius gave a halfhearted tail wag.

"Okay. You can come with me, but you have to be nice to Detective Sumner. He's a friend." I waggled a finger at him.

Sirius didn't growl but stuck close to me, whuffling quietly as I led Gary into the kitchen. He eyed the bat I laid across the table.

"Can I get you something to drink?"

"No." Gary stood in the middle of the kitchen, hands on hips, his brow furrowed. "I thought we talked about not answering the door."

"We did. He pissed me off." I busied myself, opening the refrigerator, pretending to look for something.

"He's dangerous, Sophie."

The door closed with a thump and I sighed. "I know. I know. I'm sorry." I scuffled to the pantry and pulled out a Milk-Bone for Sirius. His tail gave a full-on waggle in appreciation. The treat flipped through the air, and he caught it with a snap of his jaw. "He was yelling about owning Holly. Like she was his slave. I guess I just lost it."

Sirius plopped down on the floor to crunch his treat, and I brushed a stray hair out of my eyes.

Gary's grim whiskey brown eyes regarded me. "You can't play with a man like that. He's not kidding. The officer said he threatened you. Is that true?"

I sighed. "Yes."

"You can get a temporary restraining order, too."

"I'll think about it. If I press charges, how long do you think he'll spend in the pokey?"

"I can probably have him held overnight, but if he can post bail, he'll be out tomorrow."

"I figured. He'll be able to post bail." I scrubbed my eyes. "I'll need to talk to my sister. She hasn't told Mom yet, but I want her to do it today. Omar knows the restraining order was issued in California, so I'm pretty sure he'll stay here. However, I want my mom to be warned in case he decides to check for Holly in Arizona." The calendar on the refrigerator caught my eye. "Ah jeez. Mom's supposed to fly in on Wednesday for Thanksgiving." My fingers threaded through my messy mane.

The cell sang, *Let's Get this Party Started.* Poppy. I sent her to voice mail.

She'd spent the morning at Ian's, where she and my sister grilled me about my relationship with him. I confessed our intimate relationship, but none of their coaxing persuaded me to dish about all the bedroom antics. "Let's just say the sex is fiery hot," I'd hedged. However, I did tell them how Ian had romantically carried me up the stairs after Poppy's party, a move that won him approval from both the ladies. As much as I'd groused about them ganging up on me, Poppy's presence brought levity to our little group. Something Holly and I greatly needed.

"Do I have to come down to the station to press charges, or what?"

"No, I can take the report here. I'll need to take pictures of the glass and get a statement from Officer Kettlewell."

"Okay. Do you mind if I sit. I'm suddenly feeling a little shaky." I held out a wobbly hand.

"It's the adrenaline wearing off. By the way, what were you planning to do with the bat?"

"I thought I'd start with his man parts, and, while he writhed on the ground, I'd move to his thick skull." I sank into the wooden kitchen chair.

"Be careful, Sophie. Self-defense is one thing. Murder is entirely different. Taking a man's life in either regard will change your own life forever." Gary's voice held a warning.

I mashed my lips together and considered his words. It was strange how bloodthirsty I felt toward this belly crawling serpent. I'd never thought of myself as a violent person, but an image of my sister's sunken eyes and bruised body brought out a protective Mama Bear reaction. I could never commit cold-blooded murder, but in the heat of rage ...

Gary wrote down my statement. Afterward, he spoke with Kettlewell and took photos while I returned Poppy's call.

"Hey, girl, I'm free tonight. How about a drink? Smoke City Market?"

"I'd love to, but I don't think I can."

"Why not? You got a date with Mr. Hottie McHotpants?"

"Not exactly." I explained Omar's attempt to break down my door.

"Dear Lord! You poor thing. Are you freaking out?"

"A little."

"Are you going to stay at Ian's tonight?"

"I'm not sure. I have Sirius to consider. I've just finished his place. It's not really pet friendly."

"You're both welcome to stay with me."

Poppy lived in a swanky two-bedroom townhome in North Hollywood. The thought of Sirius's dark hair attaching itself to her white on white furniture made me cringe.

"Thanks, doll, but your fancy house is no place for a big lug like Sirius either."

"Are you kidding? He's a good boy. Really, it's no trouble."

"I'll keep that in mind. It will probably be fine if I stay here tonight. Gary thinks Omar will be in jail until tomorrow."

Gary came back into the kitchen.

"Do you want me to come over? Strength in numbers and all that."

"No. Maybe. I don't know. Let me get back to you. 'K?"

"'K."

I hung up. "What's the four-one-one, Detective?"

"I've got everything I need. Are you staying here alone tonight?"

"That's what I'm trying to figure out. I don't want to leave Sirius alone."

He stroked the dog's head. "Do me a favor and text me when you decide."

"I'll let you know."

Gary let himself out, and I dialed Ian.

"Ian's phone."

"Brittany?"

"Hi, Sophie. Ian wanted me to man his phone in case you called."

"Is he available?"

"He's on set right now. Is it important?"

"Sort of. If they take a break, can you have him call me?"

"Sure thing. Are you okay?"

"Yes. I'm fine. Just have him call me as soon as he can. Thanks."

My next call was to Holly. She answered on the third ring, and I gave her a run-down on the situation.

"Soph, I'm so sorry."

"It's not your fault. But, listen, you and Eva need to be on lockdown. Don't go for walks around the neighborhood like you did yesterday. Stay inside Ian's property. I can't take you out. If you need something, call me and I'll bring it over."

"You should come stay the night. I don't think it's safe for you to stay there."

"I agree. I need to make arrangements for Sirius." The call waiting beeped. "That's Ian, I'll call you back."

• • •

Ian walked off set to find Brittany waving his phone in the air. "Sophie called you a few minutes ago," she whispered.

A thrill flashed through him as he strode into his trailer and pressed the call back button on the mobile. Maybe she'd finally decided to spend the night at his place. So far they'd not seen hide nor hair of Holly's husband, but Ian would still feel more comfortable if Sophie moved in until things got cleared up. Besides the safety benefit, having Sophie in his bed would allow Ian to help her release some of the tension Holly's situation had produced. He could tell Sophie was wound tight as a drum over all this shite, and, after all, it was a medical fact that sex was an excellent stress reliever. As a matter of fact, now that he thought about it, having Sophie move in permanently might not be a bad idea; between his work schedule, her work schedule, and Holly's ex-husband, they'd hardly had a moment alone. "Hello, luv. Did you finally come to your senses and decide to stay at my place?"

"Well, there's been a development." Her voice sounded shaky.

Fear gripped his gut. "What's going on?"

"Omar stopped by a few minutes ago."

The statement met dead air as Ian fought to get a handle on his temper.

"Ian?"

"What happened? Exactly." He carefully enunciated each syllable.

Sophie briefly explained the altercation.

White hot anger flashed through his whole body and made him want to explode. Instead, he punched the wall leaving a hole. "Fuckin' 'ell! I had a feeling that bloody wanker was going to show his rat-arsed face."

His explosion met silence.

"Sophie Hartland, if you don't get your cute bottom directly over to my house, I'll come and physically stuff you into the car myself." He said through gritted teeth.

"Whoa, whoa, Tarzan. Relax. I plan to come over. I just need to figure out what to do with Sirius. I don't want him staying here without me, and it's not safe to have my teenager looking after him. He and Omar took a dislike to each other. I need to see if I can find a place to board him tonight."

"I told you, pack up the dog food and bring him over. It's no problem." He continued through his teeth.

"Are you sure? He sheds and sometimes slobbers and I just finished decorating with nice things that aren't exactly pet friendly."

Ian ran a hand down his face. Unbelievable, a psycho practically breaks down her door, threatens to kill her, and she's worried about furniture. He counted to ten and forced himself to temper his tone. He knew if he yelled at her, that stubborn pride would come out, and she wouldn't do what they both knew was best for her. "Who cares about furniture? If he ruins it, we'll buy something new. Look, I'm a dog lover. When I grew up, we always had one or two mutts scuttlin' 'round the house. The only reason I don't have one now is because of my insane work schedule."

"If you're sure."

"Pack a bag and get over to the house. I should be home in an hour. I expect to see you there."

"On my way."

After Ian hung up, he scrolled through his contacts and dialed a number he should have dialed the moment Holly moved into his house. "Ziggy? It's Ian. Listen man, I've got a job for you."

Chapter 20

Holly waited for me in the waning daylight at the top of the driveway while Eva played with her Barbie in the front yard. I stepped out of the car to be enveloped in her tight embrace.

"Thank heavens you're okay. I'd never forgive myself if he hurt you."

Sirius hung his head out of the back window and barked, the gate rolled open and Ian's Mustang revved up the drive, followed by a black Lincoln Navigator. Ian pulled into the garage. The SUV parked behind my Honda, and a bald-headed man the size of a Stegosaurus stepped out. His russet complexion and dark eyes spoke of island decent, either Hawaiian or Philippine, and the bulky muscles bulging out of the baggy, navy and white checked shirt reminded me of a pro-wrestler. Holly's chin dropped to her chest as we eyed the newcomer warily. Legs wide, he crossed his arms; his gaze darted from the two of us to Eva, scrolled over the house, grounds and fence line then swung back to the garage as Ian ambled out.

"Who's the dinosaur?" Holly whispered in my ear.

You could tell we were sisters; our minds tended to run along the same veins. I gave an imperceptible shrug.

"Ladies, meet Ziggy." Ian said.

I'd always thought Ian was a fairly large guy. However, he was completely dwarfed by Ziggy's girth and height, which I guessed to be about six-five. Ziggy and Ian walked over to where we stood. Sirius barked and Ian stopped to scratch behind his ears.

"Hiya, mate."

My dog melted under his nimble fingers.

"Ziggy, this is Holly and Sophie."

"Nice to meet you." Ziggy's platter-sized hand swallowed mine in a firm but not painful handshake.

"You too," I gulped.

"Ma'am." He nodded at Holly, who had retreated and closed the gap between the men and Eva.

Ian came to my side and slung his arm over my shoulders. "Ziggy's going to be keeping an eye on you girls over the next couple of days."

My eyes zinged back and forth between Ian and Ziggy. "You hired a bodyguard?"

"Sort of. Ziggy used to be a bouncer at the Roxbury when I worked there for a bit."

"What do you do now?"

"Private investigator. I provide security protection when needed." Ziggy pulled a business card out of his back pocket and, using two fingers, passed it over.

The business card read "Kaihe Zigarelli, Investigative and Security Services." I could see why he went by Ziggy. "So, basically, you're a bodyguard."

"You could say that."

"I'm going to take Eva inside while you guys hash this out." She picked up Eva and her toys and slipped in the front door.

"Nothing personal, Ziggy, but you're not very … " I swished my hands in an effort to think of an unoffending adjective, "inconspicuous."

"That's the whole point, luv. If this wanker that's after Holly sees Ziggy here watching out for her, he'll think twice about making a nuisance of himself.

"I suppose." I bit my lip, uncertain about this turn of events.

"Ziggy's going to be here in the morning as soon as I leave. If you need to go out, Ziggy can take you."

"You mean Holly. He's here to watch Holly. Right?" I pinned Ian with my gaze.

"Um, well both of you."

My mouth turned up in a great big fake smile. "Ziggy, would you excuse us for a moment. I need to discuss something with Ian."

"No problem. I'm going to check out the perimeter." He lumbered off to the fence line and soon disappeared behind the garage.

Sirius barked and scratched at the door, desperate to get out. "Sirius, quiet."

I grabbed a wad of Ian's shirt and pulled him under the front portico. "Ian, I can't take that mammoth with me to clients' homes. He'll freak them out." I hissed. "Now, I appreciate your concern over Holly and Eva, but we have a restraining order to keep Omar away. He'll never find them here.

"As you witnessed today, Omar has no intention of honoring the restraining order, luv. I'm not worried when you're in my home because it's secure. "

My shoulders sank. Ian was right. Omar was hell-bent on finding Holly.

"Okay, Ziggy can watch them, take them to the mall and drive them wherever they need, but I can't have him following *me* around."

Ian's hand closed around mine, and I released his shirt. "Sophie, like it or not, you've become a target. Your safety is important to me. When I'm working, I can't be with you to protect you, and it's difficult to concentrate on my job if I'm worried about your safety. Ziggy can protect you and give me peace of mind. "

Ulk. Crazy abusive husbands, gated security, bodyguards…when did my life turn into an action movie farce? Ian's arguments were sound. I just hated the fact that once again I was an imposition on him. As soon as I came up with a plan to move my sister, he'd probably reprogram his security codes and change his phone number. I sighed and shifted my weight. "How much will Ziggy's services cost?"

"Erm … we've negotiated a deal."

"What kind of deal?"

Ian looked down, drew a thumb across his scruff and dusted a piece of lint off his shirt. "He gets a walk-on part in one of the episodes of *LA Heat* and I promised him *Likertikz*," he mumbled.

"What?"

His gaze fleetingly met mine then glanced away. "I promised him courtside seats to a Lakers game."

"Jeez, Ian. How can you swing that?"

He produced a shrug. "Star power."

I rolled my eyes. "How much?"

"It doesn't matter."

"It does matter. How much?"

"Not sure yet. I have Brittany working on it." He rubbed his neck.

"How much?"

"Seriously, Soph. I don't know. A couple grand I guess. Ask me in a few days. What's the big deal?"

"Ian, you've already gone out of your way to allow my sister and her kid to move into your house. Now I'm horning in your place with my dog." I flicked a hand toward Sirius. "You can't hire and pay for a bodyguard for us. If my sister needs a bodyguard, I'll pay for it." I stabbed my chest. "I can't continue taking advantage of your generosity. I feel like a heel."

He gripped my shoulders. "Isn't it my prerogative as your boyfriend to let you take advantage of me? And to be concerned about your welfare?"

My breath caught. *Did he just say what I think he said?* "Ian … "

"Don't you understand? I'll pay whatever it takes to keep you safe." He gave me a shake then enveloped me in a tight embrace.

"Christ, Soph. Don't you get how frightened and furious it made me to hear what he'd done at your place."

"Sorry," I mumbled into his chest.

"And don't think for a moment I don't know you kept a few details from me. I rang your detective friend to let him know you'd be staying here and he filled me in on some of the things you neglected to tell me."

"Oops." I looked up.

He kissed my forehead. "I heard about the bat. Who do you think you are? Al Capone?"

"A Louisville Slugger can be a girl's best friend." My arms looped around his neck, and I tickled the soft curls at the nape.

He rolled his eyes but accepted the invitation. His lips came down hard. There was no tenderness in the contact. It was fierce, full of frustration and barely suppressed anger. His tongue probed my soft folds, and I opened to allow him access to plunder. His fingers tightened, pulling me close, and gripping my shirt with his fists. Sirius' whining finally released us from the tumultuous kiss.

Ian rested his forehead against mine. "How is it, a woman as stubborn as you, can drive me so nutty?"

Sirius barked.

"I guess we've both had a hell of a day. I'm sorry, Ian. I didn't realize how much this was affecting you. I didn't realize … "

"How much I care?"

"Yes," I breathed.

"Sophie, Sophie, Sophie." His head moved back and forth, taking mine with it. "When are you going to realize? This isn't a game, and you're not some tabloid fling?"

I gulped. "I … I don't know. I thought … you were just having fun. And suddenly my life has gotten so complicated, and somehow I've put you in the middle of it."

"You didn't put me in the middle of it. I did. It's where I want to be. In the middle of your life, not the periphery. Just as I want you to be in the middle of mine. Understand?"

"Does this mean I'm Ian O'Connor's girlfriend?"

"I sure as hell hope so."

A smile split my face. "Okay."

"Okay?"

"Okay."

"So Ziggy can stay?"

I sighed. "Yes. If it gives you peace of mind, Ziggy can stay. But I'll pay for the Lakers tickets."

"We'll work that out later. In the meantime, we'd better let your dog out before he rips apart your car."

I opened the back door to allow Sirius to leap down. He scrambled off into the yard sniffing and peeing on every plant, rock and bush he could find, marking his territory. Ziggy loped around front. For such a big guy, it surprised me how quietly he moved.

"Everything looks good, man. What time do you need me here tomorrow?"

"Come on in, and we'll talk about it." Ian opened the lift gate on my CR-V and hefted Sirius' bed onto his shoulder. Ziggy grabbed my duffel, which left a few odds and ends for me to carry. I whistled. Sirius tilted his head and considered me for a moment, trying to decide if the front yard or inside the house would be more interesting. In the end, he chose to follow his person. He pushed past me, clicking across the marble tiled foyer, through the kitchen and into the great room.

"Come here, mate. Where do you want your bed, buddy. Hm?"

Closing my eyes, I grimaced as his nails scrabbled along the newly installed hardwoods in response to Ian's inquiry. I entered the room to find Ian on his knees in front of the fireplace, roughhousing with my dog. Sirius was in hog heaven, talking to

Ian with little groans and grunts. Ziggy had dropped my duffel on the kitchen counter and exited through the rear door. Holly and Eva were absent, but the hall light shone brightly.

"If you really want to have fun, take his collar off and put it on your head. It drives him nuts."

"You want to play?" Ian slipped Sirius' red collar over his head and whipped it behind his back. The K-9 dashed around to find it, but Ian's hands were too quick. He plopped the collar on his head and held up his empty hands for the dog to see. "Where is it, fella? Where's your collar? Hm? Where'd it go?"

God, he was adorable. My heart soared over Ian's playfulness with my dog. It occurred to me that I could never be with a man who didn't love dogs. Sirius stuck his nose in Ian's armpit, on the hunt to locate his clothing. I left the two of them to play and headed down the hall to Holly's room.

"Holly? Can we talk?" I tapped on the door.

"Come on in."

The two of them lay bundled up in bed, watching the antics of *Curious George*. Eva wore her nightgown and her soft curls splayed across the pillow. Holly's eye was healing. The purpley bruising had turned to brownish yellow, and the shadows beneath her lashes had receded.

"Hi, pumpkin, whatcha doin'?"

"Hi, Aunt Sophie. We watchin' the monkey."

"I see that." I caressed her curls and squatted to her level. "Listen, Aunt Sophie's doggie is going to have to stay with us for a little while, but if you're scared of him, we'll make sure to keep him out of your way. Okay?"

"I not scared." She put on a brave face then whispered, "Is the big man staying?"

I shook my head. "Not today, but he'll be here tomorrow."

"Why?"

I looked at Holly, unsure how to answer.

"He's a friend of Aunt Sophie and Mr. O'Conner, and he's going to be around to keep us company. 'K sweetie?"

"He's not mean like Daddy, is he?"

My stomach plummeted and my heart welled with pity. Children were so much more perceptive than we gave them credit for.

Holly's mouth turned down. "No, baby. He's nice."

"Like Mr. Conner?"

"Yes. Just like Mr. O'Conner. He's the best of men. Isn't he, Aunt Sophie?" My sister's eyes danced at me.

Did she witness our smooch by the front door? "The very best."

"Eva, stay here and finish watching *Curious George*." She climbed off the bed. "I'm going out with your aunt. Come and get me when it's over and I'll read to you."

"Can Mr. Conner read?"

I nodded. "Absolutely."

"Can he read Cinderella?"

"You bet." I pinched her cheek.

She grinned and refocused on the television.

Ian was snuggled on the sofa with Sirius' big head lying across his lap, flipping through channels.

"Sirius, down," I ordered.

Obeying my command, he slunk off the sofa and over to his bed by the fireplace.

"It's okay, luv. He can get up on the sofa. I don't mind."

My sensibilities blanched at the thought of Sirius shedding and slobbering all over Ian's brand new furniture. If only I could be as laid back as he. "I'm sorry, Ian. He's not allowed on the furniture in my house. It's a slippery slope if I allow him to do it here."

He shrugged.

"Please respect my wishes on this subject." I shook a finger at him. "No sneaking him up when I'm not around."

He snatched my finger and his lips touched the pad. "Promise."

"Where's Ziggy?" I curled up next to him, pulling his arm around my shoulder. He tucked me into his side.

"He's gone. I have to leave by six tomorrow. Ziggy's going to be here before I go."

"I have almost a thousand dollars left from the jewelry to pay him." Holly flopped into the recliner and flipped up the footrest.

"Don't worry about it. I'll take care of Ziggy."

"Sophie, I'm an adult now. I can take care of this."

Ian and I exchanged a look. "She's almost as bad as you are."

"We're very independent women."

"Well, at least I know what I'm getting into." He said.

"What?" Holly closed the footrest and the chair lunged forward. "Getting into what?"

"Nothing," he and I said together and laughed.

"Are you two keeping secrets from me?"

"No, Holly. Don't worry about Ziggy. We'll work everything out later. Right now, let's just take it one day at a time."

"That's all I seem to be able to do."

"Aw, sweetie, everything's going to work out. Now he knows where you are, we can access your accounts. We should probably print down your banking info and transfer some money before he closes you out."

"Do you think he'd do that?" Ian asked.

"I don't know," Holly mused.

"You bet your ass I do. He wants to control you. Money is part of that control." I frowned.

"She's right. I'd better get some money out while the getting is good."

"Mommy, the monkey show is over." Eva stood in her pink nightgown, her shabby blanket dragging behind.

"Okay, sweetie."

Eva padded over to Ian and climbed onto his lap. He adjusted to accommodate her toddler body. Her little hand patted his cheek. "You're nice."

"Well thank you, pet." He grinned and tapped her button nose.

A maternal tug pulled at my heartstrings. *He'll make a great father.* Whoa! That was dangerous thinking. I needed to halt that line of thought immediately. We may be boyfriend-girlfriend, but I couldn't allow myself to think further than that. Not right now, at least.

"Read to me, Mr. Connor?"

"Of course." He stood, and she wrapped her arms around his neck and her legs around his torso. "What shall we read?"

"*Cinderella!*"

"That's a long book. I'm not sure I can read all of that."

She giggled. "Silly."

They moseyed down the hall, discussing the merits of *Cinderella.* Holly waited until she heard the door close with a quiet click before she pounced.

"I swear to God, you need to lock that man down. If he looked at me the way he looks at you, I'd drag him to Vegas and marry him at the Little White Chapel drive-thru tomorrow."

"Oh, yeah, that's real romantic," I scoffed.

"Big Sis, you can't do much better than Ian."

"I'm well aware. Just so you know, we've only just moved into labeling ourselves 'girlfriend and boyfriend.'" I used finger quotes. "It's a long way from girlfriend status to wife. Besides, I need to take my time. Michael and I were young and impetuous and moved too quickly. I think I'll be happy testing out the relationship waters for a while yet."

"Okay." She gave a shrug. "Just remember your eggs aren't getting any younger."

"First of all, I don't even know if Ian wants kids. Second, what is it with you and Mom worrying about my eggs?" I threw a pillow at her.

Holly caught it and laughed. "Last time Mom called, she told me your eggs were getting dusty. I snorted tea through my nose. You'd think you were as old as Methuselah the way she was talking."

I stared openmouthed.

"Don't worry, I've got your back. I assured her a woman of your age could still have perfectly good babies."

"Gee, thanks." *Squawk! Pick up the phone.* "Speak of the devil. Did you call Mom yet?"

Holly shook her head.

"Hi, Mom."

"Hi, honey. I wanted to find out if you'd like to cook or go out for Thanksgiving dinner? I mean, if it's just the two of us, we don't need to do all that cooking. Maybe we should make reservations."

"Hm, well, it looks like Holly's going to be in town to join us. Actually, she's right here."

Holly's head shook from side to side, and she mouthed: *I'm not here.* However, I'd had enough. It was time my sister came clean with Mom. Personally, I thought the truth, as awful as it was, was better than having her think Holly was a drug addict.

"Here, Mom, let me hand the phone over so you two can talk. Holly has some things she needs to tell you." I grabbed one of my sisters flailing hands and slapped the cell into her palm. "You need to tell her. *Now.*"

Holly shot me a dirty look, rose from her chair and paced over to the back door. "Hi, Mom … yup I'm here in LA with Sophie … No, everything's not all right." Her voice broke. She opened the door and stepped out onto the back patio. "Mom, I need to tell you something." She faded away as she walked out of earshot.

Sirius laid, his head on his paws, staring at me with droopy eyes. "Come here, pup."

Loping over to me, he shook and his collar jingled. His wet snout pushed at my hand and I stroked his soft fur. "We've had quite a day, haven't we? You were a good boy today. You growled at the bad man, didn't you? I bet you would've taken a bite out of him if I'd given you a chance. Good dog, Sirius."

His hindquarters plopped down and a big sigh blew across my leg. That's how Ian found us when he returned from reading duty.

"Where's your sister?"

I jerked my head toward the back door. "On the phone with Mom."

"Everything okay?"

"It will be."

"I'm ready to go up, are you?" He pulled at my top and snuck a peek down the front.

"Not very subtle, are you?"

In one swift move, Ian seized my right arm and slung me over his shoulder. My derriere pointed to the ceiling, not far from his cheek.

"Ian!" I shrieked.

Sirius jumped up, tail wagging, and barked an interest in the new game.

"Quiet!" We both commanded.

The back door slid open. "What's going on?" a teary-eyed Holly asked.

"Nothing. We're playing Tarzan and Jane." Ian beat his chest with his free hand and turned around.

My head now flopped next to Sirius and his tongue licked at my hair. "Ian, put me down," I hissed and completely blew all semblance of severity by giggling. I pushed against Ian's back so I could view my sister from this ignoble position. "Can you make sure Sirius goes potty before locking up tonight?"

She gave me a thumbs-up and a watery smile. Ian hauled me up the stairs, my rear bouncing all the way. "When I said, 'it turned me on when you carried me,' I didn't mean fireman style."

"I believe you called me Tarzan over the phone earlier. I'm an actor playing out my role." He plunked me on the bed.

"I don't remember Tarzan wearing so many clothes," I tittered and plucked at his shirt.

"I don't remember Jane being so mouthy."

His hard length covered my body and soon Tarzan and Jane's clothes were disposed of in jungle style fashion.

Chapter 21

The bedroom was grey with pre-dawn light, as she peacefully slumbered in the big bed. Ian hated to wake her, but they needed to talk logistics. Besides, he figured he'd have the upper hand, and meet little resistance if she was half asleep.

"Wakie, wakie, luv." Little nibbles worked their way down her jawline. His clothes smelled of fresh laundry, and a drip of water from his wet hair dribbled down her flawless cheek.

A mewling sound escaped and she buried her head in the pillow.

"Luv, I need to talk to you before I leave." Butterfly kisses touched her closed lids, and they drifted open.

"What time is it?" She gave a sexy feline stretch.

"Quarter to six."

Her hand drifted across his denim-clad knee. "Pooh. You're already dressed."

A whisper of laughter floated through the darkened chamber. "Ziggy's going to be here by six."

"Do I need to let him in?"

"No. He'll be patrolling the perimeter. I've programmed his number into your cell phone. He doesn't come in the house unless you need him."

"That seems kind of harsh."

"It's his job, luv. I've given him a photo of your sister's husband so he knows what to look for. If you need to go out, have Ziggy drive you. His car has blackened windows in case any paparazzi happen to be about. If the damn rags figure out you're staying here, the jig is up and he'll know exactly where to look for your sister."

"You're right. I'd forgotten about the photographers."

"I've been trying to keep a low profile since our last encounter. I'm hopeful they'll leave me alone for a bit. I'm sorry, but I'm afraid our dinner at Spago tonight will have to be canceled. We can't be seen together in public until your sister leaves, or this situation gets sorted."

"I'd completely forgotten about our dinner tonight, but you're absolutely right. It's too dangerous for me to stay here. I'll need to move back into my house."

A fist clenched in his gut at the thought of her leaving. There was no way he could allow that to happen. "Forget it, luv. I won't get a wink of sleep with you alone at that house."

"But you just said I need to distance myself from you right now. It's safer for Holly if Omar can't connect you and me. As long as you're just another client, he won't look any further," she argued.

"Either you sleep here, or I sleep there. Pick one. Holly's not the only one who needs protection right now. Don't forget that, Soph. And don't think for a minute I don't see through you. I know damn well you want to get another chance to take a swing at him. I understand your anger. I wouldn't mind kicking his arse, too. From what you've told me, he's not helpless, and God forbid he brings a gun. You Americans seem to be able to buy one at the corner drug."

His arguments made her pause. Perhaps he was finally getting through to her.

"Okay. I'll think about it. Maybe I can come up with a better solution."

Over my dead body.

She reached up and pulled him down, planting her lips against his before he could make another argument. They rubbed across his unshaven, rough, morning scruff up to the soft lobe of his ear. She gently sucked the nub.

His groin quickened and he moaned. Jeez, this woman could get him hard with a wink and a crooked finger.

"Luv, I need to get going." He pushed himself up.

Her hand worked its way up the heavy jeans encasing his thigh to brush fingertips across his hardening manhood.

"Are you sure you don't have a few minutes?" She playfully tugged at the button fly and pulled his other arm out from underneath the warm covers. The blanket fell away, exposing a pearly breast, its nipple tight and hard. She smelled like lavender and sex and her soft body beckoned.

"Mmm … " He nuzzled the hollow at her neck. "You're all warm and toasty under there, aren't you?"

"Mm, hm."

He glanced over at the bedside clock. "Screw it. I'll phone in late."

• • •

A few hours later, Holly and I sat at the kitchen counter working on her Last Will and Testament. I'd found a lovely website called Getyourshittogether.com, which basically provided a fill-in-the-blank form. It was simplistic, but it got the job done.

At ten thirty I called Ziggy. "Hi, Ziggy, it's Sophie."

"Yes, ma'am. What can I do for you?"

I felt like an idiot calling a guy on the phone who was probably no more than fifty feet away. "We need to run a few errands, and Ian told me he wants you to drive us."

"Yes, ma'am."

"Can you be ready to leave in about fifteen minutes?"

"Of course."

Ziggy was a man of few words.

"Thanks."

"We're going in Ziggy's car?" my sister asked.

"Yes. The windows are blacked out, and if there's any press around, they won't be able to see inside. My car has tinted windows, but they aren't as dark as Ziggy's. Besides, I'm not sure he'd fit in my car."

Holly snorted. "You certainly have a point there."

Ziggy had the Navigator running when we stepped out. Eva's car seat was in the center of the middle row bench; Holly strapped her in. The little girl hugged her Barbie backpack to her chest and stared with wide eyes at the creased folds of the back of Ziggy's head.

"Where to, ladies?

I gave him directions to Bank of America, where Holly had her accounts. Our seat belts snapped into place and Ziggy rolled out of Ian's driveway. To everyone's relief, no photographers awaited us.

It was a little past one. Holly, Eva and I had stepped out of the lawyer's office when the call came in.

"He's out."

"Thanks, Gary. Any idea where he went?"

"Just a sec." Gary came back on the line. His voice echoed, sounding like he was in an empty room or tunnel. "I followed him to a car rental service. He got on Interstate 15 heading North. I'd say he was going back to Vegas."

"Good." I breathed a sigh of relief."

"Mommy, I'm huunngry," Eva started whining.

"I know, sweetie. We'll get something to eat soon."

"But I'm hungry now."

I wandered a few paces away while my sister placated her. "Where are you? It sounds like a tunnel."

"Men's room. Technically, I shouldn't be following Omar."

"I see. Thanks for doing it. We're leaving the lawyer's now. The papers will be filed by the end of the day."

"Remain on your guard. This mess may heat up and get ugly before it gets better. Your boyfriend told me he hired a bodyguard for the two of you."

"Yes. Ziggy's pulling up now. He's in charge of driving us around for the day."

"Good. It's for the best. Stay in touch." He rang off.

Ziggy's Navigator pulled out of traffic and swung up to the curb's loading zone. Holly helped Eva climb in while I went around to the opposite side.

"No! I don't wanna sit here. I wanna sit there." Eva pointed at my seat, pushing Holly's hands away.

"Eva, you know you have to sit in your special seat. It's the rules."

"I wanna go home!" her little toddler voice demanded at top volume while she crossed her arms defiantly.

Ziggy turned. "Anyone interested in ice cream?" His big mitt held up a Dove bar.

Eva's eyes lit up, and she clapped her hands. "I cream! I cream!"

I took the frozen treat out of his hand. "Thank you, Ziggy. I think you've just diverted a full-on meltdown."

After the first few licks, the Eva became cooperative again and allowed her mother to strap her into the seat.

"Where to?" Ziggy's eyes met mine in the rearview mirror.

I glanced down at Eva licking a sticky, chocolaty finger. The poor kid had been stuck playing with adults or on her own since she arrived. "There's an indoor playground on Colorado Boulevard. Why don't we find someplace to eat around there and take Eva to play afterward?"

Holly's head lay back against the headrest with her eyes shut. She yawned. "That's fine with me.

Chapter 22

The truck's rumbly engine silenced with a twist of the key.

"Stay here. I'll only be a few minutes." I hopped out of the cab. Sirius barked and followed me down. "See," I shot him a cheesy smile, "I'll take my trusty guard dog to keep me safe."

Ian rolled his eyes but remained in the cab, tapping away on his cell. We'd shared a NATO level debate about whether or not I should return to pick up a few things from my house. I'd argued back and forth, insisting I needed my glasses and iPad. Ian asserted Ziggy could pick those items up for me, until I came clean about the real reason I was so hot to get back home by confessing I'd forgotten my birth control pills. Ian's arguments stopped like a faucet being shut off.

"I'll drive."

We spent the past fifteen minutes cruising around my neighborhood on the lookout for Omar and any suspicious characters or vehicles in the area. As I pointed out to Ian, nothing says "inconspicuous" like cruising around in a huge black pickup truck. After he was satisfied the coast was clear, he pulled into my driveway.

The security company hadn't reported any alarms, and the comforting sound of beep, beep met my ears as I keyed into the house. Sirius trotted through the foyer to his water dish by the back door. There was a package on my porch and the mailbox overflowed. I left the box in the front hall, and, after a cursory shuffle through the mail, dropped it on the foyer table to deal with later. My glasses lay willy-nilly on my office desk, and I put them on top of my head. I shifted through folders and papers on the desk, but the iPad was not to be found. I must have left it in the kitchen.

Sirius' growl sent a prickle of unease to the nape of my neck, and my heart dropped. The snarl was a warning something wasn't right. Through the office doorway, the kitchen table and a portion of the island were in view, but Sirius wasn't in my line of sight. On top of the table rested the Slugger. Women's intuition had my red Keds slapping down the hall. I snatched up the bat and hefted it over my shoulder, ready to swing. It took only a second for my eyes to dart around and locate Omar. His silhouette stood in the dim hallway that led to the bedrooms. Sirius stood by the refrigerator, hackles raised. He continued to emit a low rumble.

Omar stepped in the light of the kitchen, and I realized, I'd made a dreadful miscalculation. I'd brought a bat to a gun fight. The deadly silver tip pointed directly at my chest. The Slugger dropped to my side and hung limp.

"Where is she?" The long barrel revolver looked like something you'd find in an old western.

I did something stupid, guaranteed to piss Omar off, but I couldn't seem to help myself. Fear must have disconnected my brain from my mouth. "Who are you supposed to be? Dirty Harry?" Hysterical giggles burst forth.

Sirius barked. Quick as lightening, the gun shifted to him.

"*No,*" I screeched. My heart ratcheted up another notch, but I didn't shift any closer to Omar. The game had become deadly.

"Call him off, or I shoot."

"Sirius, *sit!*" I yelped. Unfortunately, fear threaded through my voice.

Sirius whined and took a small step forward. Omar cocked the gun.

"Sirius, *stay! Sit!*" I commanded again with force, trying to eliminate the panic.

His eyes turned to me, and he tilted his head, as if to say, "Are you sure?"

"Sit, boy," I wheedled.

His hindquarters lowered to the ground but stopped short and barely hovered above the tile.

Omar must have been satisfied because the gun returned to me. He stepped past Sirius closing the gap between us; the lethal weapon remained steady, never wavering. As the head of security for a Vegas casino, I had no illusions about his ability to accurately use the revolver he wielded. He stopped no more than six feet away; if he fired, he'd probably blow me across the room. Icy blood pumped through my veins, and my brain was having difficulty processing the next step.

"Where … is … she?" his baritone voice asked slowly and deliberately.

My mouth bobbed like a Simian monkey. I couldn't take my eyes off the firearm.

"Where is she?"

I jumped back a step and looked up at his distorted, flushed face. "Sh … she's not here."

"I know that!" he gritted out through clenched teeth.

"I … I … told you. Sh … she's at a sssafe house."

"Bitch, you will tell me where she is or … "

He never got to finish that thought. While we spoke, Sirius slunk around the corner. It only took an instant and his teeth latched onto the back of Omar's calf. He bellowed and tried shake the dog loose. I saw my opening and took it. The Slugger swung straight up, smacking the hand holding the revolver. A shot rang out, and I registered pain in my rear. It felt like a bee sting. I couldn't believe in the midst of all this, a stupid bee stung me. The weapon arced through the air and clattered somewhere on the other side of the island.

Omar backhanded Sirius. The dog's bite disconnected and he slid across the tile with a whine.

"Why you … " Fury flashed and I hefted the bat.

A strong arm shoved me aside. My upper torso pancaked onto the counter, the bat flew across the room and my glasses slipped off my head to be crushed under foot. "Oof."

Ian led with a powerful right hook that Omar just barely blocked with his arm. Omar threw a punch which Ian ducked, but he landed a jab to the kidney. The fight was on. Ian distributed his weight evenly, striking swiftly and shifting like a karate master. Omar kept his elbows in and hands closer to his face, bouncing on his toes, similar to a boxer's stance. Though their styles differed, their skills seemed evenly matched. Omar shifted back a step, still swinging, and caught a lucky shot, grazing Ian's chin.

The sounds of flesh smacking flesh and masculine grunts filled the room as the two pummeled away at each other in the tight space. My gaze searched for Omar's hand cannon. I caught sight of the corner of the brown handgrip in the prep sink on the island. I launched up and belly surfed across the granite. The gun handle was warm and heavier than I'd expected. I took a moment to send up a prayer to my father for teaching me how to use his .22 revolver.

My gaze returned to the fight. Ian landed a swift right and then a palm-fisted upper cut to Omar's chin. His head snapped back and Ian produced a fancy Kung Fu move to his knee. A pop rent the air. Omar collapsed at Ian's feet with a bloodcurdling scream. He rolled to his right side, clutching the wounded leg.

Rising atop the counter, I planted my feet, shoulder width apart, my rubber soles gripping the stone. I steadied the gun with both hands, cocked it, and pointed down at the injured man. The trigger curved into the pad of my right pointer finger.

"Stand back. I've got him covered," I hollered.

Rubbing a spot of blood from his lip, Ian looked at me.

"There's duct tape in the drawer next to the dishwasher. Use it to tie him up."

The drawer opened and closed with a snap, but I kept my eyes on the writhing man. Ian leaned over, and, lickety-split, hog-tied Omar's hands and feet, which produced more howling and cursing.

"Cripes," I grimaced. "Tape his mouth, too."

The howling quieted to a dull moan. Ian tossed the tape over his shoulder and came to where I stood. I gripped the weapon so tightly my fist began to cramp and shake.

"Hand me the gun, luv." He held out a hand, but I couldn't get my fingers to release the weapon. "It's okay now."

His warm fingers closed around mine and gradually the muscles relaxed. He uncocked the firearm, flipped the safety, and laid it aside.

"C'mon, Annie Oakley, let's get you down." A strong grip encircled my waist, and I clutched his broad shoulders to steady myself. Once my feet hit the ground, he enclosed me in a gut-crushing hug.

"Oof." I tapped his shoulder and wheezed, "Too tight."

He loosened his grip and held my biceps. His mouth worked, and I could see he held back strong emotions in an effort not to lambast me.

"Uh. You might have been right. Coming back to the house was a bad idea."

"Lady, you're going to be the death of me." He gave me a shake.

Sirius whined and we both turned. Ian released me and I stepped around Omar to crouch down where the pup lay, licking his paw, emitting pathetic little whimpers.

"Hey, good boy. What's wrong?" I rubbed his head.

His tail flopped once. Gently I picked up his paw. One nail was missing and another lay at a funny angle. Blood oozed from the wounds.

"Poor baby. You broke a toe."

"Sophie, I think you're bleeding."

I glanced over my shoulder. Ian wiped two fingers across the counter and held them up. Deep red streaks stained the digits.

"No, I'm not. It must be you." I shook my head.

His brows furrowed and his eyes followed a trail of blood drops over to where I crouched.

"Stand up, luv."

I rose.

"Your backside is bleeding. I think you've been shot."

I remembered the bee. "No, a bee stung me."

My fingers rubbed the painful sting and came away with more blood. My eyes widened.

Ian pointed to a metal piece of art that hung lopsided on the wall. A new coppery ding marred the surface. "Ricochet."

"Son of a bitch." The sound of the ocean filled my ears, my vision tunneled, and then I did something completely useless. I passed out. Ian told me later that he caught me before I fell atop Omar.

Chapter 23

"I think she's coming around. Sophie? Can you hear me?" *Thank God*. Her baby blues fluttered open, providing Ian a modicum of relief.

She lay on her stomach, a cheek mashed against the couch cushion where he had carried her after she passed out—a move that frightened him half to death. He'd searched her body for further injuries and couldn't find anything. He hoped the reason she fainted was from the shock of Omar's intrusion and getting shot, but he took a moment to dial Gary to request an ambulance and notify him of the situation. After that everything seemed to move like a speeding train. He found a kitchen towel to press against the oozing wound, and it took only a few minutes for Gary to arrive. Then more cops showed up. But to Ian's frustration, they still waited on the bloody ambulance.

Footsteps, voices, and moans of pain came from the kitchen area. Ian ignored them as he sat on the coffee table, his scraped and bruised fingers covering her hand. Gary crouched to the side, staring at her with a frown and furrowed brow.

"Can you show me some of your Kung Fu moves?" she croaked.

Ian blew out a breath, relieved that her humor remained intact. "It's Tae-Kwando, and yes, I'll show you sometime. How are you feeling?"

"Hmm … kinda lightheaded." She pressed a hand to her temple.

"You passed out."

"An ambulance should be here any minute," Gary chimed in.

"Someone call for an ambulance?"

"Speak of the devil," Ian murmured.

"In here." Gary straightened his legs.

A twenty-something, uniformed EMT, with a large white and orange box, crouched next to her head. "What's the problem?"

"I got shot in the ass, and it hurts like a bitch."

That's my Sophie. Ian bit the inside of his lip to keep from laughing.

"I'll bet it does." The tech grinned and winked at her as he pulled on a pair of rubber gloves.

Ian moved out of the way to allow the medic access. He took his hand away from the towel and the medic lifted it up to view the wound.

"How'd you manage this?"

"Ricochet." She gritted her teeth as the EMT probed the wound. Her muscles tensed, and it took all of Ian's self-control to keep from grabbing the EMT by the collar and tossing him out the door. He knew the guy was only doing his job, but it flippin' killed him to see her in pain.

"We have something to help with the pain. Do you have allergies to any drugs?"

"No. Give me the juice, Doc."

"Just a moment. I need to check your vitals first." He placed a pressure cuff on her arm and hooked a stethoscope into his ears.

"Just give me the meds," she groaned and clenched her jaw.

"Your vitals look okay. Hope these aren't your favorite jeans."

He took an L-shaped pair of scissors with rounded tips out of his medical box and proceeded to cut her jeans, revealing a pair of lavender panties underneath that were coated in blood. Sophie's facial cheeks went up in flames of mortification. The rip of the whisper soft nylon made her tuck her head under her arm as the EMT finished cutting. Gary had tactfully stepped away. Ian moved to the other side in an effort to block the view and provide a modicum of privacy from any one of the many cops wandering the scene.

"You'll feel a little pinch ... " the EMT said.

"Yipe!"

Ian's eyes flashed over to her.

"Now we're going to put a bandage on to keep the blood flow down." The medic pulled out some gauze and tape from his kit and went to work. He was putting pressure on the wound, but Sophie had relaxed somewhat as the pain meds kicked in.

"Okay, time to get you to the hospital. The bullet fragment is still in there. *Chuck?*"

A second EMT in the kitchen answered, "We've got a torn-up knee in here, lacerations, and bruises. Gonna need X-rays."

Gary stepped back into the room and assessed the situation. "Take her in the ambulance. I've called for a second truck to take the other prisoner. Sophie, I've contacted your sister and she'll meet you at the hospital."

Sophie's lids closed and she seemed to fade out as the EMTs brought the stretcher next to the couch and loaded her on to it.

"Wait." Her eyes popped open as she grabbed the EMT's arm. "Ian!"

"Right here, luv." He stepped into her line of sight.

She started to shiver, big quaking shakes that shuddered through her whole body.

His shoulders tensed and the knot of pressure in his stomach tightened up again. "What's wrong with her? Why is she shaking?"

"It's just the medication. Nothing to worry about," the EMT explained.

"Take Sirius to the vet for me, please." She paused as the next shiver eased off. "His regular one is closed on Saturdays, so just take him to any local animal hospital, okay? I'll pay for everything."

A police officer placed a blanket over her.

The woman was unbelievable. Here she was with a bullet in her ass and she was worrying about the dog. "I'll find someone to take Sirius. I'll come with you."

"*No*," she said sharply. Everyone looked over at her. She softened her voice when she spoke. "Please, Ian. I need someone I trust to take care of him. My sister will be at the hospital, they'll take care of me just fine. Please, he's hurt. Please, take care of Sirius." Tears glistened in her eyes as she begged.

He could see this meant a lot to Sophie, and even though he wanted to be with her, he realized she needed him to do this instead. "All right, luv. Don't worry about anything." He patted her hand in assurance. "You get better. I'll come to the hospital after I see to Sirius." He kissed her nose. "*A ghra mo chroi.*"

"Thank you. Someday you need to tell me what that means." She tapped the EMTs hand. "We can go now. Wait! I need my purse."

Ian scooped it up from the foyer table and plopped it between her legs, and then she closed her eyes as the EMT rolled her out.

He walked back into the kitchen where a young police officer, with a K-9 patch on his shoulder, sat on the floor comforting Sirius. Ian could see why Sophie was so attached to the big lug. He owed that dog a dinosaur-sized bone. Sirius had effectively saved Sophie's life.

"Officer, if you can help me get him wrapped up with some towels and get him in my truck, I'll take him to get fixed up."

• • •

"What's going on here?"

My eyes snapped open as the stretcher bounced along the grass.

"I had to park the car halfway down the block. Oh my goodness. Sophie? Is that you?"

"Ma'am, please step back."

"Get out of my way. That's my daughter! Sophie!"

"Mom? Let her through." I raised my voice above the din.

My mother's beloved face came into view, her grey-green eyes clouded with concern. "I'm here, baby. What happened?" Thick fingers tightly clenched my hand as she trotted next to the stretcher.

"I got shot in the butt, Mom." I shuddered. "What are you doing here?"

"Does it hurt?" she called as the EMTs loaded me into the ambulance.

I rolled my eyes. "Yes."

She hopped in after the EMT and sat next to him.

He gave her a strange look.

"Young man, I'm her mother. I'm coming with you to the hospital." She shook her finger at him to emphasize her point.

The EMT, whose name tag read Steve, winked at me. "No problem, ma'am."

"What are you doing here, Mom?"

"After I spoke with your sister on Thursday night, I keep thinking about the problem and decided I shouldn't wait to come until next week. So, I got online last night and booked a flight. Why is she shaking?"

"Reaction to the medicine or the trauma. Coming down from the rush." Steve placed a pair of fingers on my wrist.

"I'm fine, Mom. Did you take a cab?"

"No, I rented a car. Hertz had a good deal for triple A members. I wasn't sure if Holly had something to drive, so I decided it'd be best if I rented a car so we'd have two vehicles between the three of us. I got this cute little Chevy something. And the flight, oh you wouldn't believe. It was packed. I ended up sitting next to a woman with two children … " She rambled on.

"Mom!"

"Yes?"

"Tell me about it later. Okay? Just … be here … for now."

"Of course." She closed her mouth and made a zipper motion across it.

I closed my eyes, feeling every bump and shift of the ambulance. The pressure of Steve's fingers comforted me and the shivers eased off. I fell into a half dream-world state. My mother and Steve spoke in hushed tones, but I couldn't make out exactly what they were saying, and soon enough we reached the hospital and they were unloading me.

"Sophie!" My sister's voice echoed down the hallway.

"Holly?" Mother responded.

"Mom?"

"Where's Eva?"

"With Ziggy, getting ice cream. What are you doing here?"

Above the cacophony of my mother's and sibling's discussion, Steve, the EMT, rattled off my vitals to two females wearing green scrubs. Both walked at a fast clip next to the gurney as we rolled down the hall.

"Who's Ziggy?"

"My bodyguard."

"You hired a bodyguard?"

"Ian did."

"Which one's Ian."

"Yo! Girls!" I interrupted.

Everyone went silent and the gurney came to a halt. "Mom, why don't you and Holly do your best to fill out the forms? Take my handbag, you'll find my insurance cards in the wallet."

"Are you going to be alright without me?"

"Yes. The doctors will take good care of me." I reached out to pat my mother's arm, and shot Holly a "help me" look. "You'd be a big help by filling out the paperwork for me."

"If you're sure."

"Absolutely."

"You take good care of my baby," she said to the medical staff.

"We'll do our best," answered one of the green scrubs.

"Come on, Mom. Soph's in good hands." Holly hefted my purse onto her shoulder and threaded her arm through Mom's.

The gurney continued its course into an empty medical room.

"My name is Stephanie. I'm a physician assistant and I'll be removing the bullet fragment. This is Claire. She's an RN, and she'll be assisting me. We'll get an X-ray, and I'll be back in a few minutes to perform the procedure."

Procedure. I loved how they considered digging a bullet fragment out of my derriere a procedure. An hour later, I was bullet free, wearing a lovely blue hospital sack, when they wheeled me into a recovery room. They'd also given me a shot for the pain. I lay on my side, hugging a pillow, flipping channels, when my mom breezed in.

"Hello, hello. How are you feeling?"

"Pretty good," I slurred.

She brushed my hair back. "You gave us all a good scare today. Don't worry. I'm here to stay until you get back on your feet."

"Me too, big Sis." Holly stood in the doorway with Eva peeking around her legs. She looked hesitant to enter.

"Come on in." I gave a lopsided grin.

She shuffled in.

"Hi, Eva."

"You sick, Aunt Sophie?" The little girl scrunched her nose and gave me a serious stare.

"Nope." My head rocked back and forth "Not sick. I got hurt. The doctors fix-sed me up good."

"'K."

"You wanna watch toons?" I found the Disney channel.

Eva plopped herself in one of the two guest chairs and zoned out.

"Anything I can do to help?" Ziggy's enormous body obstructed the entire doorway.

"Zigs! Wha's up man? Thanks for bringing my sistah!" I gave a thumbs-up.

"No problem." He lumbered into the room and stood at the foot of the bed.

I needed to ask somebody something important, but my mind couldn't focus. My thoughts seemed all floaty and jumbled up.

"*Sophie.*"

My googly eyes zoomed in on Mom. "Huh?"

"Do you know if they're going to release you?"

"Dunno. Don't care," I sang.

"They must have given her something for the pain." My mother and sister stood on either side of me at the head of the bed, talking over me.

"Soph?" My sister leaned in to me.

"Whoa!" I put a hand on her cheek and pushed it away. "You've got sooome fun-ky coffee breath, girl."

"Did they give you some pain pills?"

I gave a slow grin. "Shot. Ss … good stuff." I lowered my voice, "better 'n pot." Hissing giggles escaped through my teeth.

Holly smiled and slapped a hand over her mouth. Mom seemed to be fighting a grin. Ziggy shook his head and a big toothy smile split his face.

"Zigs knows what I'm talkin' 'bout. Doncha, my man?" I held up my left hand for a high five. "Don't leave me hangin', dude."

He gave me a light smack.

"Mom!"

"What dear?" She tucked a hank of blondish grey hair behind her ear.

"You meet the Zigman?"

"Yes, dear. We met in the waiting room."

"Zig's the man. Right? No one's gonna mess with this dude."

"That's right, dear."

"Holly!" I whipped my head back to face her.

"I'm here."

"You okay?"

"Fine."

"What 'bout that dude Ian karate-chopped?" I scrunched my eyes. I couldn't think of his name.

"He's fine, too." Her eyes shot over to Eva.

"'K."

"Is there room for one more?" Ian stepped into the small space.

"Hi, Mr. Connor." Eva waved at him from her chair. "I watchin' Micksey Mouse."

"That's great, Eva."

My sister began to ease away, but I grabbed her shirt sleeve. "Hey, that's my boyfriend."

"I know, Soph." She disengaged my fingers.

"Mom," I wiggled my eyebrows. "Whaddyathink?"

"Hello, I'm Dorothy Hartland." She walked over and held out her sturdy suntanned hand.

"Ian O'Connor." He shook her hand. "It's lovely to meet you. I can see the family resemblance."

My mother gave a girlish giggle and preened. "I believe I have you to thank for saving both my girls' lives."

"My pleasure."

He exchanged places with Mom, and took hold of my fingers in his warm hand. A greenish black bruise marred the left side of his beautiful jawline. "How are you feeling?"

I gave him an enormous smile. "Better that you're here now."

"They gave her a shot," Holly explained.

"I see."

"A really good one." I tried to wink, but both eyes closed.

Half of his mouth curved up on the uninjured side. "The vet is keeping Sirius overnight. They've wrapped up his foot. They had to remove two broken nails and he has a hairline fracture in one of the bones on his foot, but it'll heal. They're concerned he's got a badly bruised shoulder, and they want to keep an eye on him."

I sucked in a breath. Sirius. That's what my mind couldn't remember. Thank heavens for Ian. "You're the be-est. Don't know what I'd do without you." I kissed his battered hand. "We should put some ice on this." My forefinger gently grazed the bruised knuckles.

Sea blue peepers gazed at me and a small crease formed above the bridge of his nose.

His eyes remind me of something…what was it? Oh! "When Irish eyes are smi-ling," I burst into song. "Sure, it's like the morn in spring. Something, something, something. You can hear the angels sssing … I forget the rest."

Ian smashed his lips together, and his shoulders shook.

"Are you laughing at me?"

"Never." A grin broke loose. "I need to talk to Ziggy for a minute. We'll step outside."

"Okey dokey, smo-okey."

A brunette nurse wearing purple scrubs walked in, her rubber shoes squeaking along the industrial grey tiles. "Good afternoon. I'm Missy." She erased the wipe board on the wall opposite the bed and wrote Missy across the top then flipped through the clipboard tucked into the holder next to the board. "So, how are we doing? On a level from one to ten, how's your pain?"

"S' not bad. Maybe a three or four." I grinned.

"Mm. I need to take your temperature and check your vitals."

Mom and Holly drifted away from the bed to allow Missy access. Ian walked in while the pressure cuff was strangling my arm like a boa constrictor. Even in my drug-hazed mind, his masculinity took my breath away. Missy glanced over her shoulder then did a double take. She dropped the stethoscope.

"Did anyone ever tell you, you look a lot like that Ryder guy on *LA Heat*?"

"Yes. I get that all the time," He deadpanned.

Missy returned to cutting off the circulation in my arm.

"So, when do you think she'll be getting out of here?" Ian asked.

The nurse shrugged. "Not sure. The doctor should be back in an hour or so to tell you more." The Velcro ripped open, releasing my arm, and Missy slung the stethoscope around her neck. "Everything looks good. I'll check back with you in a bit. Buzz the nurse's station if you need anything else."

Ian closed the door behind her then returned to the head of the bed.

"Luv, I have some bad news," he said quietly.

Mom and Holly approached the other side of the bed.

"What's going on?" Holly asked. "Is it Omar?"

"No. The press saw me leave your place with Sirius, and they followed me to the vet and here to the hospital. This place is crawling with bloody reporters, looking for a story." He whispered in accents too low for Eva to hear over the television.

"Maybe I should go talk to them," was my mother's brilliant suggestion.

Holly grabbed her arm. "No, Mom. I don't think that's a good idea."

I shook my head in an effort to clear the fuzz out of my brain. I could comprehend the concern, but, for the life of me, I couldn't figure out a way to handle it. "Oh my god. You didn't tell them I was shot in the ass?" I hissed.

His brow furrowed. "Of course not. I didn't tell them anything. Look, I've spoken to Ziggy and when you're released, we're going to sneak you out the back door, while I go to the front and distract them."

"Shouldn't you release a statement or something? What's to stop them from pestering her at the house?" Holly asked.

Ian ran a hand through his dark waves. "Ziggy's going to take all of you back to my place."

"And where do you live, Ian?" Mom asked.

The thought of Dorothy Hartland along with Holly, Eva and me all staying at Ian's made me cringe. Even though he had his game face on, I had no doubt it made him cringe, too.

"Mom, can you get me a soda? My tummy feels a bit icky."

"Yes, of course, dear." She patted my hand. "What kind would you like?"

"Ginger ale if they have it."

"I saw a Coke machine by the waiting room," Holly offered.

"I'll be right back." Mom scooped up her brown handbag and hustled to the door. "Eva, sweetie, do you want to come with Nana and get a drink too?"

Eva nodded, skipped over and tucked her hand trustingly into Mom's.

Once they left, I rubbed my eyes and pushed against my temples. My head cleared slightly and I spoke with slow deliberation. "We can't invade your house, Ian. Now that Omar is incapacitated, we're safe. As much as I appreciate your generosity, we can't continue to impose on you any longer. My mother and sister will move back into my house."

His lips thinned and turned down. "What about the press?"

"How bad can it be? Really? It's not me they're interested in. Get your manager to make a statement on your behalf and they'll go away. Like last time."

Ian closed his eyes and pinched the bridge of his nose. "I don't think you understand, Sophie. It isn't just the tabloids this time. I was involved in a shooting at your home. The major news channels are in on it."

My mouth rounded into an O, but nothing came out.

"Hell," my sister muttered. "Damn Omar. I am *so* sorry about this, you two. I can't believe I brought this down on your house,

Sophie. And now you've been shot and your dog's hurt. I never should have come here." She scrubbed her eyes, and her voice notched up a few registers.

"Don't worry. It's not your fault." Ian and I both comforted her.

"Right now, what's most important is you and Eva are safe."

"I have an idea." Her head popped up and I visualized a light bulb flickering on above it. "Why don't you and Mom come back to Vegas with us? Like you said, now Omar is incapacitated, it'll be safe for me to return home."

Ian shook his head. "I don't think Sophie's going to be able to travel far with her injury."

I wrinkled my nose. "Ian's right. I won't be able to sit for the ride. I'm sure it'll be fine for all of us to go back to my place. We'll have Thanksgiving here in LA and talk about your next course of action. Besides, the press is like a five year old with ADHD. They'll tire of my story and be onto the next. Dontcha you think?" My gaze returned to Ian.

He shrugged. "Maybe."

The door opened and I expected to see Mom and Eva returning. Instead, a flashbulb blinded me. I struggled to pull the blanket over my head.

"Fuckin' 'ell!"

"Sophia Hartland, tell us about your relationship with Ian O'Connor. Who shot you? Is there a love triangle between your sister and Ian O'Connor? Mr. O'Connor, who are … "

The obnoxious reporter didn't get to finish his question. Ian bodily shoved him out and slammed the door in his face. He jammed the toe of his black Timberland into the corner to keep it shut and pulled his phone from his pocket.

While Ian dealt with the reporter, Holly rang the nurse's station and was speaking into the intercom. "Get security down here now, damn it! A reporter just forced his way into my sister's room."

"Ziggy, get back up here. Now! I'm going to need you to stand guard outside Sophie's room. A bloody reporter just pushed his way in," His voice rumbled. "Yes, I'm fuckin' pissed."

Ian looked over at me. "You two okay?"

"We're fine," Holly replied.

Our eyes locked. Ian's stormy, mine wide and upset. "I swear, if there are any pictures of me in this stupid getup, I'm going to hunt that prick down and strangle him." I shifted, trying to find a different position.

Ian let out a breath of laughter. "You and me both, luv. You and me both." He rubbed his hand along his jawline. "I think you're correct. We're going to have to make some sort of statement to the press."

Muffled by the door, we heard feet slapping along the tile, more running, and a voice called out, "Hey you! Stop!"

"Better call your manager," I said.

All was silent outside the door, which is why we were suddenly startled by a knock. "Hello? Did somebody lock the door?" My mother tapped a little beat.

Ian swung the door open to allow Mom and Eva in. "Here you go, dear. They had some ginger ale." Mom handed the ice cold can to me and helped Eva climb back into her chair, clasping a Minute Maid lemonade to her chest.

"What's wrong?" Mom glanced at me then looked significantly at Ian, who casually but firmly leaned against the door, keeping it closed.

"A reporter just snuck in here, Mom," Holly answered for us.

"My goodness, Sophie. You do lead an exciting life out here in LA, don't you?"

"It would seem so," I muttered.

There was a rap, then a pause, two more raps, a pause, then three more staccato raps at the door. Ian opened to Ziggy.

"I've spoken to security. They'll place more guards on the floor. You're not going to like hearing this, but there must be more than a dozen reporters down there."

Mom and Holly left my side to huddle in the doorway with Ian and Ziggy. They all lowered their voices and spoke in hushed whispers. I only caught a few words of their conversation.

"What's a porter, Aunt Sophie?" While I'd watched the football huddle at the door, Eva had silently wandered over to the bed.

"A reporter is a person who works for the news."

"Huh."

"Would you like to sit on the bed with me?"

She nodded, placing her can of lemonade on the floor. She held her arms up and I lifted her petite body next to mine.

"Are you going to be okay, Aunt Sophie."

"Yes, of course. In a few weeks, I'll be right as rain."

"Can we come live with you and Mr. Connor, forever?" Her wide eyes pleaded with me.

"Don't you want to go back home?"

She shook her head and frowned. "Daddy's mean. He yells at mommy. Can't we stay with you?"

My eyes teared up, and I pulled her to my chest. "Yes, of course, you can stay with me at my house. As long as you need."

"Do you think Mr. Conner would give us the Minnie Mouse kitchen?"

I gave a wet smile. "I think he might."

She snuggled into the curve of my body. My eyes drifted shut and the fatigue I'd been fighting since receiving the shot finally overtook me.

• • •

I woke to silence and a dull throbbing ache. I groaned and shifted, rolling onto my side.

"How are you feeling, dear?" Mom sat on one of the guest chairs, a *People* magazine in her lap, her half-moon glasses pushed up on her forehead, pulling back her short bob.

"Mom? Where is everyone?" The pink shadows of evening dusk drifted through the slatted blinds. I must have been asleep for a few hours.

"Some girl named Brittany took your sister and Eva out for a bite to eat. Ziggy's in the hall guarding your door, and I'm here." She ticked off her fingers.

"And Ian?"

"I'm not sure. He hasn't returned from the press conference yet."

"The what?" I sat forward and immediately regretted my actions. White lights flashed around the edges of my vision. "Ouch! Son of a monkey's uncle!"

The magazine dropped to the floor as my mother hurried to my side. "Relax, dear." Her cool hand pressed against my shoulder. "Everything's been sorted out. That shot they gave you must have worn off."

"What exactly have you sorted out?" I asked through gritted teeth as I cautiously rolled back onto my uninjured side.

"Ian spoke with his manager, and it was decided the best course of action was to come clean. So, they worked with the police to make a statement. Then Ian made a statement, but he didn't answer questions."

"When did this happen?"

"About an hour ago."

"What did he say?"

Mom's gaze didn't meet my gaze. "Just reiterated what the police said. Oh!" Her faded blue eyes snapped back to me. "He did request the press stop hounding you and respect your privacy during your recovery. The police backed him up on that."

She was holding something back. "Anything else?"

"Yes. A freckled detective named … "

"Sumner?" I supplied.

"Yes, that's it. Detective Sumner came by to check on you before the press conference. Really, Sophie. I can't tell you what an exciting day it's been."

"Mm. I'm sure. Can you hand me my purse, Mom?"

"What do you need?"

"My phone. I'd better call my crew and Poppy. Let them know I'm okay. They're probably going crazy since it's been in the press."

She dug around the oversized bag and handed me my iPhone.

"If you don't mind, I'm going to step out for a moment and stretch while you make your calls."

"That's fine. Why don't you go get yourself something to eat?" I waved her out the door. "Jeez. What the hell?" There were twenty calls and over forty new texts. I scrolled through the texts. Most of them were from strangers, reporters, if I had to guess. I cleared them all and called Poppy first.

"Girl, what is going on with you? The press is going crazy. The police said an intruder shot you and Ian incapacitated him. Ian said you're okay and under his protection. What does that mean, 'under his protection'? It sounded like you were engaged or something. Was it Omar?"

"It was Omar. Ian karate chopped him, and I got shot in the butt."

"What? Did you just say you got shot in the butt. As in the ass?"

"As in the ass."

She went off into a peal of laughter. After a moment, I joined her mirth, wincing as the giggles jiggled my injured tush.

"Oh my God. This is not funny." She giggled again. "Are you going to be okay?"

"Yes. I'll heal. Right now it hurts like hell. Listen, can you do me a favor and contact my crew and let them know I'm okay."

A lab-coated doctor walked in and pulled the chart off the wall.

"How long are you going to be at the hospital? Should I come by tomorrow?"

"Not sure. I'll let you know. The doc just walked in, so I've gotta go."

"You've stirred up quite a beehive of activity, Ms. Hartland. All my nurses are swooning over your fiancé." The overhead lights reflected off his shiny bald head as he looked at me through rimless glasses. "How's the pain?"

"Manageable." My brows puckered and the corners of my mouth turned down.

He frowned. "Your vitals look good. You're not running a fever. So, we're going to release you."

"I'm not spending the night?"

"Not tonight." He pulled out a square pad. "I'm giving you a prescription for the pain and one for antibiotics." He rattled off instructions, as if memorized by rote, then ripped off two sheets from his prescription pad, and handed the illegible scribble to me. "Any questions?"

I shook my head.

"Okay. Ms. Hartland, good luck to you." He exited the room, passing by Ian without uttering a word.

"You're awake." Ian said.

"And apparently leaving."

"You're being released?"

I nodded.

Ian hiked a hip onto the side of the bed and pushed a lock of hair behind my ear. He gazed at me; tension lines radiated around the edges and his jaw muscles flexed. "We had a press conference."

"I heard."

"Did you watch it?"

"No. Mom told me. Apparently, I'm 'under your protection.'"

Ian nodded. "My manager wanted me to tell everyone we were engaged to quash the love triangle rumors, but I didn't think that was fair to you."

"You either." I looked down at my fingers, plucking at the thin white cotton blanket. "Ian, we'll be perfectly safe staying at my house."

"Why don't you spend tonight with me? Then return to your place tomorrow." A finger lifted my chin. "That way I'll know your safe, and we can keep the reporters out."

I sighed. As much as I wanted to be independent and stop imposing on Ian, I was too tired to argue and any semblance of fight left me. "Fine. We'll do it your way, but I warn you, my mom can be a lot to take."

The tension lines eased. "I consider myself duly warned."

"Warned about what?" Mom swept the door wide.

"Warned we're apparently invading Ian's house tonight."

"Of course, dear. We already settled that while you were asleep."

My eyes shot back to Ian. He shrugged and grinned like an impudent schoolboy.

Chapter 24

The fire pit crackled and danced in the waning evening sun. Its warmth toasted my front side, keeping the cool November breeze at bay. I pulled up a small ottoman, adjusted the donut under my bum to a more comfortable position, and laid my head back against the outdoor love seat to observe nature's spectacle of color. A rainbow display of hues ranging from pinks to oranges played along the clouds as the sun set. This was probably the first time I'd been alone with my thoughts since leaving the hospital.

I'd left Mom and Holly in the kitchen, debating whether or not Ian's wineglasses could go in the dishwasher. Poppy and Ian were sitting at the dining room table planning a Christmas party Ian wanted to throw for the cast and crew of *LA Heat*. While Poppy's unexpected plus one for today's Thanksgiving dinner, Rich, sat on the floor playing with Eva and her Minnie Mouse kitchen. Apparently, while my life was going to hell in a handbag, she and Rich were … well, I'm not sure what she and Rich were doing. But, it surprised all of us when she showed up at the door with him in tow. I have to say, Poppy must have had a mellowing effect on him. In the past two hours, he hadn't said or done anything that made me want to slap him. Although, it might also have had something to do with the quick discussion Ian pulled him aside for soon after their arrival.

The days since my visit to the hospital were nothing less than exhausting. After Ziggy and Ian snuck us out a back alley door of the hospital, we were driven to Ian's home where we stayed for the first night. Sunday afternoon, Ian and I visited the police precinct to make our official statements about Omar's invasion and found out how he was able to get past my security system. It was all very technical, but from what Gary told us, Omar pieced together some sort of equipment which hacked my system and allowed him to reset it, so I wouldn't suspect anything when I arrived home.

On Sunday, against Ian's verbose wishes, I insisted we return to my house. The paparazzi, for the most part, had decamped from the neighborhood. A few stragglers hung around both Ian's and my places, but Ziggy was able to "encourage" them to leave. Gary, also sent a cruiser around the community regularly. I rescheduled two consultations to the following week and Michelle finished the job we'd been working on. Between shopping and visiting with the girls, I spent the next few days running invoices, paying bills, responding to e-mails, and prepping for the following week's consultations.

LA Heat production was on break for Thanksgiving, so Ian had this week off. He flew east on the red-eye for an interview with the *Good Morning America* show. He went on *GMA* to promote *LA Heat* and talk about Doctors Without Borders, a charity near and dear to his heart. I missed him. It was an unusual emotion for me. It had been such a long time since I'd been in a relationship; I wasn't used to missing someone.

Holly and I tuned into *Good Morning America* together Monday morning. Ian looked fabulous, as usual. I ground my teeth as the hostess flirted with him. The flair of jealousy was another unusual sensation for me. She quizzed him about Saturday's debacle, but Ian easily deflected her inquiries, keeping the discussion to his show and Doctors Without Borders. We spoke on the phone Monday evening, and Ian told me he planned to visit his father and stepmother while in New York. I assumed he meant he'd be spending Thanksgiving with them. Since I didn't want to sound like a needy girlfriend, even though I'd hoped he'd be home to share the holiday together, I wished him well and suggested we get together when he returned. When he arrived on my doorstep Wednesday night, I gaped at him like a dime store guppy.

"Did you miss me, luv?" He sent me one of his deadly smiles, and as usual, my heart fluttered.

"What are you doing here?"

"Well, that's a nice greeting for your long lost boyfriend."

I blushed and pulled him into the house by the lapels of his coat. "I'm just shocked to see you. I thought you were spending Thanksgiving with your family in New York."

"Not at all. Didn't your mother tell you? We're having Thanksgiving over at my place. You girls are supposed to cook up a turkey with cranberries."

Irritation flashed through me. Once again, I was out of the loop. Mom and Holly had gone grocery shopping for holiday dinner, but I assumed we'd be eating at my house. Poppy was supposed to join us. I figured the girls would keep me company and my mind off Ian's absence. "*Mom!*"

"Yes, dear?" Mom bustled in from the kitchen.

"Where are we eating Thanksgiving?"

"Well, hello, Ian. I didn't hear you come in. It's lovely to see you again. How was your trip?"

"Good, good. How have you been, Dorothy?"

"Mom," I ground out. "Where are we eating Thanksgiving?"

"At Ian's, of course."

"How come nobody told me?"

"It must have been an oversight. I thought you knew. Ian invited us at the hospital. He has that lovely big dining room table you installed. We'll all fit comfortably there."

I rolled my eyes and said sarcastically, "I'm so glad my life is in good hands."

"Well, really, dear," my mother huffed with exasperation. "We're just trying to make it easy for you, so you can focus on recovering."

I was duly chastised. "I'm sorry. You're right. I appreciate not having to plan everything."

Mom patted my cheek. "You don't like it when you're not in control of everything. I know. You're just like your father. Now take Ian into the living room, and I'll fix us something to drink."

I looked at Ian, who stood silent on the sidelines. "You see what you're getting yourself into, don't you?"

He pulled me close and kissed the top of my head. "Wouldn't have it any other way." Then he lowered his voice and his breath drifted across my ear. "So, how is my favorite derriere?"

"Sore."

"Perhaps I can do something to make it feel better."

• • •

The sliding door closed behind me, and I glanced over my shoulder. Ian came around and joined me on the love seat.

"Everything settled with the party?"

"So it seems. Your friend Poppy is very efficient. What are you doing out here all by yourself?" He slipped an arm over my shoulders. His body heat seeped through my lightweight jacket, warming me.

"Admiring your view. I think I could look at it for hours and hours and never get tired of it."

"So, you like my house?"

"Yes. You really picked a lovely spot."

"Hmm. What are your sister's plans? Will she be returning to Las Vegas?"

"I'm not sure. She's thinking of staying in LA. She has some art gallery contacts here and she thinks she'll be able to get a job. I'd like her to start seeing a therapist. I think Omar screwed with her mind."

"Will she and Eva stay with you?" Ian poked the fire with a stick. Embers showered, and the fire flamed. The charred wood fragrance filled the area.

"Probably for a while. Although, she said something about finding an apartment," I mused. "Really, she should probably just move in with me. I'm in a decent neighborhood with good schools."

"Sophie, would you say you like the renovations you've done to my house?"

I frowned. *That was off topic.* "Of course. I always do good work. The real question is, do *you* like it? After all, it's your house."

"It's brilliant, but would you decorate it this way if it were your place."

I frowned. "Me? Maybe not exactly like this. I have a different style of living, and I always have to take Sirius into consideration. I tried to tailor it to your likes. That's my job. Why? Is there something you're not happy with? I'm sure I can change it."

"Not at all. I love what you've done. This isn't coming out right at all." Ian rubbed his jaw. "Let me back up. When I sat down, you said you'd never get tired of this view."

I snuggled into his side. "Who could?"

"What if you were able to look at it every day?"

"Ian, I told you before. My family can't impose on you," I said firmly. Really, we'd been through this already. I thought Ian had accepted that. "Plus, everything seems to be fine at my house now. I mean, we'll probably have media coming around for a while, but it'll eventually go away."

"I'm not talking about your family. I'm talking about you. Living here. With me."

"You mean like cohabitating?"

"Something like that."

I scoffed. "What would your Irish Catholic mother have to say about that? I can just imagine. I'd be the slut sleeping with her good boy."

"She wouldn't say anything of the sort if you were wearing a ring on your finger."

My heartbeat sped up and I froze. *Did he just say what I think he said?* My neck, bit by bit, turned on its axis, the sound of the Gore-Tex material scraping against my chin sounded loud in my ears. I met Ian's unblinking gaze. "Ian O'Connor, what exactly are you implying?"

"*A ghra mo chroi.*" His thumb drifted across my cheek.

The Gaelic momentarily sidetracked my thoughts. "What does that mean?"

"It means, love of my heart."

I gulped; our intense gazes never shifted. "Do you mean it?"

"Yes," he murmured. "Marry me."

"I can't."

"Why not?"

"I ... I ... " I scrambled to find a cohesive argument.

"Do you love me, Soph?"

"Yes, of course. How could I not?" I whimpered.

"Say it."

"I love you."

He pulled me into a crushing embrace. "Then marry me."

Oh, how my pitty-patty little heart wanted to say yes. However, my hard head prevailed. We barely knew each other. I'd married my first husband too young. I didn't want to make a similar mistake by marrying Ian without getting to know him fully. I pulled back to search his face.

"Is it the celebrity life I lead that causes you hesitation?"

Is it? "No. Well, yes, the press does sort of bother me, but that's not why I'm saying no." I held up a hand. "And I'm not saying no, not ever. Just ... no ... not right now. We don't know each other well enough."

"I know you're the only woman who's led me on a merry chase and scared the living daylights out of me by almost getting herself killed by a psychopath."

"Hey! That wasn't my fault ... exactly."

"You're smart, sexy, funny and beautiful. You've climbed into my heart, and I can't get you out. I don't want to get you out. I have this need to protect you, even when your stubbornness is driving me up a wall. You're also the first woman I've dated, since my New York days, who hasn't tried to utilize my status to get a leg up in her career."

I grimaced. "Uh … Ian … that's not exactly true. I shamefully used your status at Sheila's party to diffuse a situation. And … I kind of hoped you'd let your friends know about me." I ducked my head in shame.

"First," he placed a finger under my chin, forcing me to look up. "You didn't use me. I helped you out because I love you. Second, of course, I'm telling all my friends about your brilliant capabilities as an interior designer. That's why I'm having a party, to show off your work. I'm proud of the wonderful changes you've made. I still can't believe the difference. I think everyone should use your crew. I'm talking about the people who only see me as a means to getting her face on television."

"Oh. You don't have to worry about that. I hate having my picture taken."

His soft lips gently touched mine. "That's what I mean. You're not mixed up in the Hollywood business rat race. You're my grounded rock, keeping me sane. You're outside of it all. I need you, luv."

"I don't know, Ian. We hardly know each other. I don't want to make the same mistakes I made with Michael."

"I'm not Michael, and I take my wedding vows very seriously." He gave a distinct frown.

"Okay, okay. I'm not saying you're a cheater." I patted his hand. *Sheesh I didn't want to rehash that argument again.* "What I'm saying is, we can't just jump into this. We don't know enough about each other. For instance, what about kids? Hmm? We've never even discussed kids."

"Love 'em. Want a passel of them." He grinned.

"I should tell you, I've had a miscarriage. I don't know if I can carry to term." I crossed my arms. "And this isn't me caving in to you. Just providing information."

"Then we'll adopt. We'll be like Brad Pitt and Angelina Jolie. We'll wander Africa adopting kids along the way."

My stomach panicked at the thought of half a dozen kids. "I only want two!"

"Two it is," he agreed readily.

"Ian," I groaned.

"Look, our first compromise."

"I'm not ready to take that step again." My emotions swung in so many different directions, it felt like I was on an amusement park Tilt-a-Whirl ride. Ian's sudden proposal put my brain and heart at odds. I fidgeted with my watch as I debated. Did I want to be with Ian? *Yes*, my heart screamed. Was I willing to leap off that cliff without looking? No, my brain stood strong. I'd done that in my past and my relationship with Ian, though still new, was too important to me to rush. I needed time, and, whether he believed it or not, he needed time to get to know me as well. My immature relationship with my ex had taught me a life lesson. One I couldn't forget, even for my amazing new boyfriend. I wasn't ready for another marriage, so my head and heart decided to compromise.

"Can't we just live together in sin?"

He gave me a hard stare, which I returned, refusing to back down.

"All right, Soph. You don't have to be ready right now. I've got time. Move in with me. Let your sister and Eva live at your place." He squeezed my leg and gave a self-satisfied smile.

He got exactly what he wanted. Didn't he? I rolled my eyes. "I can't believe I've just agreed to this. Don't think I don't know what you're doing." I shook a finger in his face. "You're trying to wear me down. Like when I started this reno and wouldn't date you."

An eyebrow winged up. He grabbed the finger and kissed the tip. "Let's just say, if I see your resistance weakening, I will take advantage."

"Arrgh!"

Chapter 25

Three Months Later

"Good morning, my darling Valentine." Ian's voice grumbled over the Bluetooth headset.

It was ten past eight and the gates closed behind me as I headed to the nearest Starbuck's, before proceeding to my latest job in Beverly Hills. "Good morning, Valentine. What time did you leave? I didn't hear you."

"Quarter to six. You were dead to the world."

"I'm planning to cook a delicious Valentine meal for you tonight, so don't be late."

"I should be home by seven."

"Perfect."

"Marry me, luv."

The question wasn't out of left field. Ian had been asking me to marry him at least once or twice a week since Thanksgiving. Sometimes as we fell asleep, or at meal-time, over the phone, attached to a bouquet of flowers, or via text. I'd laughingly told him not yet, every time. He took it in stride and continued throwing the question out at odd moments, knowing it was only a matter of time before he wore down my resistance. Only, today was going to be different.

"Yes."

"What?"

"Yes."

"Yes, you'll marry me?"

"Yes, Ian O'Connor. I'll marry you." A wide smile split my face.

"You're not screwing with me, are you, Sophia?" His voice held a warning.

"I'm not screwing with you."

"Bloody brilliant! Did you hear that mates?" His voice faded a bit. "She finally said yes. I'm getting married."

The background noise of celebration and congratulations lit up the phone line.

I giggled.

"Why didn't you wait until tonight? Now I have to wait all day to see you."

"Because you asked me now. Why didn't you wait to ask?" My cheeks puffed up in glee.

"Because I'm a bloody git. Come by the set today. I must see you."

"I'll swing by at lunchtime."

"I'll make sure they have your name at the gate. I'm going to be utter rubbish today. I can't remember any of my lines."

"You'll be fine. I'll see you at lunchtime."

"Lunch. *A ghra mo chroi.*"

"I love you, too, Valentine."

About the Author

Ellen Butler lives with her family in the Virginia suburbs of Washington, DC. She holds a Master's Degree in Public Administration and Policy, and her history includes a long list of writing and editing for dry but illuminating professional newsletters, and windy papers on public policy. The leap to novel writing was simply a creative outlet for Ellen's overactive imagination. Her genre is women's fiction and romance. She likes to provide strong female characters and suspense in her novels. Professionally, she belongs to the Virginia Writer's Club, the Northern Virginia Writer's club, and Write by the Rails. Ellen is an admitted chocoholic and confesses to a penchant for shoe shopping. You can find her first two novels, *Poplar Place* and *Second Chance Christmas,* at major online book retailers. For more information visit Ellen at: *www.ellenbutler.net,* and on Facebook at Ellen Butler Books. View her blogs at Tempting Romance, *temptingromance.blogspot.com.*

A Sneak Peek from Crimson Romance
(From *Naked Truth* by Tami Lund)

Kennedy St. George stepped up behind her cousin who stood in front of an ornate full-length mirror, staring at the big, white dress reflected there. "Hey, you coming? We can't exactly have a wedding without the bride."

Sabrina blinked rapidly until her eyes focused, until, Kennedy suspected, the tears receded. "How are you doing?" her cousin asked instead of answering the question.

"I should have known better," Kennedy murmured. No point in pretending she didn't know what the bride was asking. "There were hurricane warnings on my wedding day."

"The weather is not an accurate predictor of happily ever after," Sabrina gently chided. Kennedy pointedly looked at the window, which framed a gloriously beautiful, late spring day. Sabrina rolled her eyes.

"You and Cullen are perfect for each other," Kennedy responded. "Jerry and I … weren't."

"We are hardly perfect for one another, although Cullen is the perfect guy." She absently twisted the engagement ring on her finger, a dreamy smile on her lips.

Cullen was often gruff, swore like a sailor, and quite possibly did not own a razor. He was lousy at small talk and awkward at family functions. But he was loyal to a fault, adored Sabrina to the point of obsession, and if one liked scruffy guys, he was definitely handsome.

Sabrina laughed. "You don't think so. I can tell. Which is okay, because he's about to be my husband, not yours. What's your version of the perfect guy?"

"No guy is perfect."

"Fair enough, but what type of guy would make you happy?"

"Anyone besides Jerry."

That earned her a stern look from Sabrina's reflection in the mirror.

"Okay, okay," Kennedy relented. "I'll play your game. Let's see … perfect guy …"

"Someone who doesn't cheat."

"That's a given," Kennedy pointed out, although she understood why her cousin mentioned it.

"What else?"

"This is hard." She pondered the question. "I guess I'd like someone who proves he cares by his actions instead of just saying it all the time."

"That's reasonable."

"And I'd like someone who has his own life, too. You know I work a lot of hours at the hospital, and I like what I do. I imagine I'd come to resent a guy who expects me to work a nine-to-five schedule just because it fits his needs."

"Considering I'm marrying an FBI agent, and agents definitely don't work regular hours, I get that. Anything else?"

"I'm not into going out on the town all the time, clubbing and such. So when we would get to spend time together, I'd want to do it at home, cooking together or watching a movie or, I don't know, just hanging out—that's my idea of a perfect evening."

"So no party animals for you."

"Nope. But he still has to be—" she cut herself off.

"Good in bed?" They shared a laugh. Sabrina abruptly sobered and said, "I think you should start dating again. In fact, Joey, one of the groomsmen, is single, and he's really sweet. Good looking, too. I bet he fits at least some of your criteria."

"Don't even think about setting me up at your wedding."

"Weddings are the perfect place to meet someone."

"Weddings are the perfect place to meet a one-night stand, and if I'm not interested in dating, I'm sure as heck not interested in *that*."

"Why not? Not about the one-night stand necessarily, but about dating at all?"

Sabrina's earnestness invited an honest response. But Kennedy didn't know how to respond. Five years ago, she'd married a man who'd swept her off her feet, who'd given her empty promises about rainbows and unicorns. Two years later, he'd stolen every last nickel and charged her credit cards to the max before disappearing out of her life.

The official story was that he'd cheated on her, so she'd demanded the divorce. That was humiliating enough, but she figured if everyone knew the truth—that he'd literally stolen everything while she'd been stupidly unaware—that would be ten times worse. Cheating was, unfortunately, a fact of life. It happened, you moved on, and you hoped to find someone new, someone who wouldn't cheat. But your own husband leaving you with literally no recourse whatsoever? There was something far more … embarrassing about that, at least in Kennedy's mind.

"How can I?" Kennedy asked, sticking with the lie she'd told everyone, even her cousin and best friend. "How can I trust someone again?"

Sabrina adjusted her veil and squeezed her fist around the white-with-blue-embroidery handkerchief in her hand. "You just do. I don't know how to explain it. You just reach a point where you realize this man is the one, and you are going to put all of your trust in him because you are so in love you don't really have a choice."

"I did that with Jerry, remember?"

"Did you, really?" Kennedy averted her eyes. What her cousin implied was right. The hurricane on the day of her wedding hadn't been the only warning sign. She had just been a fool and refused to pay attention.

"I won't ever make that mistake again," she vowed.

"Certainly not if you never date again."

She smirked. "It's safer that way."

"Safe isn't fun. Live a little. Enjoy yourself today. Dance with Joey. Flirt with him. See where it leads." Before Kennedy could protest again, Sabrina turned away from the mirror and lifted the billowing, white skirt. "Now come on, I want to get married."

Kennedy grabbed the train to make it easier for Sabrina to walk. *I can't take the chance*, she thought as she followed her cousin out of the bride's room.

• • •

They met the groomsmen in the lobby, just outside the chapel. Cullen's brother, Marshall, was the best man, a less scruffy and slightly shorter version of the groom. When he saw the bride, he smiled widely and spread his arms as if he intended to hug her, but caught himself and squeezed her hand instead, murmuring that she was beautiful and Cullen was a hell of a lucky guy.

Cullen's FBI agent partner, Jack Boudreaux, wasn't nearly so couth. When he saw the bride, he gave a loud wolf whistle and pulled her into a bear hug, lifting her off her feet and causing her to squeal. Kennedy expected the bride's uptight sister, Vanessa, to snap at him for crushing the bride's dress, but she simpered instead.

Kennedy supposed she could understand. Cullen's partner was an incredibly attractive man. Although Cullen and Sabrina had been dating for a year now, Kennedy hadn't yet met his closest friend. Now that she was admiring him from only a few feet away, she was sort of glad she hadn't. He was James Bond with thick, blond hair and a clean-shaven jawline, and he looked damn good in a tux.

Damn good.

It wasn't like she hadn't come across hot guys throughout the course of the last three years, so why was her heart racing? Why did she feel flushed? She forced herself not to fan her face, even as she worried that she was breaking out in a sweat and might ruin her makeup.

Not going there. Jerry had been good-looking, too, and look where that had gotten her.

He wasn't this good-looking.

Kennedy wanted to tell her inner voice to shut the hell up. Besides, Joey was the groomsman Sabrina had suggested she get to know better. Sabrina had said precious little about Jack over the course of her and Cullen's courtship, other than the occasional comment about him being a playboy. Which explained why she wouldn't have suggested Kennedy break free of her self-induced, nun-like lifestyle with him. Another cheater wasn't on the agenda.

"I was just informed that you and I are walking into the chapel together."

Kennedy shifted her focus to the man who was speaking, the very man she had just been salivating over. "Uh, we are?"

He did that slow perusal thing with his eyes that guys did when they wanted a girl to know they liked what they saw. A slow smile curved his lips. "Yep."

She recognized that look. She may have been out of the dating game for far too long, but she still understood the process. What she didn't know was how to respond.

"No, no," Vanessa interrupted, as she wedged herself between them. "You and I should walk down the aisle together." She batted thickly mascaraed lashes and smiled coyly. Kennedy resisted the urge to stick her finger into her mouth in a gagging motion. They weren't in high school anymore, even if Vanessa was acting like a lovesick teenager.

"Cullen told me he'll kick my ass if I don't do what the wedding planner tells me," Jack commented. "And she said I'm supposed to walk in with the hot brunette."

Hot brunette? Was he talking about her?

Vanessa brushed a perfectly coifed blond curl off her shoulder and lifted her chin. With an audible sniff, she said, "The pictures will look better if you and I are in them together."

Jack arched his brows. "I could've sworn this wedding was about Cullen and Sabrina. Not you."

Vanessa opened her mouth to retort, but the wedding planner grabbed her arm in a vise-like grip and dragged her away to stand alone at the end of the processional.

"Where's the best man?" Kennedy asked, as she watched Vanessa argue with the wedding planner.

"Already inside with the groom. Cullen was looking a little panicked, so the priest suggested his brother be up there for moral support."

"Oh no. He isn't having second thoughts, is he?"

Jack chuckled. "Hell no. If he could've had his way, Cullen would've carted her off to Vegas a year ago. Sabrina wanted this dog and pony show, and he's doing it because he loves her, but he hates being in the spotlight like this." He abruptly changed the subject. "So Cullen tells me you're the bride's BFF."

"Yes. We're cousins as well."

"How come stalker woman is the maid of honor?"

"You mean Vanessa? She's Sabrina's sister." Kennedy giggled, taking herself by surprise. When was the last time she'd giggled in the presence of someone of the opposite sex who wasn't related to her?

"She's scary as hell. I haven't been pursued like that in a long time."

"Vanessa has been pursuing you?"

Jack nodded. "She practically attacked me as soon as I walked into the church. I'm not really into that. I'm into more subtle women."

She ignored the last bit and blurted, "She's married."

Jack arched those sleek, blond brows again. "Now I'm really glad I didn't let her catch me. I'm not into married women either."

He gave Kennedy's left hand a pointed look. She squeezed her bouquet until she was afraid she would snap the stems on the burgundy and cream-colored roses. She was so lousy at this game. Besides the fact she wasn't even sure she wanted to play it in the first place.

"What about divorced women?" *Oh my God, did I just say that out loud?*

Jack shrugged. "I like single women. Divorced is single."

Kennedy's chest heaved as she sucked in air. "I'm not—" She lost her train of thought when he reached over, cupped her wrist, and pulled her arm through the crook of his, resting her hand on his forearm. Not only did he look amazing in the tux, but he felt good, too.

Not good.

"Showtime," Jack murmured, and Kennedy realized that the doors to the chapel were open and the music started, indicating it was time for the processional to begin.

She struggled to fill her lungs. Jack gave her a concerned look. "You okay?"

Kennedy shook her head and focused on breathing. In and out. That's it. This wasn't *her* wedding. It was Sabrina's, and Sabrina was marrying the man of her dreams. The right man. Her forever happily ever after.

"I just don't like weddings as a rule."

"Why not?"

"My own was a disaster."

Jack watched Kennedy watch the bride. A slow, sad smile spread across her face as Sabrina began to make her way down the aisle. He turned his attention to the bride, too.

She looked like a frigging princess in that big, white gown. Her smile was so wide that he was half-afraid her face would split in two. He glanced at his partner and best friend. The deer-in-the-headlights look that had been on his face since early this morning was gone, replaced by adoration, as his eyes never left his almost-wife. Cullen was hooked, no doubt about it. Sabrina was, and now always would be, the center of his world.

Lucky bastard, Jack thought, even as he followed that thought with, *I couldn't imagine being so beholden to another person*. It worked for Cullen—which was a hell of a surprise, frankly—but he knew marriage wasn't for everyone.

Kennedy was married?

He shifted his gaze to watch the hot bridesmaid standing across the aisle, who was now watching the bride and groom with rapt attention. He'd missed that little tidbit of information somewhere along the way. She wasn't wearing a ring. He'd noticed that because he'd been scoping out the various options for a little after-reception female companionship.

Weddings were a great place to pick up a one-night stand, but you had to be careful to pick a woman who didn't have forever on her mind at the moment. The good thing was, the generous pours at the open bar tended to make almost anyone forget about forever, at least until the next morning. And Jack was good at slipping out of bed and out of their lives before they could even suggest exchanging phone numbers, let alone talk about a second—or hell, how about a first?—date.

He'd narrowed his focus to Kennedy, and had assumed she was single. While dodging the maid of honor, he'd caught sight of the willowy, brunette bridesmaid and his interest had immediately been piqued. He could tell she was one of those women who didn't demand to be the center of attention, who was probably more of a wallflower. In his experience, women like that tended to be wildcats in the sack. Perfect for a temporary wedding pickup.

Whether she preferred to duck the spotlight or not, she was definitely sexy. Besides that thick, chestnut-brown hair that trailed halfway down her back, she had expressive, green, doe eyes set into a heart-shaped face, along with Cupid's bow pink lips that caused his imagination to wander into seriously smutty places.

She wore the bridesmaid dress well, too. It was a simple number in a bronze color, with a halter neckline that emphasized the top swell of breasts that were neither too small nor too large. All things considered, his choice of a bed partner for the night hadn't been difficult at all.

Except for the whole marriage bit. He wasn't into married women, no matter how attractive they were. He'd hooked up with a handful of married women throughout his misspent youth, and each time had been a disaster—an emotional roller coaster for the women and mediocre sex for him. It was hard to get excited when a woman either cried or talked about another man constantly. In his experience, women who cheated didn't really want to cheat; they just wanted their significant other to notice them.

The roar of applause, catcalls, and wolf whistles indicated that the ceremony was at an end, and Jack shifted his focus to watch the groom bend his bride over his arm and kiss her with such enthusiasm that the priest blushed.

* * *

Kennedy felt a pang of jealousy combined with regret as she watched her cousin and new husband make out on the altar. Five years previously, she'd received no more than a chaste peck on the cheek from her groom. Two years later, she'd sat in her living room and cried frustrated tears and thought, *I should have known it wouldn't last.*

As Cullen and Sabrina posed for the photographer before proceeding down the aisle after being pronounced husband and wife, Kennedy tortured herself by comparing the ratio of couples to individuals in the church. She realized the number of married couples far outweighed the number of single people. Those couples were happy, too, as far as she could tell, which only added to her misery. Kennedy wanted to be happy.

She eyed her wedding counterpart. Jack was single, and he seemed happy. Maybe he knew something she didn't.

"Stay away from him," Sabrina had warned her a half dozen times. "The women love him, but he only wants one thing."

Considering how just the simplest touch from Jack had spiked her blood pressure, she suspected it was not difficult at all for him to pick up women when he was in the mood for a little action.

Was that the key to happiness as a single person? Occasional one-night stands, with no other expectations? Jack looked, at the very least, content and comfortable in his own skin.

Kennedy certainly wasn't happy, and neither did she feel comfortable in her own skin half the time. She tended to dress down, to hide herself, to try to avoid being noticed by the opposite sex. It was easier that way. Otherwise, she might have to be forced to address unwanted attentions from men like Jack.

They were unwanted, weren't they?

Since her divorce three years ago, Kennedy had not dated at all. She was too afraid. She'd fallen for her lying ex-husband, let him talk her into moving from her comfort zone—her hometown of Dallas—to New Orleans, a town that was an entirely different world. She'd let him talk her into marrying him. And then he'd taken everything, including her pride, right from under her nose.

She glanced at Jack again, caught him watching her, and averted her eyes.

Kennedy's experience with one-night stands was limited to two times in her entire life. There was that one time in college, when the guy had bet his friends that he could convince her to sleep with him. She thought he wanted to date her, wanted so much more, until the next morning when he laughed while he pulled his shorts over his thighs and said, "Thanks for that, Kennedy. I'm strapped for cash right now and that twenty bucks will sure come in handy."

The other time had been a stupid mistake she'd made with the divorce attorney she'd hired when her ex stole all her money. So she probably shouldn't be open to attempting another one-night stand.

Except that, honestly, wasn't it different if she knew about it up front? If both parties had the same expectation? While the outcome had been humiliating, she could admit that the sex with the attorney had been good, at least while she'd been in the moment.

Maybe it had been good *because* it was a one-night stand.

She eyed Jack again. He certainly looked like he could please a woman in bed. Those big hands, with lean, nimble fingers. What would they feel like, caressing her breasts, sliding down her belly to the apex of her thighs?

Those full, slightly pouty lips trailing kisses along her throat, over her chest, suckling her nipples. His tongue darting out to tease her skin as he continued his downward path, until his lips were pressed against that part of her body that hadn't felt the touch of a man's lips in …

"Almost done," Jack murmured, pulling her abruptly from the impromptu fantasy. His chocolate-brown eyes watched her from under hooded lids.

She turned her head slightly away. The man looked as if the rented tux had been made specifically for him, whereas Cullen looked faintly uncomfortable in the fancy duds.

Jack stepped in front of the altar and offered the crook of his arm. Kennedy slipped her hand through and let it rest lightly on his forearm as they both turned and posed for the photographer.

"Don't be gentle, baby," he teased, which caused a surprised giggle to burst from her mouth just as the camera clicked.

She lightly slapped his arm with her other hand. "You just ruined that picture," she scolded as they walked down the aisle.

"By making you laugh? How do you figure?"

Kennedy shook her head as she kept a smile plastered onto her face in case someone was still taking pictures. "I don't photograph well," she explained. "Especially when I laugh."

"That is one of the weirdest things I have ever heard," he remarked, just as they reached the end of the procession and were tugged apart by the wedding planner.

After greeting the guests and promising to see them at the reception, then smiling for another multitude of pictures, it was finally time to pile into the limo. Since Vanessa was doing a lousy job of managing her maid of honor duties, Kennedy picked up the slack and herded everyone into the back seat before rushing into the church to ensure they hadn't left anything behind in the bride's room.

When she returned, the driver took the three bags she carried and placed them in the trunk, and then held the door open while Kennedy tried to duck into the back in a dress that wasn't terribly accommodating to such activity.

The limo was full. "Oh," Kennedy said. "I guess I'll sit in front."

"You can't," Sabrina said. "Cullen's grandma is up there. She said she wanted to flirt with the driver." She giggled as she lifted a half empty bottle of champagne and drank straight from the bottle. Cullen shook his head, looking faintly embarrassed by his grandmother's actions. The driver cleared his throat, his eyes lifting to look at the almost cloudless sky.

"There's plenty of room," Jack announced, and before Kennedy could react, he slipped his arm around her waist and hauled her into his lap.

"No!" Kennedy struggled, twisting her body, pushing against Jack's chest, trying to shift into a less compromising position, even as the door slammed shut and the rest of the crowd in the limo laughed.

Jack's arms wrapped around her body, effectively trapping her arms against her sides and forcing her to sit still. "Relax," he whispered next to her ear. "It's a short ride to the reception, and you shouldn't be left out just because you were helping the bride."

Kennedy tried to force herself to relax. He hadn't been hitting on her; he had only tried to help. Just because sitting in his lap elevated her own body temperature was no reason to assume the guy was a sleaze. Besides, twenty minutes ago she had been giving serious consideration to the idea of having a one-night stand with him.

As she became aware of the size of the erection pressing into her backside, her thoughts plummeted into the gutter. Guess she was back to considering shagging him, even if she knew damn well it would only happen once.

Jack loosened his hold, and then cupped her waist and adjusted her in his lap. "Sorry," he murmured. "That was feeling a little too good."

Cullen shoved his shoulder. "Lay off the bridesmaid, Jack."

Hey, what's the problem?" Jack teased. "We're both consenting adults. If she wants to sit in my lap, she has every right to do so."

"There wasn't anywhere else to sit," Kennedy protested, feeling the need to defend herself. "And you pulled me into your lap."

"Aw, that hurt. Are you saying you would have been happy riding in any old lap that was handy?"

"No!"

Kennedy could relate to Cullen's reluctance to being in the spotlight. She hated knowing everyone in the limo was watching her, was laughing at her obvious discomfort. Jack thought he was helping, but truthfully she would have preferred to have ridden to the reception by herself, even if it would have meant missing out on the feel of his muscular chest against her back, his impressive erection against her ass.

Damn, she was becoming a harlot in her own head. It really had been too long since she'd enjoyed skin-to-skin contact with a man.

"I'm sorry," she muttered, her eyes closed, her body tense as she focused every bit of attention on the effort not to move.

"Don't apologize," Jack admonished. "I was just teasing you."

They arrived at the reception site, and Kennedy bolted from the vehicle almost before it came to a complete stop. As she reached for the front door, she turned her head, glanced over her shoulder—and saw Jack, standing next to the limo, a contemplative expression on his face. Kennedy wondered why he appeared so pensive.

• • •

"It's beautiful," Sabrina declared as she and Cullen stepped into the ballroom, greeted by a round of applause and catcalls from their guests.

"You're beautiful," Cullen murmured, using the opportunity to nuzzle her ear. Sabrina giggled and did not push him away.

"Marriage seems to agree with Cullen," Jack commented as he and Kennedy stood side by side, next to the head table, watching as the new bride and groom were introduced.

"Cullen agrees with Sabrina," Kennedy responded.

"They're good for each other. She brings out the best in him."

"And he balances her."

"Match made in heaven," Jack said, his voice light with sarcasm.

Kennedy chuckled. "Hardly. They're practically opposites. But they do prove the old adage that opposites attract."

Cullen and Sabrina moved onto the dance floor as the band struck up the cords of "Just the Way You Are" by Billy Joel. Kennedy glanced at Jack, and they burst out laughing.

"Our turn," Jack murmured, and then he led her out onto the dance floor.

As it turned out, he was a good dancer. He exuded a certain confidence and grace that was both slightly intimidating and overwhelming for someone like her, who hadn't had a great deal of self-confidence even before she'd allowed her ex to walk all over her.

"You're a good dancer," Jack remarked as they swayed to the music. One hand rested lightly on the small of her back, while the other clasped her hand, gently guiding her around the dance floor.

"Thanks. It's because I have a good partner."

"We fit together well," Jack said, and he sent her into a twirl before catching her and resuming the dance again.

"Oh," she gasped.

Jack winked. "Stick with me, babe. I'm full of surprises."

The song ended, and the wedding party left the dance floor and made their way to the head table so that dinner could be announced.

• • •

Dinner led to the cake-cutting ceremony and an endless stream of toasts. Kennedy gave her own tearful tribute, thanking Sabrina for being there for her own wedding and for giving Kennedy the opportunity to do the same for her.

Jack whispered to Cullen, "I didn't realize she's married."

"Was. She's been divorced a while. Three years, I think."

"What? Was she sixteen when she got married?"

"Twenty-five, actually."

"How long did it last?"

"Couple years. He cheated on her, so she left him."

Jack studied Kennedy's tearful performance. "She doesn't look like the type a guy would cheat on."

Cullen shrugged. "Some guys like variety, I guess, regardless of how good the catch they have. Oh hell, now they're both crying." He stood up to comfort his wife, who was hugging Kennedy and openly sobbing. Jack stood up and pulled the microphone from Kennedy's hand.

"I guess that's my cue," he said as he offered her a cloth napkin to dab her eyes. "Kennedy's good at the sappy stuff; I'm good at the funny stuff."

That elicited a round of appreciative chuckles, and then he launched into the first of several amusing stories about some of his partner's less-than-stellar moments in life. Cullen's brother stood up and joined him at the mic, and within a few short minutes, they had the crowd roaring with laughter, all at the groom's expense.

He took it good-naturedly, though, lifting his drink in mock toast and saying, "I'm pretty sure I finally got it right now," just before he dipped his head and kissed his smiling wife.

"Thanks for taking over," Kennedy said as Jack dropped into the chair next to her. "I didn't mean to get so emotional up there. I guess I've had a little too much to drink."

"Haven't we all?" He lifted his glass and drained it. "Isn't that what you're supposed to do at a wedding?"

She smiled and took another sip from her champagne glass. "I'm not sure "supposed to" is necessarily accurate. Although you're right that it is pretty common."

"More champagne or something else?" he asked.

"I like the champagne," she admitted. "But I don't know if there is any left."

"Sure there is," he said, and he stood up and left the table. When he returned, he held a bottle of champagne in one hand and a glass of bourbon and Coke in the other. He filled her glass and stuffed the bottle into the ice bucket sitting at her elbow.

"Where'd you get it?" Kennedy asked as she sipped at her drink.

"Charmed it off one of the waitresses."

She shook her head. "Why am I not surprised?"

Jack wanted to sleep with her, but he was not interested in anything more than a quick fling. Still, it irritated him that she thought he was *that* guy. Especially now that he knew her ex-husband had cheated on her. He didn't want her to believe all guys were like her ex. Even though he intended for their affair to be brief, he wanted her to understand that she was special for that short time. Jack prided himself on the fact that none of his liaisons left the experience with a bitter taste in their mouth.

"Come on, let's mingle." He held out his hand in invitation. She placed her hand into his, and he tugged her to her feet, leading her away from the table without releasing her hand.

"Are you and Sabrina the only ones in the family who live in New Orleans?" he inquired as they walked.

Kennedy nodded. "Practically everyone else lives in Dallas. That's why Sabrina got married here, instead of in New Orleans."

"Is that what you'll do, when you get married someday?"

She shook her head. "Not getting married again."

Her tone bothered him. It was as if she were giving up on something without ever having given it a chance in the first place. Even though she had been married once before, he determined that one didn't count. She hadn't had any control in the way it ended.

Whatever she might have replied was lost when she smiled fondly, clearly pleased about something. He was momentarily bowled over by the way the smile lit up her face before he shook it off and shifted his gaze to determine what caused her such obvious joy.

"Who's that?" he asked, nodding at the older couple and young man who were standing near the edge of the dance floor, talking animatedly. The woman in the group waved enthusiastically in their direction.

Kennedy's smile widened and she lifted her hand to wave back. "My parents. And my brother, Carter."

"Carter?" Jack arched his blond brow.

Kennedy giggled. "My parents have a thing for presidential names."

"I'll say."

"You have a problem with that, Jack?"

"Actually, my name is Jackson." He grinned cheekily when she continued giggling. He liked the sound of her giggle. He had the sense she didn't do it often, and he felt a moment of pride that he was able to elicit the reaction so easily. He glanced at the half-empty champagne glass in her hand and decided to pretend she was so relaxed because of him, not the alcohol.

"Let's go say hi," he suggested. As they walked toward the group, his gaze swept the room.

"What are you looking for?"

"The maid of honor."

"Still having issues with Vanessa?"

"She's drunk and she keeps hitting on me. And by the way, I'm definitely throwing off *not interested* vibes."

He liked the relieved look that flashed in her eyes. He liked that he was able to put it there.

By the time they reached the gathering, another woman had joined them, wrapping her arms around Kennedy's brother from behind, and resting her chin on his shoulder. He looked faintly embarrassed by the public display of affection.

"That's Sheryl, my brother's girlfriend," Kennedy whispered just before they stepped to within hearing distance of the small family gathering. "She's a little much to take when you first meet her," she warned.

Kennedy's parents were typical warm and friendly Southern folk. Both greeted Jack warmly, complimented him on his amusing speech, and thanked him for watching out for their daughter. Kennedy rolled her eyes.

"He isn't even my date, Mom," she protested. "We just happened to be in the wedding party together."

Mrs. St. George eyed Jack in a way that would make a lesser man uncomfortable. "You two sure looked good walking down the aisle together."

"Mo-o-o-m."

Kennedy's annoyance at her mother's broad hint made it easier for him to take it in stride. Otherwise, he might have gone running in the other direction. Matchmaking Mamas ranked up there with married women on his *not interested* list.

"Maybe it's just him," Kennedy's brother's girlfriend purred. She straightened away from Carter and strutted over, surprising everyone by enveloping Jack in a full-body hug.

Jack disengaged himself and chuckled. "Well, that's a hell of a greeting."

Sheryl smiled coyly and batted heavily made-up blue eyes. "There's more where that came from."

Carter scowled. His mother tried to divert everyone's attention by speaking overly loudly about how lovely the wedding was, and how delicious the food was, and how adorable the bride and groom were.

"Honey, we're going to have to consider moving to New Orleans at this rate," she said to her husband. "It seems every time one of the children on your side of the family gets married, that's where they end up."

"Vanessa still lives in Dallas," her husband remarked. "What about you, Carter? You going to move to New Orleans when you get married?"

"Not getting married," he said distractedly.

Jack found it curious that both siblings were so anti-marriage when their parents appeared to have a healthy, loving relationship. Was he curious enough to ask Kennedy about it, or would that lead her to the wrong conclusion about what he expected out of today?

Sheryl continued to flirt with him, making it easy to banish any thoughts regarding marriage and futures. Jack figured if Carter ever did want to get married, this was definitely not the right choice.

Kennedy, he noticed, was assessing the situation. He suspected she was trying to determine a way to help her brother out of this embarrassing predicament. Before Jack could ascertain what she planned to do, she wrapped her arms around his bicep and said, "Come on, Jack. Dance with me."

He tossed her an amused look and politely excused them both before leading her out to the dance floor. "Sacrificing yourself for your brother's happiness?" he teased.

"It's not really a sacrifice. But that was pretty bold of her to flirt with you right under Carter's nose."

"She was just flirting."

"*Just flirting* more often than not leads to other activities."

Her tone was icy. It took Jack a few seconds to realize why.

"Sorry. I forgot. About your ex, I mean."

She shook her head. "It's not me I'm worried about," she explained. "I don't want my brother to get hurt, that's all."

He didn't believe her, not entirely, but he was wise enough to let the subject drop. Instead, he pulled her close, wrapped his arms around her waist, nuzzled her ear.

"This isn't a slow song," she pointed out. Her voice sounded awfully breathy.

"Yeah, I know. But I like holding you in my arms. It feels good."

"Oh."

•••

Kennedy wished she were wittier. It seemed all she could ever say around Jack was "oh." Not exactly stimulating responses.

Jack was certainly stimulated. They were close enough that she could feel his erection pressing into her belly. He wasn't trying to hide it, either. When he nuzzled her ear, she tilted her head to give him better access. And then she realized what was happening.

"What are you doing?" she asked.

"Hitting on you. Is it working?"

"Um …"

"Want to go somewhere more private?"

"Umm …"

He twirled her away, pulled her back, and caught her, squeezing her more tightly than he had been a moment before. Kennedy forgot to breathe. She was distantly aware of the fact that he was backing her off the dance floor. She knew she should, but she made no move to stop him. Sabrina's warning echoed in her head, but all she could think was, *I deserve to have fun tonight. I can handle a one-night stand.*

I want a one-night stand.

A few minutes later, he led her up a set of stairs that climbed from a hallway near the kitchen to the second floor.

"How did you know these stairs were even here?" she wondered as she held his hand and followed.

"I scoped out the place when we first arrived. Force of habit," he admitted. She knew he was talking about his job, not his past liaisons, which she appreciated. For the moment, she wanted to pretend she was the only one. Otherwise, she might back out.

At the top of the stairs, he paused to flash her a grin over his shoulder. She gave him a wobbly smile in return. He tugged her hand, leading her to the bride's room.

Where they found Cullen and Sabrina prematurely sealing their wedding vows.

"Guess they can't get it annulled now," Jack remarked as he quietly pulled the door closed.

She shook her head, as reason pushed through the haze of alcohol and lust. "This is a bad idea. Sabrina says I'm supposed to stay away from you."

"I'm going to have a talk with Sabrina about interfering with my sex life," Jack muttered. "Why did she say that?"

Kennedy shrugged. "You're a player."

"Are you looking for forever, Kennedy?"

She gasped and vehemently shook her head. Been there, done that, she almost said out loud.

"Me neither. So how is this a bad thing again?"

"Umm ..."

"I'm usually pretty good with the intuition thing. And my intuition is telling me that you are attracted to me."

Kennedy cleared her throat. "I—I think your intuition is correct."

Jack grinned. "I thought so. And I'm sure it's pretty damn obvious that I'm attracted to you."

To prove his point, he backed her up to the wall, pressed his palms against the wallpaper, and dipped his head to nibble at her throat. She made a small, strangled noise and grabbed his shoulders to keep herself from falling when her knees buckled.

Jack sucked her earlobe into his mouth. "I promise, babe, you won't regret it. I'm a very attentive lover."

"Oh God."

"I want to hear you scream that."

"Limo," she gasped, and she grabbed his hand and dragged him back down the hall to the stairs. She had no idea what caused her to think of the stretched vehicle out in the parking lot; all she knew was that three years of self-enforced celibacy had pushed her libido to the limit. She wanted to break her fast, and she wanted to do it right now, with this man.

Whatever happened tomorrow didn't matter. Whatever happened in two hours wouldn't matter. She just needed right now, and she needed it to involve her and Jack and a distinct lack of clothing.

The driver sat in the front seat, reading a newspaper and tapping his foot to the beat of a country song blaring from the speakers. Jack handed him a wad of cash and tucked Kennedy into the back of the limo. As soon as they were inside, the car lurched into motion, sending her tumbling into the groomsman's lap. He pushed the button to raise the darkened glass that separated them from the front.

"We aren't really doing this, are we?" she asked as Jack smoothed her skirt up her legs so she could straddle his lap without tearing her dress.

"Hell yes, we are. You don't want to know how much I just paid that guy to drive around in circles for half an hour."

"Half an hour?"

"Trust me, babe." He flipped her onto her back on the plush leather seat.

"What?"

He laid down on top of her, his body nestled between her thighs as he propped himself up on his elbows. "Have you ever had sex in a limo before?"

She shook her head, staring up at him.

"It's fun," he promised, and he dipped his head and kissed her.

Kennedy was embarrassed that the driver knew precisely what they were doing back there while he drove aimlessly around town. She wasn't this sort of woman. She'd slept with precious few men before meeting her ex-husband, and she'd only slept with one since asking for the divorce. And that decision had been a knee-jerk reaction when the lawyer she'd consulted about the divorce had promised to retrieve her money—even offered a reduced fee—if she would sleep with him. She'd been so distraught and confused, she'd done it. Except afterward she'd been too mortified to face him again, so she'd sent him an email letting him know she no longer required his services. She then went to a far more expensive female lawyer who was no less intimidating, but at least she hadn't hit on Kennedy.

"I don't normally do this," she breathed as he slowly made his way down her body, kissing every inch of exposed flesh along the way. The fantasies she'd had at the wedding flashed through her mind. The real thing was so much better.

He pushed the dress over her shoulders and tugged at the bodice, revealing her bronze-colored bra. He pursed his lips around one lace-covered breast and exhaled. Hot, moist air puckered the nipple. Kennedy arched into his touch and made another strangled noise of pleasure.

"Glad to hear it," Jack said as he focused his attention on the other breast. "I like the idea of being your first."

She arched again, threaded her fingers into his hair and squeezed. "I mean this," she gasped. "Sex. Mindless. No commitments."

Jack paused in his ministrations and lifted his head to look at her face. "Do you want me to stop?"

"Oh God, no," she said before she could think, could possibly utter another answer. Not that she would at this point. Every nerve ending in her body was screaming with anticipation. If he stopped now, she was certain she would self-combust.

He gave her a lazy smile. "You can handle this, babe. No strings. No worries. Just let me pleasure you."

"O-okay."

He dipped his head, kissed her cleavage, and then continued his downward path until his elbows were pressed into the leather seats and his hands cupped her thighs, holding her steady while he laved at her as if she were the tastiest ice cream cone. Her fingers stayed threaded in his hair as she urged him on with gentle pushes.

Her hips bucked. She chanted, "Oh God, oh God, oh God," and then she exploded, the orgasm so intense her back bowed off the seat.

Jack sat back on his haunches, fighting with the clasp on his tuxedo pants, fumbling in his urgency to be inside her.

And then he was, leaning forward, pressing into her, his arms around her back, his hands cupping her head. He kissed her and thrust, and kissed her and thrust, again and again and—. Suddenly he pushed away and pulled out.

Kennedy's eyes shot open, and she blinked dazedly as he sat on his haunches and contorted his body, struggling to reach something in the pants that were twisted around his knees.

"What are you doing?" she asked, confused.

"Damn it," Jack muttered. He finally managed to pull his wallet out of his pants. "I can't believe I almost forgot to use protection. Shit. I never do that."

Kennedy lay back against the seat and breathed a sigh of relief. She watched him struggle to open the condom package, and then attempt to sheath his erection. His hands shook so badly, he couldn't seem to get it right. It was oddly thrilling.

She finally took pity on him. "Our half hour is running out." She pushed his hands away and quickly and efficiently rolled the condom over his erection. He closed his eyes and let her do it, making a noise of desire deep in his throat.

"Okay," she said, and she opened her arms. "Come here."

"Anything you say, babe." He moved over her, positioned his erection, and thrust again. "Yeah," he grunted as he pulled out and thrust again. And again. And again.

"Oh God." She began the chant; her insides began to coil round and round, tighter and tighter, in a paradox of pleasure combined with the edge of pain. She arched against him, dropped her hands to grab his butt, and pulled him more tightly against her.

He responded by thrusting harder and faster, grunting between kisses. "Come on, baby," he crooned. "Come with me. Come on."

"Yes!"

She exploded. Jack let out a yell of his own as he chased her over the edge, filling the condom before collapsing on top of her.

"I don't think I can move," he muttered a few moments later.

"I hope that changes quickly, because I can't breathe."

Jack shifted onto his side, taking Kennedy with him so that they faced one another on the seat.

"You okay?" he asked as he let his hand wander, smoothing over the dress that still covered half her body.

She smiled. Her smile wasn't wobbly anymore. Amazing what great sex could do for a woman. "Quite. This is a little embarrassing to admit, but it's been a while."

He rolled his hips. "Give me a few minutes, and I bet I can manage another go-round."

The limo lurched to a stop. She struggled into a seated position as she frantically began pulling herself together. Jack used a napkin to dispose of the used condom, and then tugged his pants over his hips and tucked his shirt into the waistband. The driver knocked on the window, and Jack pressed the button to roll it down just enough to let the man know they would be out in a moment.

"This is so embarrassing," she moaned while Jack helped her adjust her dress.

"You're embarrassed that you just had sex with me?"

"I'm embarrassed that he knows we just had sex." She jabbed her thumb at the door.

"Relax, babe. He sees this stuff all the time."

He did not give her a chance to respond. He pushed open the door, climbed out, and then bent and helped her out of the limo. Kennedy turned to look at her reflection in the mirrored windows.

"I look terrible."

"You look hot."

"I look like I just had sex."

"Which is hot."

She rolled her eyes and tried to fix her hair. In contrast, Jack simply ran a hand through his and apparently considered himself good to go. She focused on her own disheveled locks again.

"I don't think I can go back into the reception," she protested.

He glanced at his watch. "It's almost over anyway. Want the limo to take you back to the hotel?"

"What are you going to do?"

"Go inside and let Sabrina and your parents know that you left, so they won't worry."

The gesture was curiously endearing. "Thanks. Really. I mean, thanks. That was … great."

He leaned into her, tucked an errant strand of hair behind her ear, and brushed a kiss over her lips. "You're right. It was great."

And then he was gone, striding across the parking lot toward the reception hall. Without looking the driver in the eye, Kennedy asked him to take her to the hotel, and then climbed back into the limo. She sank into the seat and blew out another deep breath.

Oh my God, she'd just had sex with renowned playboy Jack Boudreaux.

And she'd liked it. A lot.